Dreams In Ash

A Firefighter's Story of the Great Chicago Fire

By

H. Scott Walker

Dreams in Ash by H. Scott Walker

ParkWood Creative
2912 ParkWood Drive
Quincy Illinois, 62305

ISBN: 979-8-9865898-4-8

Note: All images within this text are either original files, or in the public domain. No copyrighted material has been utilized.

Dedication

This book is dedicated to the brave men and women of the fire service who risk their lives, and well being in the protection of others.

*Greater love has no one than this, that he lay
down his life for his friends.*

John 15:13

In particular, I wish to thank my wife,   Dr. Karen Sears. Without her help and guidance this novel would never have come to be.

Introduction

This is a work of historical fiction. Like other works in the genre, it weaves a fictional narrative around actual historic events – here, the Great Chicago Fire of 1871. The fire is etched in American history and folklore, yet much of the story isn't well known. History is told in the language of facts, and much has been written detailing the events of the fire – its origin, its size, the losses, and the incredible rebuilding effort. But the essential truth of any disaster is found in the experiences of those who face them. At its best, historical fiction provides a deeper sense of events by humanizing their impact. In this telling of the fire's story, the author endeavors to put a human face on the tragedy by focusing on a fictional firefighter and his family as they navigate the tragedy. It hopes to fill in the blanks by providing context, a picture of sorts of Chicago in 1871.

On balance, the novel is a fair telling of the fire story, and of the socio=cultural influences of the time. That said, the academic still living within the author cautions the reader that while this novel is well researched, it is not intended as a reference text. The depiction of the actual fire is mostly accurate. However, for narrative purposes, the author occasionally employed literary license on some minor details.

A challenge in historical fiction is the unintended blurring of fact and fiction. Several of the characters in the novel were actual people associated with the events of October, 1871 – Catherine O'Leary and Mike McDonald are examples. Conversely, all the main characters are fictitious, including the entire Collins family. To help the reader sort history from fiction, the author has included an addendum reviewing the story's historical accuracy chapter by chapter.
For those readers interested in an academic study of the fire, the addendum also lists references used in creating this novel.

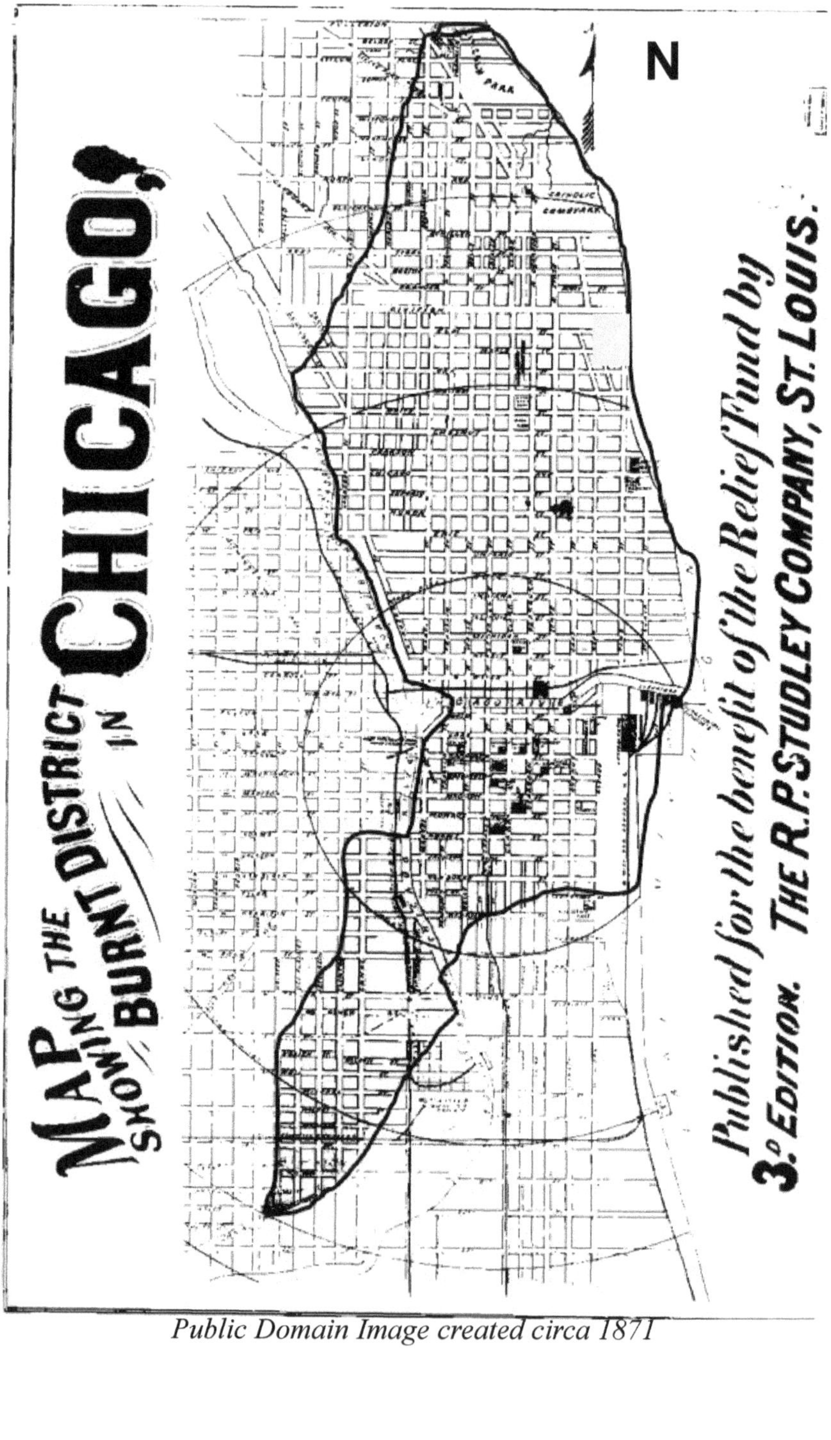

Public Domain Image created circa 1871

Part One

Tinder

The O'Leary Dairy Barn
circa 1871, unknown author

September 30, 1871

Chicago Illinois

Chapter 1

The smoke and heat seemed relentless – it always did. Eyes watering, and desperately sucking air through the bandana around his face, Sean Collins drove his pike pole into a crease between the slats. He twisted, then pulled with all the dwindling strength left in him; Patty did the same. Their efforts were not in vain; a six-foot section of the wall came crashing down. Sheets of flame and a cloud of black smoke engulfed the two men. Both firefighters instinctively turned away from the onslaught until a hose stream knocked down the fire. They caught their breath a moment before moving to the next section of wall.

The work was simple enough – pull down the outside walls of the building so the hose streams could penetrate. Simple, but exhausting. The fire had already claimed the east building of the Burlington Warehouse. The fight to save the west building had turned desperate. In the mind of every firefighter stood the genuine fear that if the fire wasn't stopped quickly, it would rampage unchecked through several additional blocks. And so, though exhausted, they toiled on.

They moved down to the next wall section. "Patty, mind that hornet's nest in the eaves. They'll put a tickle on us if you roust them," said the bigger of the two men.

The shorter man studied the nest for a moment, and said, "They're gone – smoked out. Smarter than us, sure enough. Tell me again why we're doing this."

"We're not paid for our smarts. You should be thankful for that; you would be a poor man indeed."

With a chuckle, Patty replied. "And if it were good looks that mattered, I would be rich."

When the wall came down, a swarm of angry bees poured out of the so-called *empty* nest. Luckily for the two men, the erupting flames quickly destroyed the nest and its occupants – almost.

Patty, rubbing the sting on his forehead, said, "Well maybe there were a few left."

Sean simply shook his head.

Firefighters Sean Collins and Patrick "Patty" Doyle had just pulled down the last section of wall when Patty dropped his pike and went to a knee in exhaustion. He said, "Sean, I would trade my left leg for a cold drink and warm bed."

"You think too little of your leg then,".

"I tell you plain, I like a good fire fight as much as the next man, but I'm nearly at my end. This is the third monster in as many days."

Even Sean, a tall, broad shouldered bull of man looked done in as leaned heavily on his pike. "Aye, it's been Hercules' own labors for a while now, but glory be, it looks like we got this one whipped."

The two men half walked, half stumbled to the rail bed running between the two buildings, and sat on a track.

Patty used his gritty sleeve to wipe his grittier face. "This can't go on much longer. Sooner or later, one of these bastards will get the better of us and the whole damn town will burn."

Sean patted his friend on the back. "You worry too much."

"If you say so, but I tell you now, if we don't get rain soon, there will be the devil to pay."

"It'll be October and with it, the winds will shift from the north. Rain will come then."

Patty shook his head. "It's the wind that scares me. If we had gusts today, we'd be chasing this fire all across town."

"The river would stop it. Never seen a fire that could swim."

"The river is a good six blocks to the West and a mile to the North. Can you imagine it, Sean? That would be near a quarter of the city. It's unthinkable, it is."

"It'll never happen Patty. As I said, you worry too much."

"And what's to stop it but us. Any manner of ills can happen when you're not looking."

"I suppose you're not wrong, but there is nothing gained by worry. We won today – that's enough."

"Is it? I hear tell some poor bastard died in the east building. Worse, the fire took a warehouse full of whiskey and corn mash. There is a sin against nature if ever there was one."

"Lost whiskey is worse than a man's death? You're a ghoul Patty."

The wry grin Sean knew so well spread across his friend's face. "Depends on the man, now doesn't it? The whisky too, I suppose. But you know what I mean, we're done in. And what have we got to show for it but a burnt-out building?"

A wave of heat induced dizziness washed over Sean; he laid back with his head propped on the tracks. "Those houses across the street are still standing, at least for now. That's victory enough for me."

Chicago had grown fast and chaotically. The previous 40 years saw thousands of immigrants (mostly Irish and Polish) move to the city in search of a better life. Buildings went up quickly and space had long since become scarce, pushing the working poor into overcrowded slums intermixed with commercial properties. Much of the city was a hodgepodge of homes, sheds, barns, animal pens, factories, slaughterhouses, and shops all haphazardly wedged together. Most were shabby and poorly constructed, nearly all were wood.

Fire had always plagued Chicago, but never more than in the fall of 1871. A long, hot summer with precious little rain had left the city a virtual tinder box. The draught had caused the trees to drop their leaves early. And, mixed with tons of trash, the yards and alleys were blanketed with flammable litter. A discarded cigarette or unattended cooking fire easily found fuel to grow. The Burlington Warehouse fire was but one of many fires fought in the early fall.

"I tell you, Sean, I am bone weary. Tomorrow morning can't come soon enough."

"We all are. It's been tough going for a while now. Too many fires, too much suffering."

They fell into a moment of exhausted silence that Sean relished. Sean thought, *Patty will talk soon, he can't help it. He has the curse of gab.*

"You know, Sean, it's Sunday tomorrow."

And there it is. "What of it?"

With a sly smile, Patty nudged his friend. "Will you be visiting Danny's widow for a bit?"

"I suppose I will check on her – see if she needs anything."

Making an obscene gesture, Patty teased. "I'm sure you'll give her what she needs."

Sean gave Patty a stern look. "Don't make it sound lewd. She's a proper woman."

"Of course she is. I meant no disrespect. Still, she is a bonnie lass."

"I suppose she is, but don't be spreading gossip. It won't do no good for anyone."

"Gossip? Me? I am the very sole of discretion, I am. Still, a young woman gets lonely. And, your proper lady does work in a whore…"

Sean fixed a hard stare on his friend. "Choose your words careful Patty."

"All right Sean, don't get blood in your eye. I am only having a jab at you. It's a fine thing that you look after her and the kids."

"I owe it to Danny."

Patty sighed, "No – you don't. It wasn't your fault. I was there, I saw what happened. There was nothing you or anybody else could do."

"So you keep telling me, but the man is dead. Anyway, I don't mind looking after them. The girls are a joy. I always wanted a daughter, you know."

"Just wait, soon enough Liam will be giving you some grandbabies."

Sean groaned as he sat up. "Not at the rate he's going."

"Are you schweinhunds done with your nap?" Sean knew the voice without looking up. It was Deputy Chief Snider, a burly German with a foul temper. Legend had it he once broke a man's ribs with an axe handle for nothing worse than talking back to him.

"Just catching our breath, Chief," answered Patty

The German growled, "There is a building on fire behind you. I'll put a boot in your teeth if you don't get to moving. Schnell!"

Patty said, "Right away, any orders?"

Sean appraised the man. He thought, *He has no axe handle with him now, does he? I wouldn't mind putting this pike up his arse. I wouldn't mind that one bit.*

As if reading his mind, the big German glared at Sean. The two stared at each other, neither moved nor spoke. Finally, Snider pointed at the east building. "The owner says there is a small safe on the first floor, near the stairs. Go bring it out. - das foreman's body too if you see it. The building won't stand much longer. It'd be good if his widow had something to bury."

Sean studied the building; she was a sturdy old girl. Like most warehouses, it was a *Mill Construction.* She had brick walls and massive beams, eight by eight or bigger, supporting the floors and roof. Sean knew mill construction stood up to fire well, but the blaze had had its way with her for 3 hours now. The first floor had all but burnt itself out, but the attic was burning like hell itself. *Even a tough old building had limits. Sooner or later, she'll crumble - sooner, more likely,* he thought.

Patty said, "We'll see to it." Sean only nodded.

"And don't think you will be hiding in there goldbricking. I'll be looking for you two scherst fort."

"Scherst fort?" asked Patty.

The big German paused and thought, then replied. "Scheisse! … er… soon." The chief turned and marched off. They heard him mumble, "Damn lazy Irish, no better than the darkies."

Sean said, "Why provoke him? You knew what he meant."

Patty glared at the man's back. "I've had my fill of his kind."

"Ain't no sense to getting your back up," said Sean. "There is an endless supply of the ignorant. Kill one and two new ones show up at the funeral. Now, let's go about getting that safe before we're wearing the roof as a hat."

The two men walked across the tracks toward the burning building. Climbing a short stair to an elevated loading dock, they peered inside. The fire lines had put nearly a foot of water on the floor. Through a thick haze of blue smoke, they could just make out a large open space divided by stone walls every 30 feet or so. The walls contained arched passages connecting several rooms. Piles of twisted plows and field harrows were scattered about the first room. The fire's heat deformed the farm implements into near unrecognizable shapes.

Sean said, "Come along. The office is likely in the center of the building, near one of those stonewalls. I'll wager the foreman will be close by too."

"That would be as good a place as any to start, I guess," said Patty as he moved into the room.

Sean clutched his friend's shoulder, stopping him. "Mind your steps. There're likely floor hatches for moving stock to the basement. It won't do to fall in one and drown." With that, he grabbed a broom sitting next to the door. He put the end in the water in front of him, sweeping it from side to side as he walked. "Stay right behind me."

Slowly, the two firefighters waded across the darkened first room and into the second. Only the sound of sloshing at their feet marked their progress. As they went deeper into the building, the rumble of fire hoses pouring water into the attic and the steady echo of water cascading through holes in the floor above grew louder.

Just inside the second room, Sean's broom handle prodded something soft. When he pushed, the gloomy light revealed a body half floating in the shallow water. He said, "I am guessing this poor fellow would be the foreman."

Patty stepped forward and turned the man over. "I suppose so. Being close to this arch, it will be easy enough to find him on the way out. Which way do you think the safe is?"

"To hell with the safe. If it's well built, it will survive whatever the afternoon brings. If not, whatever's in there is already buggered. Either way, I'm in no particular mood to risk my life for some well-to-do's business papers. Let's get this poor bloke out of here."

"I don't know about that, Sean. The big Hun won't like us not getting that safe."

"Well, he can come back with us to look for it then. But right now, I am getting this fellow out of here and home to those who'll claim him. Grab his arms, I'll take his legs."

It was then that Sean heard it. A deep groan overhead, followed by a distinct cracking. Instinctively, he grabbed his friend and pulled him against the wall inside of one of the stone arches. A deafening crash resonated through the building, and Sean felt his legs kicked out from underneath him. Stunned, it took a few seconds for him to realize what had happened. The entire second floor had collapsed on either side of the stone archway. Rubble buried his arm, but he managed to pull it out without effort. His shoulder hurt, but it was tolerable. *I'll be damned*, he thought. *Somehow, I survived a collapse with little more than a few bruises.* He looked over and saw his partner on the ground, buried to his waist in debris. "Patty, how are you?"

"I've been better. I think my leg is broken, Sean."

Sean looked up at what was left of the second-floor ceiling, fire raged in the attic above. "This whole place will crumble quick enough. Do you think you can get out?"

"I won't be walking anytime soon, I'm afraid," said Patty.

"All right then, climb on my back and we'll get you out of here."

"Are you daft? There's an ocean of fallen rubble between us and the door. You can't crawl over all of this damned wreckage with me on your back. Leave me here and get yourself back to Maggie and Liam. I'll be fine."

Sean grabbed his friend. "Stop the nobility act. We both know you're a selfish prick. Now get on my back and let's get out of here before this place falls on our heads."

"It's true; I am a selfish prick, but I am not a fool. This building is about to come down, and only one of us can get out of here alive. Now get going."

"For the love of St. Peter, stop being a stubborn mick and get on my back. I'm not leaving you and we can't stay here. So, stop arguing and let's go."

"All right then," said Patty. "But if we both die, I am telling Saint Peter that I died of bad luck, and you died of stupidity."

Sean grumbled, "The saints protect the foolish, it's why you're still alive." He lay flat, and Patty half rolled - half climbed onto his back. He heard a pitiful groan when his friend moved the leg. Patrick wrapped his arms around Sean's neck and centered himself for balance. With effort, Sean raised himself to his hands and knees. He said, "And what makes you think you'll be seeing Saint Peter with me? You're more apt to be arguing with old Beelzebub, as I see it."

"Because," said Patty, "I'll still be clinging to your back like a tick. You made your bed, now you're stuck with me all the way up Jacob's ladder."

Despite the grim circumstances and the weight of Patrick on his back, Sean couldn't help but laugh. "Like I said, you're a selfish prick." Sean crawled out of the archway.

"And what does it say about you… (he winced in pain) … that a man such as me is your only friend?" A burning board from the attic above fell a few feet from them. "If we're going to go, I suggest we do it soon, and quickly."

Sean scaled the debris pile that had been the second floor. With great effort, he picked his way across the heap, being careful to test stability before committing his full weight to any part of the tangled mess. A few feet in, another burning chunk of roof fell close by. The crash made Sean flinch. The pile shifted, rolling Sean, with Patty on his back, down and over. Patty screamed as his broken leg hit a piece of iron.

"Jesus, Mary and Joseph, that hurt!" muttered Patty. He noticed the fallen board had ignited some debris. It was a small fire, but burning steadily. "This is no good, Sean. It'll take a lifetime to pull me out of here. Go on ahead and find some help – if there be any close by."

Sean again rolled flat on his stomach. "Let's not start with that again. Shut up and scramble on quick as you can."

"No, Sean. I won't do it. Get out of here before we both get killed."

"Do you want a broken jaw to go with that leg? I told you before, we both go, or neither of us does. Now stop your infernal nonsense and get on."

Patty grumbled, "Damned if you're not as stubborn as a Missouri mule."

Together, they continued the painfully slow crawl across the pile. Precious minutes slipped by as Sean toiled to get halfway through the wreckage. Lumber from the attic, some of it quite large, continued to fall from above. The whole while, Patty watched the growing fire behind them. Sean paused to catch his breath.

Patty said, "So, which do you think it will be that does us in – the fire behind us or something crashing down from above?"

Still catching his breath, Sean replied, "Dammed if you're not… a gloomy one… and heavy too. Maybe you were right… I should have left your portly ass back there."

They were surprised by a call from in front of them. "Hey who goes there? Where are you?"

Sean answered back. "Here! We're over here and in need of a wee bit of assistance."

Two firefighters scrambled across the pile toward them. Sean recognized them as Sammy Dougan, the other an odd fellow everyone called *The Preacher*. Sean didn't know his Christian name.

The Preacher said, "We saw you two go inside – why I can't fathom – and thought we would take a quick look for you in case you survived. And I'll be dipped in manure if you aren't here in one piece. It's God's work, it is."

Sean took a moment to catch his breath, then said, "He has a broken leg. We could use your help."

Sam Dougan said, "And you shall have it, but let's dispense with the pleasantries and get moving. This place doesn't look very friendly."

With difficulty, they got Patty out of the building within a few minutes. Once out, they carried him to a shaded area across the tracks. The four of them remained silent for several minutes as they caught their breath. Sean was about to speak when another loud groan emanated from the building. Moments later, the entire structure collapsed. The men watched helplessly as a wave of bricks and debris tumbled and rolled towards them. They reflexively covered their heads to ward off the onslaught.

As quickly as it started, it was over. Several bricks had struck Sean on the arms and legs. He pushed the debris off of him, and checked himself for injury. Every movement hurt, but all seemed functional. He knew he would be bruised, but was thankful nothing felt broken.

"That was far too close," said the Preacher as he tossed off a brick.

Sammy said, "I've earned a bruise or two, but I'm all right. How are you, Preacher?"

The Preacher dusted himself off and said, "Not a scratch. Lucifer missed me again. I need a drink."

Sammy Dougan pointed at the burning heap that had been a building. "I hear tell there are dozens of whiskey kegs in the basement. Perhaps you should salvage some."

"That loss is pure tragedy," said the Preacher. "But I believe I have tempted fate enough for one day. It's always the bars, warehouses, and hotels that burn. Have you ever noticed that the whorehouses never get touched?"

"And what have you against whorehouses?" asked Sammy.

With a chuckle, the Preacher answered. "Nothing at all. I may just start sleeping in one just to play it safe."

"Is that so? And tell me again why they call you the Preacher?" asked Sean.

Sammy laughed. "Well, it's not because he found the Lord, I'll tell you that. One time we was…"

Sean heard a gasp from Patty and saw that he had gotten the worst of it. Bricks covered the man, several of them lay on his broken leg.

"Are you all right Patty?" asked Sean.

Patty groaned and tried to move – he couldn't. "Do you believe it? Right on my damned broken leg. It feels as though I broke it again."

"The gods of misfortune seem to be after you, my friend. I think I should stay away from…"

Sammy nodded at the bull of a man coming at them. To Patty, he said, "Here comes Snider, to check on us. I think it's time me and the Preacher got back to our own company."

Sean replied, "It appears you saved our lives. I owe you a debt."

"It's the job, isn't it so? Take care, you two." With that, they moved down the tracks toward one of the hose wagons"

Sean had hoped Snider had something more important to do than check on them. But he didn't.

"Well, I see the Lord has seen fit to spare you two. Why, I can't say. Did you get the safe?"

"No," said Sean. "The second floor collapsed on us before we found it. We found the foreman, though."

"Where is he?"

"Still in there. Like I said, the ceiling collapsed. It broke Patty's leg."

Deputy Chief Snider looked at the smoldering pile that was once the Burlington Warehouse. "Well, it will be hell finding anything in there now."

Sean snapped, "Did you hear me? Patty broke his damned leg."

"I heard you. I'll have some boys come to fetch him. It would have been better had you gotten the job done, is all."

"It would have been better if we hadn't been in there at all."

"And whose fault was that but the Almighty? No one but him could have known the building would come down so quick."

Sean stood to face the big man. "And no one but you and the devil could care less."

"Mind yourself, or I'll add to your bruises. Wait here with your friend till they fetch him. Then find your captain and see if he has use for you." Snider took another look at the building, shook his head, and walked off.

They sat in silence for a while. Sean worried about Patty's leg and he contemplated how close at hand their death had come. He wondered how Patty's family would get on had they died. Would someone look after them? He didn't worry about his own family. Liam was almost a man now – a troubled young man, but a survivor. As for Maggie? He hated to admit it, but he wasn't entirely sure he cared.

"Sean," panted Patty. "I haven't had time to thank you. I'd be dead for sure."

"You would do the same for me."

"I'd like to think so. Still…"

"Still, nothing. It's over. Leave it be."

Patty gingerly pulled his pant leg up. He looked at his mangled leg and grimaced. "It looks like something I saw at Shiloh. Do you think I'll lose it?"

Sean inspected the leg. Patty was right; it looked like a battlefield wound. The ragged end of his shin bone had pushed through the skin in two places. "I won't lie. It looks bad, but I've seen worse. I don't think it'll cost you the leg. Still, you'll limp for a while."

Patty hung his head. "That's generous, I'm afraid. From the looks of it, my firefighting is done. Now I'll be just one more poor crippled bastard looking for work where there is none – as if the war hasn't left enough of them around. Maybe you done me wrong by bringing me out, now that I think on it."

Sean patted his friend's shoulder. "There you go again, being all gloomy. See the doctor before you go pickin' out your beggar's corner." Inwardly, he thought, *He likely ain't wrong though.*

Chapter 2

Exhausted, Sean trudged down Clinton Street. After the warehouse fire, he had climbed in his cot around eight. An alarm had come in around midnight. It wasn't much of a fire, just a machine shed, but it was enough to keep him up all night. *If I had any sense, I'd go home and to bed. But I promised the girls.* He smiled at the thought of Kerry and Mary joyfully bounding about. Then an image of Katie came to him; her green eyes sparkled as she smiled – smiled for him. He pushed the fantasy aside. *A few more hours awake won't matter.* As he walked, he rubbed his shoulder, trying to loosen it up. He groaned. "Blazes that hurts."

The collapse of the warehouse had left him bruised and sore; especially his right shoulder. *That'll be a bother for a week or more,* he thought. Then chastised himself. *Don't be complaining, Patty would trade places with you now wouldn't he, and the both of us came close enough to meeting the Almighty, and that's the truth of it. You're lucky to be breathing, Sean. Remember that.* He shook his head dismissively. "The luck of the Irish, Patty called it."

A few hours' sleep and a quiet day will set me right. He groaned. *Maggie will be looking for me to go to Sunday service with her. If I'm late, we'll argue, and she'll be at me the rest of the day. If I go with her, then go to visit the girls, she'll be put out as well, and I'll be without sleep. Either way, Maggie will be on her war horse. I'd gladly visit the Lord's dinner party if he could dull that sharp tongue of hers.*

As he passed Wright Street, his reverie was interrupted by the sound of heaving. He saw a man, obviously still drunk on all fours in his yard – not an uncommon sight on a Sunday morning. A little boy sat on a stoop watching as his father fell face down in his vomit. *Poor bastard likely slept it off in the yard. He did well to stumble home; I guess. No doubt there's more than a few sleeping in the alleys behind the saloons and whorehouses in the District this morning.*

The neighborhood always looked its shabbiest in the gray of morning. The street was crowded with little cottages – shacks really – some were barely standing, all needed paint. Wedged in among them were coal sheds, privies, chicken coups and animal pens for pigs and sheep, mostly. Dogs, chickens and even the occasional goat wandered freely about, rooting through the piles of refuse scattered in the yards. He knew the area smelled foul, but he had learned to ignore it, unless the rare wind blew in from the southeast. Then the stench of the stockyards and slaughterhouses down by the rail depot would overpower the neighborhood. A wind from the north carried the smell of sewage from the river, and that was almost as bad.

Wind direction was a common topic in the neighborhood. Mostly, folks hoped for west winds in the summer, and no wind at all during fall and winter when it turned cold. Though over the last month, rain had come to dominate the conversations over the back fences. Normally dry weather was a blessing, as rain stirred up the insects and turned the entire neighborhood into a sea of mud. But, it had been so hot and dry for so long, fire was on everyone's mind.

Sean caught movement in the corner of his eye. A woman was stirring about inside her cottage. Sean turned away out of respect for her privacy. Privacy was a rare thing in the neighborhood. The cottages stood close and more often than not, the summerlike heat had most doors standing open, and windows uncovered for ventilation.

What upset him most – when he allowed himself to think about it– were the windows, the broken ones. Few cottages had all their windows intact, his included. They stood open like gaping wounds now, but he knew in a month or two they would be covered over with scrap lumber or feed sacks; anything to help keep the cold out. The covered windows left the already dreary interiors dark and lifeless. Rarely did a window get fixed, glass was expensive, and work was scarce. Those that could find work barely made enough to feed the kids and buy coal for heat. Windows had become a bit of a status symbol on the south side. Sean grumbled, "Now, there's the luck of the Irish for you, Patty. You hope the wind doesn't blow and you aspire to window glass."

As Sean passed DeKoven Street, he noticed the O'Leary's barn door open. *I should take the girls some milk*, he thought. He peered into the barn and saw an imposing woman feeding a calf. She wasn't heavy, but a lifetime of hard work had left her sturdy. The small dairy operation was owned by Patrick and Catherine O'Leary –although everyone knew it was really Catherine's business. Patrick helped, but spent most of his time working odd jobs at the stockyards. Those who knew Catherine, admired her. At 38 years of age, she was raising five children and running a reasonably successful business. She was as tough as nails, but friendly and generous. Sean called out, "Mrs. O'Leary, can you accommodate a customer?"

The woman looked up and beamed. "Sean Collins, you're out and about early enough. Did you work yesterday?"

"That I did."

"Well then, you had the devil's day, didn't you? I hear tell the Burlington Warehouse caught fire. Word is it took a life, and more than a few firefighters were hurt. I'm pleased to see that you're still in one piece."

"As am I," said Sean. "I wonder if I could bother you for a can of milk?"

"You can, but I don't think you need it. Mrs. Collins was here yesterday."

A little embarrassed, Sean said, "It's for the widow Sullivan's girls. They don't get milk regular. She struggles for money, I am afraid."

"It's a wonderful thing the way you firefighters take care of your own. Do you have a can?"

"Afraid not, but if you have a spare, I will return it tomorrow morning."

"Of course. Just give me a moment."

A few minutes later, a smiling Catherine O'Leary returned with a can of milk and a tiny bundle of fabric in her hand. Sean asked, "What have you there?"

"I made some hard candy for my little ones yesterday. There were a few broken pieces left over. Give them to Mrs. Sullivan's children. A little treat will do them good."

"It's generous of you. Are you sure your children won't miss it?"

"I think I raised them well enough to appreciate the value of sharing." With a grin, she added, "If not, a swat on the backside will stop their complaining quick enough."

Sean let out a rare chuckle as he handed her a nickel for the milk. "Let's hope it don't come to that. Thank you again, Mrs. O'Leary."

As he left, she called after him. "Sean, hold a moment if you would. I hope I'm not speaking out of turn, but I got something weighing on me that I think I should burden you with."

"And what is that?"

Mrs. O'Leary fixed a worried gaze on him. "A few times these last weeks, that Johnny Gallagher has been skulking around the neighborhood. Do you know of him?"

"I've heard of him," said Sean. "There's not much about him to praise, or so I hear."

"True enough. He's as mean as a rabid dog, and about as trustworthy. He's one of Big Mike McDonald's thugs, you know."

"That I haven't heard, but I can't say I'm surprised."

"Here's the thing, Sean. I hear tell that Liam is running with him. Truth is, I've seen them together myself. I thought you should know. I don't want to overstep, but no good can come of it."

Sean felt a sudden knot in his stomach. "You're not overstepping at all. I thank you for your candor."

"That's a relief," said Mrs. O'Leary. "I have been bothered about saying something, but I don't wish to see Liam fall in with those people. I've known him since he was in short pants."

Sean sighed. "I'll tell you the truth; I'm not surprised to hear it. With each day, that boy becomes more of a worry to me, and a heartbreak to his mother. Have you shared this with Maggie?"

Mrs. O'Leary shook her head. "No. I thought this a thing best for a father's ears."

"True enough, but I honestly am at my wit's end at what to do with the lad. He's too big to whip, and I've talked to him until I'm out of wind. There's no getting through to him."

"Sadly, a lot of the neighborhood boys are falling astray. It's the lure of easy money and high times, I guess."

"Maggie pesters me to pick up and leave. She thinks we should buy a farm somewhere west or south. Maybe find a place that's more like the old country."

"Ah Sean, there's nowhere as pretty as the old country… or as harsh. Anyway, there is nothing in the wilderness but Indians and Protestants and neither will look kindly on our kind settling down there."

"I've told her as much. And I reminded her how hard a farmer's life is."

"She'd do well to listen to you. Stay with your own is what I say. We're not welcome most places."

"We aren't welcome *here* either, Catherine. They all but spit on us."

"True enough, but there is safety in numbers. I hear tell our kind are run out of the country villages, sometimes worse if you know what I mean. They'll tolerate the darkies quicker than us."

"I doubt it's always so. I saw a fair bit of the country during the war; there are decent folk around everywhere. Still, I'm not of a mind to go anywhere. And even if we did pick up, I doubt Liam would follow. He's near old enough to set his own path."

"Likely not. But Liam is a good lad. It's the company he keeps is all."

"There may be something to it," said Sean. "But I am beyond making excuses for him. I thank you for telling me about it though, and thank you for the milk and candy. The girls will think it's Christmas."

"Think nothing of it," Catherine sighed. "You know, it seems just only yesterday young Liam was here with Mrs. Collins, all bashful and tongue tied. He was a shy one you might remember."

He tipped his cap and said, "Time is as relentless as a river, I suppose. We've no choice but to let it take us where it will."

Sean left the barn feeling even more tired and burdened than before. The news of Liam hardly surprised him, but it still weighed heavily on him. *My darling boy has grown sullen and impertinent and now… and now… carousing with a street criminal, so it seems. This will set Maggie off on another of her dark spells. I don't think I can bear her just now.* His thoughts of going home vanished. More than ever, he needed the comfort of seeing the girls.

It was a sense of obligation that first compelled him to look after Katie and her daughters. Now, he recognized the truth of it.

The constant bickering with Maggie and arguing with Liam had made home nearly unbearable. The little Sullivan girls brought sunshine into his otherwise dreary life. His time with them took his mind off his troubled home life, even if only for a little while. And then there was Katie. He relished his time with her. She was lively and sweet. Her smiles warmed his heart – and broke it. Being with her, seeing the love in her for her daughters, put a clear light on the coldness in his own home. But he was married and an honorable man. And Katie was a proper lady, and that was that.

Still, his mood lightened as he climbed the steps to their apartment.

Chapter 3

Katie Sullivan knocked on Mrs. Carmichael's door. She hated having Mary and Kerry sleep at the old woman's all night, but what else could she do? The eatery didn't stop serving until 10 and between cleaning up and the walk home; she was seldom in before midnight. As much as she wanted to, there was no sense in waking the girls so late, and she doubted Mrs. Carmichael would tolerate being disturbed either.

Mrs. Carmichael answered the door, and like most mornings, the questions started immediately. "So, Katie, what time did you get in last night?"

Katie knew that Mrs. Carmichael didn't approve of her working at the hotel, especially at night. But the old woman understood the necessity of her plight and helped as she could. *A mother must do what she must, to feed her children* was how she put it. "The same time as always, Mrs. Carmichael."

"I'm glad to hear it. I don't mind watching the girls if you *must* work nights. But I won't be a party to any mischief. There's no good in a proper lady being out so late."

"Of course not. I assure you I come straight home from work."

"And Katie, did you take a hackney carriage home?"

And who has the money for that? "Of course," Katie lied.

"Good, good. I worry about you, lass. It wouldn't do for you to be walking the streets at night by yourself; especially in that neighborhood. Mark my words, something awful might come of it. We women must always be careful. Men are monsters and a lone woman on the street at night is inviting trouble."

Don't I know it. Katie asked, "Did the girls behave?"

A warm smile brightened the woman's face. "They were angels, as always."

As if on cue, the two girls bounced out of the kitchen and to their mother's side. Katie said, "Thank you again. I don't know what I'd do without you."

The old woman patted Kerry on the head. "They really are no bother. Will you be taking them to St. Paul's this morning?"

"Of course, the 10 am service, as always. Will you be joining us?"

"That would be lovely, dear."

With that, Katie shepherded her daughters back across the hall.

Kerry and Mary bounded into the tiny one-room apartment and jumped on the bed, squealing. Katie scolded them. "Settle down, the both of you. You act like wild Indians." Truthfully, their exuberant laughter warmed her heart. Her girls were everything to her, her only joy. Most days, she hardly saw them. They would barely be home from school when she had to drop them off at Mrs. Carmichael's on her way to work. A few precious hours in the morning, and an hour in the afternoon, were all they had together. Except for Sunday. Sunday was always their day. On Sunday they were inseparable, and most wonderfully, they all huddled together in her bed at night.

Sunday made every other day – and the nights – tolerable. She didn't mind helping in the kitchen so much, or even serving the early evening patrons. The plates were heavy, but she had grown accustomed to that. It was the later crowd that she dreaded. As the night wore on, the men became drunker and progressively cruder. As she watched the girls rough housing she thought, y*es, this – them – is why I put up with it.* Then she shook her head dismissively. *As if you have choices, you fool.*

A knock on the door interrupted her thoughts. The girls stopped their play and ran to the door like expectant puppies. They knew who was at the door and were nearly beside themselves with excitement. Katie understood; she would never admit it, but she felt a touch of it herself. For the sake of propriety, she pulled the drape that separated the sleeping area from the rest of the apartment, then answered the door.

He had barely crossed the threshold when the girls shrieked, "Uncle Sean!" and pounced on him. The big man pretended to be overpowered and allowed himself to be pushed over. Katie watched as the three of them merrily wrestled on the floor. She often admired that no matter how rough Kerry and Mary were with him, he remained extraordinarily careful and gentle with them. Tears welled in her eyes at seeing her children so utterly happy. *How different Sean is than their father,* she thought. *Danny had little interest in our girls. Or me either, unless he was drunk, that is. Then he either turned randy or mean. Or, God help me, both.* She cringed at the memory of how he violently used her. *I'll wager Sean is a gentle lover.* She blushed and pushed the thought aside. *Shame on you for such thoughts.*

"Mary! Kerry! Let the poor man up. It's a wonder he still comes by."

Sean got to his feet. "I don't mind them a bit. Your girls are angels on earth, if ever there were any." He patted Mary on the head and said, "Give this milk to your mother."

"They adore you, no doubt of that. They so love your visits. Thank you for the milk as well. Your kindness to them – to us – is a gift."

Sean smiled. "Think nothing of it. Speaking of gifts… girls, what do you suppose I have in my pocket?" He produced the tiny bundle and handed it to Kerry. On seeing the candy, they let out that piercing but heartwarming squeal unique only to ecstatic little girls. Mary impetuously jumped into his arms. He grimaced and put the girl down. "Easy on me, lass. Your uncle Sean has a sore shoulder."

Katie said, "And what is it about your shoulder?"

"Nothing to worry about. Just a scratch and some bruises. I'll be right as rain in the day or two."

"It didn't seem like nothing. You should let me look at it."

"No, I won't bother you with it," said Sean. "It will be fine."

"It's no bother. With all you do for us, it's the least I can do."

Sean's face reddened. "I couldn't ask you to. I'd have to remove my shirt… It wouldn't be proper."

"Nonsense," said Katie. "I'll remind you I'm a widow, not a blushing sprig of a girl. I've seen men's chests often enough."

"If… If you're sure it's no bother. I… I wouldn't want to put you at unease."

"Go on then. Let's have a look." She herded the girls toward the sleeping area. "Mary, Kerry, the two of you take your candy behind the bed curtain till I tell you to come out. And mind you, I better not see any noses peeking out." When she turned back, Sean was already unbuttoning his shirt. Katie felt her cheeks burn as he removed his shirt. She had overstated her familiarity with men and their naked chests. The truth was, she had only seen her younger brother's and, of course, her husband.

She had long noticed that Sean was a stout man, near six feet and broad shouldered, but the specimen in front of her was unexpected; her brothers were young and rail thin, and Danny was portly – soft in the middle. Looking at Sean, she thought, *Good lord, it's hard to believe that he and Danny are even the same species of animal. He looks to be chiseled from stone; just like one of those Greek statues I seen in the picture books.*

Trying to hide her nerves, she sternly told him, "Don't just stand there, sit down and let me look at you… your shoulder, that is."

Sean smiled. "I don't think I ever saw you so bossy."

"You men are all the same. The best of you will take care of others, but ain't a one of you who can take care of yourself. If it wasn't for us women, you'd all be dead in a month."

"If you don't mind me saying so, Danny was a lucky man to have those darling girls and a woman such as yourself looking out for him."

"He was my husband and your friend, and I won't speak ill of him, but Danny wasn't one to count blessings*" A drunk and a bully he was. It's a wonder you even associated with Danial. How different might my life could had been if I'd met a man such as this as a girl?*

She inspected her guests' injury. An angry purple bruise covered his upper arm, shoulder, and part of his chest. She gently explored it, feeling for lumps. "I'm not hurting you, am I?" she asked.

"No, you're as gentle as a lamb, Mrs. Sullivan."

"Good, and how many times have I told you to call me Katie?"

"Yes, ma'am."

"Let me get some water and alcohol to wash that wound. It's dirty and will get infected."

As she pulled down a bottle of whiskey from a shelf, she said, "This was Danny's; I keep it to clean out scrapes and scratches. But if you'd like a nip, you're welcome."

"No. But thank you the same."

"Of course, it's too early. Danny liked a touch a in the morning after work is all."

Sean smiled. "I remember that Danny certainly liked his whiskey. Myself, I never acquired the taste. An ale now again is enough."

I could love this man. If only we had…

"What's that look?" he said. "I haven't offended you, have I? I meant no offense to Danny, I just…"

"Nonsense," she said. "Temperance is a virtue."

As she leaned in and gingerly washed his wound, his breath tickled her neck. In all the months he had been visiting, it was the first time they stood so close or that she'd ever actually touched him. The feel of his skin sent a little flutter down deep inside, and a compelling warmth she hadn't felt in a long time. Her cheeks burnt with embarrassment. To break the building spell, she set the washcloth on the table and said, "That's better. Let's have a quick look at your back and this business will be done."

As instructed, Sean leaned forward and put his elbows on his knees. Katie noticed a long-ragged scar running from under his left shoulder to the base of his neck. "Heavens," she said, "what in the world caused such a scar?"

It was Sean's turn to feel embarrassment. He attempted to cover it with his hand. "It's an ugly thing, I know."

She pushed his hand away and said, "Nonsense. Men wear scars like badges of honor – or mementos of foolishness. I'm guessing foolishness is not a habit with you. Was it from a fire?"

In a subdued voice, Sean said, "The war – the Shiloh fight. Us and a few thousand Johnny's had a bit of a disagreement about who should or shouldn't be in Tennessee. A cavalry boy slashed me with a saber to prove his point."

"From behind? There's no honor in that."

"Honor is a thing poets and politicians go on about, and always far from the fight. Truth is, there's never much honor in any battle, just butchery. Still, I came home, he didn't, so there's that I guess."

"Does it hurt?"

"Not anymore. Your touch is quite soothing."

Without realizing it, Katie had been lightly tracing the wound with her fingers, raising goosebumps on the back of his neck. Ashamed, she quickly withdrew her hand. "I'm sorry," she gushed. "I was being overly familiar."

"No apology needed. You were being kind, nothing else."

You're on dangerous ice Katie; she said to herself. *You have no business feeling what you're feeling; put a stop to it before this becomes even more inappropriate.* "Even so, we're done here. I think you're right; a few days' rest and your shoulder will be fine. But you'll be sore for a good while; there's no doubting that."

She handed him his shirt. When he had it buttoned, she called to the girls. "You two can come out now. Mr. Collins will be fine."

Kerry piped up, "Can Uncle Sean stay for breakfast?" Mary added, "Can he take us for a walk to the river, too?"

"No, darling. We have to go to church, and he has his own family to tend to. We've kept him far too long already."

Mary whined, "Please, Uncle Sean. Please stay for a while longer."

Katie thought, *they so miss having a father, even one that ignored them more than not. It's no wonder they adore Sean so.*

Sean tousled her hair and said, "You heard your mother; it's time for me to leave. But I'll be back soon enough." He looked at Katie and added, "If that's all right, of course."

She replied, "You are welcome here anytime, you know that."

Sean bent down and hugged the girls. Then he took Katie's hand and said, "Thank you for your kindness… Katie."

Her breath caught at his touch. Flustered, she withdrew her hand and moved to the door. "You are more than welcome. Now, be on your way. Your wife will be worried about you." *And I hope she knows just how fortunate she is.*

*****

Sean ambled home worried. *Katie seemed a bit off at the end. She never ushered me out like that before.* His stomach knotted. *I was too forward, that's how it was. What was I doing taking her hand as I did. I would truly miss the girls if I've gone and made myself unwelcome. Truth be told, I've grown fond of Katie too; too fond, I suppose. If she knew my thoughts, she'd show me the door for good. She's a good lass – not quick to temper. Still, I'll put my manners on a tighter leash from here on.*

He walked in to an empty house. "Well, I've gone and missed church." *That's a blessing*, he thought, *but I'll pay for it when she comes home.* He pulled off his clothes and fell into bed. Thoughts of Katie lightly touching his scar, then of Mary's little arms hugging him, drifted through his mind. Within minutes, he was sleeping.

The rattle of a skillet on the stove woke him up. Sitting on the edge of the bed, he tried to gather himself. He stretched and winced at the pain in his shoulder. He was still buttoning his pants when he walked into the kitchen. "What time is it?"

Without looking at him, Maggie said, "Past noon. Have you eaten?"

"Not a thing. I could do with a good meal."

"You'll have to make do with some ham and potatoes."

Sean sniffed. "It smells like heaven, it does. None can beat you in the kitchen, and I've said as much to any who cared to listen."

Maggie remained focused on her cooking. She coolly replied, "Sure you have, and pigs' fly. Your flattery won't excuse you're coming home late and missing church. I suppose you and the boys were celebrating yesterday's fire." She turned to confront him. "Saints preserve us – what happened to you? You're bruised from tail to nose."

"I was a little too close to the building when she fell."

Maggie's expression didn't soften, or her tone. "I'd say you were. It's a good thing you're built like an ox, because you're no smarter than one. Your foolishness will leave me a widow someday. Then where will I be?"

"Happier I guess."

Maggie waved off his comment dismissively. "Oh, don't be playing the martyr. You know every word I say is true."

"You could show a little sympathy."

"I'll give it when you deserve it. Is that where you were then this morning? Did you have a doctor look at your shoulder?"

"That wouldn't be necessary now, would it? I had errands to run is all. Speaking of it, I had a visit with Mrs. O'Leary. She tells me Liam is running with a rough crowd."

"Catherine should mind her own business. Well, I suppose it's good you stopped by the Dairy. Where is it then?"

"Where's what?"

"Are you thick? Whatever had you stop is what."

Sean paused; wanting to choose his words carefully. He didn't want to argue again, but watching Maggie's jaw set and brow furrow told him a storm was coming. She growled, "Oh, I see it now. You've been visiting that woman and her brats again."

"Now Maggie, there's no need in getting your back up."

"No? Do you understand how humiliating it is? Me going to church alone, like a widow, and all the time my husband is doing God knows what with a little trollop?"

Sean raised his hands in submission. "I am sorry I missed church, but you have no reason to talk that way. We've fought this fight before, accept the truth of it. I only looked in on Danny's little girls like I promised I would. There is nothing unholy happening between me and Katie---."

"Katie now, is it? Well, ain't that charming. Don't think me a fool. A man don't visit a woman like that out of charity alone."

"A woman like that? You mean a good and proper woman."

Maggie slammed the skillet down. "Don't be telling me what I mean. No good and proper woman spends her nights working in a brothel."

"She doesn't work in a brothel. She cooks and serves at the hotel eatery."

"That eatery is nothing more than a saloon that serves the drunks food, and you know it. And don't play naïve with me. Everyone knows what sort of business gets done on the second floor of that so-called hotel."

"I know nothing of the second floor or what goes on there, but I do know she serves food and nothing else."

"Oh, you are a fool. That little piece of Sodom and Gomorrah you call a hotel is run by big Mike McDonald. Everybody knows how things go with him. Jobs are scarce, and there's no shortage of desperate women looking for work. So, just how do you think she got that job?"

"She asked I suppose."

Maggie scoffed. "Just asked? There's a treasure. Big Mike is a whore monger if ever one walked. Don't kid yourself about your *innocent* little Katie. She got that job by spreading her legs like every other girl there; and she likely keeps it the same way. And if she ain't entertaining men on the second floor yet, she will be soon enough."

"Enough!" snapped Sean. "That's vile gossip, and it's beneath you. She's done nothing to you that deserves your scorn. She's a poor widow with hungry children to feed – nothing more."

"Maybe, maybe not. But know this: no woman *chooses* to let foul men grunt and drool on her for a living. Every one of those whores in that wicked place has some sad and troubled story. The devil preys on the desperate, and he ruins souls a little at a time. Your Mrs. Sullivan will be no different, if she's not lowered herself yet – it'll happen soon enough."

"That's hateful gossip is all, she doesn't have it in her. And even if she did, who are you to judge? You spit venom out of foolish jealousy. You think low of me. Her, nor I have done nothing to warrant your wrath."

"Jealousy? You are a dense one. I don't give a tinker's damn what you do with her. Men are what men are, and they rut where they can. If she wants to lift the burden of my wifely duties, I'm all for it. I've paid my dues, haven't I."

"A burden, is it? There's a cold thing to say."

"It's the truth now, isn't it? Since I've gone barren, there's no good reason for accommodating your base urges anymore. If she's willing to lay with you, let her have at it, I say."

"At thirty-seven? You're not barren, and you know it. You're just cold hearted."

"Am I? I've submitted to you often enough since the stillbirth. If I could conceive, I would have. It ruined me. Losing that little girl was a sorrow, but I am at least done with that awful obligation."

"If that's how you feel, then why are you so worked up over this imagined nonsense with Mrs. Sullivan?"

"Imagined? Do what you want, see if I care. But I won't be humiliated by your flaunting your sins in the light of day. If you want to see her, then skulk around the hotel at night like all her others. But you'll act proper in the light of day. And if you get her with child, you won't be taking food off my table to raise the bastard. It's bad enough that me and Liam do without that which goes to those brats."

Sean shook his head. "This is all in your imagination. You do without nothing. And I am not carrying on. I tell you she is nothing like…"

Maggie put a plate of food on the table and interrupted him. "… Nonsense, is it? We'll see how she turns out soon enough. This city is awash in filth, and crime and immorality. Live in squalor and sooner or later you get dirty; that's what I say. Look at our Liam."

"Liam is heading for trouble. There's what we should be discussing."

"What's to discuss? This city, this life, has corrupted him. We've buried three children because of this life, and now our only son is headed for a violent death or prison. If you cared about him, or me, you would take us away from this awful place, and to a proper home – a place with fresh air and green grass."

"We've been over that road and back. You're dreaming if you think there's a life for us out there in the countryside. We're better off here, with our own people – hard as it is."

"Better off? Better off, you say? Our Liam is almost lost to us. That's no one's fault but yours. We live in a big country full of opportunity, and here we sit in squalor and desperation, because you're not man enough to leave the familiar. Or is it you can't bring yourself to leave your whore?"

"Get it through your head! I look in on Danny's children, nothing more."

"Then why do you cling to this awful place when Eden is but a train ride away?"

"Maggie, you're a dreamer; God love you for it. But I've seen that country you talk about. It's mostly full of starving farmers barely scratching out a living and a few wealthy swells who would cheat you blind given the chance. The only thing they have in common is they all praise Jesus on Sunday, and spend the rest of the week hating the darkies and us Irish."

"It ain't all like that. My cousin says Quincy…"

"I'm tired of hearing about Quincy and your cousin. The truth of it is, you'd be as miserable there as here. And if we did leave, what makes you think Liam would follow?"

"You will hear me for once. Elizabeth says that Quincy is a river town, but it's clean and bustling. There's plenty of work, if you don't want to farm. There's plenty of Catholics too – mostly Germans, but some of our folk as well. She says our people are treated well enough. Sean, it's a place like the old country."

"Tis no place like the old country, not west or south or anywhere else. What you're looking for ain't to be found this side of heaven, Maggie."

"And what is that?"

"Contentment – that's what you seek, and you won't find it. Even if we went to your Quincy town, or anywhere else, we'd be packing our troubles with us. We brought them with us from

Ireland, and we toted them here from New York. Our problems aren't with this place Maggie, it's *us* making us unhappy."

"You mean me, don't you? Not *us*, it's me you're blaming."

Sean didn't want to bicker anymore. He stood to leave. "I said what I meant. Thank you for the hash. It was a fine meal."

As he went out the door, she called after him. "Well, go on then. Go to the bar with your so-called friends, or maybe go visit your precious Mrs. Sullivan. Explain to her how this city is the promised land. See what *she* has to say about it."

This page left blank

Chapter 4

It was a good plan, and it worked, Thought Liam. *I just hope Johnny doesn't muck it up now.*

He didn't care for sitting in saloons; they smelled foul, and he had little use for drunks. The waitress had said Big Mike would be down in a minute or two. That was nearly an hour ago. Liam picked at his ham and cabbage, as much to occupy himself as out of hunger.

"Remember now," said Johnny, "let me do the talkin. Mike is easy put off."

Johnny is nervous, Liam thought. *Too nervous. He claims to be friends with McDonald, but something is up his arse. Johnny is a good enough fellow, but he seems off kilter – fidgety, like a squirrel.*

The sound of laughter caught his attention. The serving woman was slapping a man's hand away from her bottom. He had been watching her work on and off for the last thirty minutes. She seemed in constant motion, bustling between the tables, the bar, and the kitchen. He wondered how she kept up the pace.

She was a pretty woman, maybe 25 or 30, with strawberry hair and a delicate complexion. Mostly, the men ignored her, except when yelling out for more beer – most, not all. A few men had tried grabbing her; when they did, she would force a smile and push their hands away. Just now, a particularly obnoxious drunk managed to pull her onto his lap. He pawed at her breast before she could escape. She looked flustered. That got a hardy laugh from the crowd.

What kind of woman works in such a place? He thought. *I wonder if she is one of the upstairs girls too? Probably, I guess. No decent woman would be here. Then again, she doesn't have that hardness about her. I know the look of an alley cat. They act all sweet and friendly, but there's always something gone dead and cold in them. She looks out of place here; but then I suppose I do too. I wonder...*

A portly man dropped heavily into a chair across the table. *And so, this is the big man everyone talks about,* thought Liam. He noticed the rosy cheeks and puffy eyes of a hard drinker. *He's bloated and short of breath – likely hasn't done a day's work in 10 years. Still, those expensive clothes and sharp eyes tell a story, now don't they. This piggy has teeth. I can see that plain enough.*

Big Mike fixed a hard glare on Liam, even as he spoke to Johnny. "Well then, Johnny Gallagher, what is it you think will interest me?"

Johnny shifted uneasily in his seat. "I know you're a busy man, so I'll get to it. I've got some goods you'll be interested in."

"Oh, have you now. I'll make this short. I've got no interest in peddling stolen property. There is plenty enough of those gents in the alleys; go bother them."

"Begging your pardon, Mr. McDonald, but as I told Liam here, this is something you will like."

"Don't be cagey, boy. What is it then?"

"Whiskey...," said Johnny. "... lots of it."

Big Mike leaned back and folded his arms above his impressive gut. "I buy my whiskey from James Shannon. I'm not interested in whatever poison you two have cooked up in your cellar."

"But that's the thing, Mr. McDonald. It is Shannon's whiskey, and we can sell it to you for half the price you're paying now."

With a laugh, the big man replied, "Is that right? You two lifted a few bottles of whiskey, have you? Ain't that just well and dandy? I'll tell you what, this one time, I'll give you 2 bits a bottle. But mind you, there won't be any talk of it. I don't want old man Shannon catching wind that I paid for some of his stolen goods. He's a good supplier, and I don't need to ruffle his feathers."

Liam thought, *Well Johnny, this ain't going to plan now, is it?*

"You're not seeing the whole of it, Mr. McDonald," said Johnny. "It ain't a few bottles, it's three cases, and we can get more each week if it suits you."

"Are you daft? Three cases? Shannon's knickers are likely on fire already. You won't get out alive breaking in again. And by the by, what will he be saying when I stop buying his whiskey, but still selling it? No boys, what I should be doing is giving the both of you to him, just to build the goodwill. He's likely to sell me three cases at cost for the favor."

Liam couldn't sit quietly any longer. "And suppose Mr. Shannon didn't know the product was missing? And suppose you could double your profit on each sale? And what if it could be done every other week? All without risk to you? Would that interest you?"

McDonald fixed his gaze on Liam. "I wondered if you had a tongue. Liam, is it?"

"It is."

"Alright Liam, you've piqued my curiosity. Exactly what are you proposing, lad?"

"It's plain enough. You buy your usual product from Mr. Shannon as always. You sell it as you always have and make whatever profit you always do. But, you also buy extra cases from us each week at half your usual cost. *Those* you sell out the backdoor for whatever price suits you."

"I see. And Shannon won't miss three cases a week? Are you turning water into whiskey like some sort of Irish messiah, or are you pulling it from a unicorn's backside?"

Liam shrugged nonchalantly. "How we get it is likely a topic best left alone – for both of us, I would think."

"You got sand boy. I'll give you that." McDonald looked over his shoulder and bellowed. "Katie, fetch us three lagers."

The woman stopped what she was doing and ran to the bar.

"Sand or not, I don't do business blind. You'll tell me what…"

The server arrived with the beer. "Here you are Mr. McDonald."

"That's a good girl, Katie. And haven't I told you to call me Mike?"

McDonald's hand snaked behind Katie when he spoke. There wasn't any doubt where it landed. She didn't push it away like she did the others. The thin smiled stayed frozen on her lips, but it didn't hide the humiliation or what Liam guessed was fear in her eyes. Big Mike swatted her bottom and told her to go back to work.

Johnny said, "There's a fine-looking woman. I'll be paying her a visit upstairs."

"Not until I've broken her in first, you won't," said McDonald.

A conspirator's smile lit up Johnny's face. "What are you waiting for?"

"Let's say she's a special project. She has a lot of smarts, and is not naive. Still, she's fool enough to think that she has choices." He took a swig of ale. "You have to be patient with that kind; let her adjust to her situation. She's all proper now, but soon enough she'll understand that there are worse fates. I'll enjoy putting her in her place, that I'll tell you."

"If anybody could turn her out for the second floor, it'd be you. You're a charmer, Mr. McDonald, everybody says so," said Johnny.

"Take your lips off my ass, boy. It ain't about charm, it's about power. And speaking of going upstairs, that's a good idea. Johnny, take your beer and go upstairs and tell Kitty that I said to give you a girl on the house."

"Liam too, I hope."

"He'll stay here with me and finish our talk."

"But…" Johnny started.

"Go on. Your Liam will be up shortly."

Johnny smiled at the prospect of what waited upstairs, thanked his host, and quickly left.

McDonald returned his attention to Liam. "Now boy, let's stop dancing. I want to know what you and Gallagher are up to."

Liam shifted uncomfortably in his seat. "Maybe you should be talking to Johnny. This was his doing, not mine. I was just along to help him out."

"Don't play me for a fool, boy. Johnny is as mean as a badger, but ain't no smarter than one either. If this was all his doing, I'd be hearing about old man Shannon's head being bashed in by robbers. No sir, whatever is going on here sounds sharp, and Johnny is a blunt tool. Now, stop the games and tell me what you two are up to."

"It ain't so much, really. Shannon ages his whiskey in big oak barrels; each one close to fifty gallons, I guess. He fills a new one every few days and bottles the stuff from the oldest ones. What we do is… we go in at night and skim some off the top of the barrel and replace it with water. Then we bottle it and melt red wax over the corks just like Shannon does. We get the whiskey and no one's the wiser. Simple enough, I figure."

McDonald laughed and said, "Simple enough, is it? What will happen when folks all over Chicago start carping about watered down whiskey?"

Liam absent mindedly tapped the table with his knuckles. "We bring our own water, and it's flavored a bit with charcoal. The trick is to not get greedy; we don't take more than a gallon at a time, and never twice from the same barrel. No one will tell the difference."

"That's clever enough. And what of the night watchman? Where is he while you're pilfering the goods?"

"I know the man. He's a good enough fellow, but a poor excuse of a watchman. We pay him to look the other way. He's happy enough."

"Shannon won't miss the bottles?" asked Mike.

"We don't use his. We collect empties in the alleys behind the saloons. You've donated a fair share, yourself."

"So, you're selling me back my own bottles, are you? Like I said before, you got some sand in you. All right, I'll buy your whiskey, two or three cases a week as you can manage, at two bits a bottle.

But I can't be risking selling unaccounted for product. For safety's sake, I think I'll ship it south to Peoria. I got associates there; in fact, you and Johnny can transport it – a little extra cash. If your game, that is."

"Who are these associates?" asked Liam.

"If you need to know a thing, I'll tell you. Remember, curiosity kills cats."

"I ain't keen on mixing in with people I don't know. Foolishness kills more than cats."

"Don't worry about it, they're with me, that's enough to keep you whole. I just want you along to handle the transactions. Johnny ain't up to that. He can provide muscle, if need be, but if you do this proper there won't be call for it." Big Mike leaned forward and added, "I like you, lad. I think I could use someone of your talents for some other things I have in mind. Come work for me."

Again, Liam shifted in his seat uncomfortably. "Johnny will be happy to hear about the whiskey. The thing is, I was only in it for some laughs – I just wanted to see if I could get away with it, you know."

"Well, you did get away with it, and fairly tidy work to boot. But it's reckless to risk so much for only laughs and a few coins. I can help you make some real money."

"What kind of work are you suggesting?"

"For one I was thinking you could visit the butcher shoppe over on LaSalle – pick me up some steaks."

Liam shrugged. "You mean run errands for you? There's money in that?"

A gleam sparkled in the fat man's eyes. "I run a restaurant and meat is pricey. I'm thinking more like what you did with the whiskey. Make a midnight visit and relieve him of a few hundred pounds of beef and pork."

Look at him, thought Liam. *He looks like a toad, grinning like that.* "Mr. McDonald – sir – I mean no disrespect. It's none of my business how you make your living, but I don't think I would feel comfortable living off other people's backs. I don't think it would set right, if you know what I mean."

"You'll steal whiskey but not meat? There's a peculiar split in your principles, boy."

Liam said, "Shannon is a prick. I got no beef with the butcher."

McDonald chuckled. "That's a good one - no beef with the butcher. You're a hypocrite lad. I thought better of you."

"Oh," said Liam, "how's that?"

"Son, living off other people's backs is the way of the world. Liking them or not has nothing to do with it. When you were a child, you lived off the sweat of your father. Old Man Shannon lives off the back of his employees. The politicians live off the back of Mr. Shannon. I tell you lad, there are only two kinds of people in the world, sheep and wolves. I won't speak for you, but being somebody's fool, don't sit with me very well. Look around you boy, you and me are Irish. We've been beaten down and taken from for generations, both here and across the water. Nothing will change until we push back, until we *take* our fair share, too."

"Again, no disrespect, but you take from your own people."

"Sheep are sheep," said McDonald. "I'm not particular about which breed I sheer. Lad, work for me or don't, I couldn't care less. But know this: eventually you'll realize that you're either going to let the powerful use you until they have ground you down to nothing, or you can make opportunities for yourself. And don't fool yourself, no one is going to help a poor Irish kid. If you want something, you'll need to take it."

"My father calls this the land of opportunity, though I ain't seen it. Still, there are laws to be obeyed."

McDonald spit on the floor and wiped his mouth with his sleeve. "The law? What do you know about the law? What you call the law is there to keep the sheep corralled. I tell you this, the men in fine suits and fancy carriages live by a different set of laws. Me, I have my own law."

"What law is that?"

"The law of nature, the strong prosper, the timid suffer."

"My pop says there's honor in hard work?"

"Is there honor in being poor, in being hungry? Tell me Liam, does your father work hard? Did his father before him? What have they to show for it? You may not like it, but the honest man never gets ahead. I know most of those so-called respectable well to do's uptown, wolves and jackals, the whole lot. That's just the way of it. The sooner you understand that, the better."

"I ain't arguing, but I need to think about it."

"Do that, Liam."

"Just out of curiosity, how much would you pay me for that meat?" asked Liam.

"A hundred pounds would be worth ten dollars. But, I'm offering you more than money. There's respect and security too. If you're with me, you'll be a prince in this city. The sheep will step aside for you on the sidewalk. There are other benefits too. Tell me, Liam, have you been with a woman before?"

Liam bristled at the question. "Sure, a few times."

"Practice makes perfect, doesn't it? While you're thinking on my offer, go on upstairs and get yourself some education."

As Liam walked away, Big Mike smiled and said to himself, "Another fish netted."

*****

Liam climbed the stairs, awash in confusion and nerves. His mouth tasted coppery, and his fingers tingled. He knew all too well what working for Mike meant. *I saw myself as one of those fella's in that Robinhood story – this ain't that. Still, what the fat fucker said made sense. Big Mike is a man to be wary of, but this could be just the thing. On my own, I won't make headway – likely get pinched too. Mike can provide protection and I could make some real money. I sure don't want to end up like my father, breaking my back working for scraps and a wife like my mother harping at me all day and night. Domestic bliss? - no thank you. It'd be easier to buy love an hour at a time and leave it there. It seems the smart play to look at the butcher shop, see what's what. If it's quick and easy, I could do well.*

As he climbed the stairs, he heard Johnny grunting like a wounded animal. He had a mind to go back downstairs, but thought it would be foolish not to at least see what his girl looked like. He stopped, gob smacked, on the foyer of the second floor. In the doorway stood the most beautiful creature he ever saw. She was young, more girl than woman, with long, flowing curls of auburn hair. Her silk robe hung open, covering little of her porcelain skin.

She glanced at him, and completely unbothered by her indecency, continued speaking with an older woman.

Liam stood transfixed as he drank in every inch of her. The spell was broken when the girl's green eyes fixed on him. "And what are you staring at?"

Liam wasn't sure where the words came from, but they came. "An angel fallen from heaven, I think."

It surprised Liam that the girl, who had seemed so unconcerned at standing near naked in front of him, blushed so at the compliment. She self-consciously gathered her robe closed and snapped, "What? Who are…."

"My name is Liam, I'm glad…."

"Well, you can put away the sweet words. For all your charm, you're still a scoundrel. A gentleman doesn't stare at a woman like she's some odd curiosity."

"And a lady doesn't parade naked in front of strangers."

"From the look of you, I'm the first you've seen." With that, she retreated to her room and slammed the door.

The old woman smiled at Liam and said, "Well boy, you put her on her heal."

"Sorry."

"Don't be. That little kitten could stand to have her claws dulled. Big Mike sent you up here, did he? Johnny said you would be up in a bit. I'll fix you up with Mary; she'll take good care of you."

Liam never took his eyes off the door. "Was that Mary just now?"

"No. That was Rose."

"Rose, is it? If it's all the same, I'd like to spend some time with her."

The old woman laughed. "I bet you would, and devils want a cold drink. Rose is Big Mike's special girl. No one touches her but Mr. McDonald himself."

"She's on the young side for being his lover, don't you think?"

That earned another chuckle from Kitty. "Lover? Boy, you are green, aren't you? Big Mike don't love nobody but Big Mike. She is more of a pet if you had to put a name on it. Now, go on down to the end of the hall. Knock and tell Mary that Kitty sent you in. You'll be happy enough."

A muffled woman's voice issued from the room where Johnny was rutting. "I told you no!"

Kitty glared at the door, then turned to Liam. "Don't be thinking you can get overly rough either. Have your fun, but I best not see any bite marks or bruises on Mary."

"I would never…"

"Sure you would never, and haven't I heard that before. Including from your friend Johnny. He's a mean one; I won't have that happening again. You remember what I say; If you hurt her, you'll get paid back double in the alley later."

"Maybe I should leave," said Liam.

"Oh, don't be putting your tail between your legs. I'm just looking out for my girls. Now go on down the hall. Mary will like entertaining you, I can tell."

Liam started down the hall, but stopped. "Mam, I was just wondering. How old is Rose?"

The old woman frowned. "She's been here near a year now; I suppose that puts her nigh on to eighteen. But, listen close, if you value your neck, you'll put her out of your head and keep a distance. Mike ain't a man to cross."

Newspaper sketch of Big Mike McDonald

Circa 1890, unknown author

This page left blank

Chapter 5

It isn't the smell that burrows into you – not that the stench of rot and shit and death isn't hard to stomach. No, it's the sounds I hate – the moans, the screams, and worse yet, the crying. After all the years since the war, the sound of a grown man crying still put an empty feeling in his gut. *If it weren't Patty,* he thought, *horses couldn't drag me in here.*

As they walked down the ward, past the long row of beds bearing the sick and dying, Sean watched Liam closely. The boy was as white as a ghost. *For all his bravado, and talk about being a wolf among sheep, the boy is still tender. This place is a palace compared to the hospital tents in Vicksburg, or Chattanooga, or Shiloh – especially Shiloh. Could Liam have come through those horrors, the screams, the piles of arms and legs everywhere, the dead stacked like cord wood? Likely not, thank God he was spared.*

"You alright boy? You look a little peaked."

Liam bristled. "I'm fine. But I don't see why you brought me to this… this place."

"Patty could do to see a friendly face or two. He's always been fond of you."

Liam continued to stare straight ahead, avoiding the despair on either side of the aisle. "I haven't seen him in years."

"You're young; a year or two seems like a long time to you. To a man Patty's age, it was just around the corner."

They found Patty lying on a cot, staring absently at some unknown thing. The sight of him unsettled Sean. The normally robust man looked deathly pale. He aged years in the few days since the accident and seemed somehow to have shrunk.

A wan smile spread across Patty's face when he recognized his friends. "Sean darlin', you've come to see your old friend. And you brought young Liam to boot."

"How goes it Patty?" asked Sean.

"It goes pretty good – all in all."

"And the leg?"

Patty pulled the sheet aside; his left leg ended just below the knee, a bloody linen bandage covered the stump. "They took the leg – said too much bone got ruined. The gangrene was inevitable had they left it on."

"Jesus!" gasped Liam.

Though in pain, Patty managed a chuckle. "Breathe easy boy, it's just a leg; I've got another. It's just the half of one at that."

Sean clasped Patty's shoulder. "I'm sorry Patty."

"Ain't no sense in sorry. I kept all my parts traipsing through Dixie; the devil wanted his due is all."

"Now there's a jolly thought, gloom and doom await." said Sean.

"Don't you worry Sean, God loves you, he does. The angels are protecting you."

Sean laughed, then said, "Are they now? They seem to throw a lot of trouble at me."

"No more than you can handle, and you can handle a lot, my friend. As for me, a leg is as good as anything to lose – better than an arm – or my wee willy, God forbid."

Liam interjected, "Pardon me for saying so, Mr. Doyle, but you seem awfully composed for a man who lost a leg. I'd be…"

"You'd be what, young Liam – bitter? Sobbing like a little girl? What's the good in any of that? If not for your father, I'd been burned alive. I'll take limping around as a blessing."

"You lost your leg, and for what? It's all…"

"Liam!" snapped Sean. "That'll be enough. I'm sorry Patty. He is overfond of speaking his mind."

"Let him speak Sean. His head is as good as most others."

"I'm sorry Mr. Doyle. But I can't help but think that you lost your leg fighting a fire in a building that fell down anyway. And you did it for some lordly hob-nobber who wouldn't spit on you if you were on fire. Ain't it all just a fool's game, and you came up short?"

Patty shifted in the bed, groaning as he pulled himself up. "A fool's game, is it? You have a narrow view lad. I suppose that's a privilege of youth. Me and your father, and all the rest of us, fought a fire that would have spread – maybe taken twenty or thirty homes. I paid a steep price, but not for nothing."

"And do any of them care a lick for you? Life is a dogfight. As I see it, a man must take care of himself first."

"Aw Liam, I know your father didn't put such nonsense in your head. I don't know the man who owned that warehouse. Maybe he's the greedy prick you suggest; maybe he's a lovely man. And I don't know the people who live in those houses we saved; some may be saints – others sinners. I don't know or need to. Many a man isn't worth the dirt he stands on. There's no shortage of liars and cheats, and people who hate others because they hate themselves. But those folks are in the minority. Most people are decent enough and help when they can."

"And what does it get them? Nothing is all."

Patty shook his head. "Why does it have to pay? Look at your father there. Do you know he brought me out of that burning building – crawling over smoldering trash and muck with me on his back – knowing he was signing his own death warrant? I begged him to leave me, but he wouldn't because he's an honorable man. A man who values others as much as himself. And those two fellas who helped us out of that place – they didn't know us from Adam, and they knew the danger, but they came on none the less. Why? Because it was the right thing to do."

 Patty reached out and took Liam's hand. "Don't you see son, If we treat life like it's a dogfight, we're no better than a dog ourselves."

Liam shook his head. "I'm sorry about your leg – I am. Still, if a man is going to make something in this world, he has to fight and scratch and claw. Nobody will put out a hand, at least that ain't holding a club. Nature has it right, there's wolves and sheep – eat or be eaten."

"Liam," said Patty. "You're right, life is hard – harder for some than others. I ain't an educated man, nor a smart one. But I know a thing or two about people. No one gets through this life alone. We all depend on the grace of each other. Those wolves, as you call them, are more like vultures. Looking for an easy meal is all. And they spread misery wherever they go. I lost my leg doing the right thing. It's a tragedy – it is. But I'll sleep at night knowing the world isn't worse off for me being in it. That's enough. Your father is a good man, better than most I've met. You would do well to learn from him. It's what you give that measures you, not what you have. Anyway, I'm just a one-legged old Mick, so what do I know?"

Sean said, "You know plenty, my friend, but you're too generous with me. Now, when can you go home to your loving wife?"

"Loving wife? Did I get a new one while I was asleep?"

"Talk like that, and she'll kick your crutches out from beneath you."

"She likely will regardless. No matter though, in a day or two they'll send me home. I hear tell that the lovely city of Chicago will pay to fit me with a peg for my leg – probably in a month."

Sean said, "You'll look like a pirate. It'll suit you."

"I'll look like every other old man clomping around. The damned war filled the countryside with them… us."

"True enough, and they seem to get on with life alright; so will you. Do you need anything?" asked Sean.

"No, but thank you the same. I'll hobble around fine."

"Have you thought about what's next for you? I'd be pleased to ask around about work. I'll give you what I can in the meantime."

"I won't be needing your charity, Sean." Patty chuckled and added, "Would you believe it, Chief Snider – the great Teutonic prick himself – came by this morning. He said he spoke with his brother-in-law – he runs a brewery you know. Anyway, he said they would find work for me; could have knocked me down with a feather. Who would have thought that mean old bastard would go out of his way to help me out?" He looked at Liam. "Like I said, people are better than you think."

Liam shrugged. "As I see it, he was responsible for what happened to you. Getting you a job at slave wages isn't much by way of restitution."

"And where did you get the notion that the Chief was responsible for my leg? He owed me nothing; getting me work was a kindness and I'll be happy to earn a fair living. There is no shortage of men looking for work."

"Liam," said Sean, "Will you wait for me outside, please? I want to talk with Patty alone for a moment."

When Liam was out of earshot, Sean asked, "Are you sure you won't be needing help? This is me talking; don't let your pride do you harm."

"You'd be doing good by me if you stopped by now and again to visit… at least until I am on my feet… er… foot. The Mrs. may have some needs you could help with too." He chuckled and added, "To be clear, not the kind of help you are giving Danny's widow, though."

"Jesus Patty, that again? I told you prior there is nothing happening…"

"… Again, I am having some fun with you, Sean. Although I suspect your Maggie is a bit nervous."

"Maggie doesn't like me enough to care, truth be told."

"I am sorry about that. A cold home is a prison, it is. And, I have to tell you, I see now why Liam worries you so. He's got things twisted up a bit."

Sean sighed. "He has a good heart buried in that puffed out chest. I suspect sooner or later he'll see the world for what it is. I just hope he doesn't hang himself before he does."

This page left blank

Chapter 6

Kerry wrinkled her nose. "Uncle Sean, you smell like smoke."

"There was another fire last night, sweetheart. Your Uncle Sean had to put it out."

"My daddy used to put out fires too… till he went away."

"That's right darling girl. Your daddy and I put out fires together."

Kerry snuggled closer against his chest. "Are you going to be our daddy someday?"

Katie looked mortified. "Kerry, we spoke about this…"

Sean hugged the little girl. "Honey, I am more like your daddy's special helper. But you and your sister are precious little angels to me."

Katie pulled her daughter away, hugged her and said, "He may think you an angel, but I know you're a little scamp." A tickle of the ribs and a light pat on the bottom elicited a giggle as Kerry ran to join her sister in the kitchen.

To Sean, Katie said, "I apologize if she made you uncomfortable."

"You never need apologize for the girls; you know that."

As was always the case, seeing him with the girls brought up feelings she knew she shouldn't have. She changed the subject. "And why were you working with a bad shoulder… would a few days off kill you?"

"No work, no pay. Besides, it's mending just fine – just a day or two more and all will be right."

She asked, "So what burnt last night?"

"Just a wood shed. The fella was splitting logs and tossed his cigar – lit off the yard and got into the shed."

"People should be more careful."

"True enough, but I never seen it so dry. It doesn't take much of a start."

Katie sat on a chair by the table. "There're too many fires these days. I worry about you."

"No need in worrying, the lord will come for me in his own time."

"Danny said the same, and he's gone now, isn't he? It would be hard on the girls to lose you too."

"And you?"

More than you'll ever know. "I wish you had different work is all."

"I could say the same." He regretted it as soon as he said it.

Her face reddened. *Oh God! He's heard, but how?* Humiliation brought on anger. "Oh, and why is that?"

"I… I know working nights is hard."

"You're worried about my sleep, are you? How lovely."

To the girls, Katie said, "Go across the hall and see Mrs. Carmichael."

Mary pouted. "We want to stay with Uncle Sean."

"Don't sass. Do as I say or I'll tan your bottom."

When the girls had sulked out, Sean said, "I've upset you, I'm sorry."

"I'm not upset, just curious. What aren't you saying?" … *please lord, don't let him know.*

"Let it be Katie. It's none of my affair."

"It *isn't* your affair, but I want you to speak your mind anyway."

"It's just that I know how things are there… I hear stories."

"Stories about me?" demanded Katie.

"No! Just stories about the hotel, about Mike…"

"What do you hear?"

"It's a rough crowd, is all. I suspect they can be disrespectful to a woman."

"And?"

"And nothing. I wish you didn't have to be around that sort."

Katie could feel her face burn in equal parts embarrassment and anger. She had made peace with what others thought of her working at the hotel. But not so with Sean, his opinion mattered – greatly. She said, "And no decent woman would expose herself to that sort. Is that it?"

"I said no such thing. You're there because you need money to take care of your children. I just wish you could find other employment."

"I wish it too, but just how do you suggest I do that? Thanks to that damn war, there are thousands of widows in this city; and wives supporting crippled husbands too. There's more than there are jobs, I can tell you."

"Katie, please don't take offense. I know all that. I only wish you had better opportunities."

"Opportunities? What world do you live in? I'm an Irish woman who never saw the inside of a schoolroom. What opportunities do you think I have? I'm lucky to have any job at all. You've no right to judge me!"

"Katie, I swear, I don't judge you. I think the world of you. You're dear to me, I worry is all."

"Worry about what?"… *Do you know?…* "And what's this about Big Mike?"

Sean sighed. "Let's let it go."

"You don't think I hear the whispers. Tell me what your wife and the other women say of me and Mike."

"I don't believe a word of it."

"Tell me," insisted Katie.

"I hear that Mike abuses the women who work for him. Makes demands of them."

There it is, he's heard somehow. "So, you think I am laying down for Mike. That I'm one of his… his whores, is that it."

"Of course not! I would never think such a thing. You're the finest woman I know. But I worry he will harm you."

And how fine a woman will you think of me when you hear that he is making those demands, and I'll likely have no choice but to submit? What then, Mr. Collins? How will I ever face you when those whispers are true? "That's a fine thing now, isn't it? You're being worried about my reputation and all."

"As I said, Katie, I worry…"

"Tell me, Mr. Collins, are you worried about what the old women whisper about us?"

"We've done nothing to be ashamed of."

"Sure, we haven't. But then a woman working where I do, I am guessing you expect we will sooner or later. Isn't that right?"

"Don't say that! I'd never take advantage of you, Katie. And I don't care what wagging tongues go on about. I've never wanted more than to take care of you and the girls."

She said, "I can take care of myself, thank you very much. I think it best you leave now."

"Will I be welcome back?"

Katie stood. "I am not sure. Let me think on it."

Sean pleaded. "Don't be angry. You and the girls are dear to me. I only spoke from worry. Please don't shut me out."

She walked him to the door. "As I said, I can look after myself."

*****

Sean walked away, confused and heartbroken. What have I done? I've never seen her like that? It was so unlike her. I can't leave things like this. I'll wait a few days and talk to her again – apologize.

*****

Once the door was shut, she sat on the floor and cried – trapped, terrified, and humiliated.

Being with Sean reminded her of the life she so desperately wanted, although she knew she couldn't have it. But at least she felt worthy of it. Now she felt dirty and trapped.

The night before, Big Mike had made a pass at her – again. She had been fending off his advances for weeks; this time was different. He had pulled her onto his lap and said, "It's time you and I discuss what's expected of you. Come see me in my private office after you're done working."

The implication was clear enough, and she had no illusions about what he expected or her situation – let him have his way or lose her job. In desperation, she confided in the two cooks, Ruth and Anna. She hoped for sympathy and advice. What she got was laughter.

The old woman, Ruth, was dismissive. "Just give him what he wants," she had said. "Ten minutes on your back or maybe on your knees, and it'd be all over. I did it; he only lasted a minute or two."

When Katie said she couldn't do it, Ruth got indignant. "Come off your high horse, princess. You're no better than me, might as well get used to it. It's a man's world, and the lot are no better than pigs. The sooner you realize that what's between our legs is the only thing they value in us, the better off you'll be. Keep your job, or don't, it's nothing to me, but don't go thinking right and fair has anything to do with it."

It was what Anna had said next that horrified Katie. "Tell her the whole of it, Ruth. She should know."

Ruth had slammed a skillet down. "Mind your tongue, Anna. You'll get the both of us in trouble."

"Katie," Anna had said, "It's best to just go along. Getting fired isn't the worst that can happen." It was then that she had told her what Big Mike and his friends had done to that poor child, Rose.

The thought of it now brought the terror out again.

Water District

Circa 1868, unknown author

This page left blank

Chapter 7

Liam felt a growing unease as they turned the corner from Clinton to DeKoven streets. "Begging your pardon Mr. McDonald, If I might ask, what are we doing here? I suspect you aren't buying milk."

"Astute as always, Liam. I am here because I have some business with the O'Learys. They won't like what I have to say. You and Johnny are here to assure there's no unpleasantness."

"I've known Mr. and Mrs. O'Leary since I was a boy. They've been good to me; if there is to be rough stuff, I'd just as soon not be party to it."

"There is the point, lad. You being here is to make it likely there *won't be* an altercation. The best way to make sure people make the right choice is to not give them one."

"And what's this business you have with them – that requires peace keepers?" asked Liam.

"It's just a disagreement about services rendered is all. Have I misjudged you, boy? Have you no sand after all?"

"I just like to know what I am walking into is all."

Big Mike McDonald eyed Liam warily. "Then do as I say. Stand by the door and don't say or do anything unless I tell you."

The three made their way to the O'Leary cottage. Big Mike knocked, but no one answered. Liam reluctantly followed as they trudged to the back of the lot and entered the dairy barn. They found Mrs. O'Leary tossing hay with a pitchfork. She stopped working when she saw them. Pointing the prongs of the pitchfork in the general direction of McDonald, she said, "So, it's you, is it? And what gives you cause to slink into my barn?"

McDonald gave Mrs. O'Leary a smile as much reptilian as human. "Would you mind pointing that fork somewhere else, Catherine? That's no way to greet an old friend, now is it?"

She didn't budge. "I think I'll be keeping it where it is. State your business and be gone."

"Don't be coy, you know why I am here. You are in arrears in your business association dues."

"So, now it's a business association; there's a laugh. Be man enough to call it what it is – extortion."

"There's an ugly word. I simply provide protection to the businesses around here, and they pay a fee in… tribute… yes, it's a tribute, it is."

"Call it what you want, you fat leach. I'll not pay you for the right to breathe."

The smile never faded from his lips. "You're taking the short view, Catherine. This is a dangerous neighborhood. Any number of unfortunate mishaps might happen without my protection."

"The only danger in this neighborhood is you and your pack of thugs. You can threaten all you want, McDonald. There will be no money from me."

"I am sorry to hear that – I am," said McDonald. "The thing is, if one business shirks their civic duty, then no one will feel the need. Then… then the neighborhood goes to hell in a handbasket. I can't have that, now can I? There must be consequences, don't you see? You will come to that truth sooner or later. You will save yourself some unpleasantness if you come to your senses now. It'd be better for both of us, but mostly for you."

Catherine O'Leary glared at Liam. "And Liam Collins, you're a party to this? Your father and mother will be ashamed of you."

Liam felt his cheeks burn. "I am sorry, Mrs. O'Leary, but it's the way of things. You're making too much of it. Save yourself the trouble and give him his due. There's no cause in fighting might."

"Might? His due? Do you hear yourself, lad?" She gestured at McDonald with the pitchfork. "This fat toad ain't no mightier than a sewer rat. Our people came to this country to escape this very thing. I'll not bow down to it, and there is nothing that him or you, or that mad dog Johnny Gallagher there can do to change my mind."

Johnny spit a wad of phlegm at her, barely missing the hem of her dress. "Mind your tongue, woman. Or I'll show you how a mad dog bites."

Liam saw Mrs. O'Leary blanch. Defiant but shaken, she said, "Step closer and I'll run you through."

Johnny snarled, "I'll be putting that pitchfork up your cunnie, you bitch."

"And you'll earn a hole in your chest for the effort." They all turned to see Patrick O'Leary standing at the barn door with a double-barreled shotgun.

Big Mike shot Johnny a harsh glare. "Stand down there Patrick. There is no reason for anybody putting holes in anyone. Johnny has a loose mouth and quick temper is all. I apologize for that. We are all just talking here."

Mr. O'Leary pulled the hammers back on the gun. "I think you've said all that's to be said. It's best if you leave."

"As you wish," said Big Mike. "Though I was hoping to come to a reasonable understanding. Patrick, why don't you come to the hotel some evening? We can talk about this like reasonable men – over a drink. Maybe play some cards." Looking at Mrs. O'Leary with an evil grin, he added, "Of course, there are other entertainments I can provide, if you catch my meaning."

Mr. O'Leary responded. "I believe I'll not be visiting that hotel of yours. There's nothing for me there, McDonald. I keep myself to my work at the stockyards; the dairy is Mrs. O'Leary's affair. She runs it and I'll not tell her what to do with it – neither will you."

"And there's the problem, you see. Letting a woman run a business is never a good idea. They don't have a head for the practical. They get worked up over what should or shouldn't be and not what is."

Catherine O'Leary waved the pitchfork in McDonald's direction, but kept her eyes on Johnny. She said, "I'll tell you what shouldn't be – you stealing from your own kind. And what should be is you swinging from a gallows pole. Now get out."

"See, Patrick, it's just as I said. There's nothing more stubborn than a self-righteous woman. You can't reason with them."

"She ain't wrong," said Patrick. "The three of you should get out. None of you are welcome here. That includes you Liam. I'm ashamed of you, boy."

Big Mike waved off the insult. "I'll leave – for now. But don't be thinking this is the end of it. We have issues to resolve. And they will be resolved one way or another."

As Liam followed Big Mike and Johnny out the door, he had to push back the bile that had risen in his throat. He had been terrified that blood would be spilled – maybe his. He said to himself, *That was a shameful thing. Sure, the O'Learys should just pay the damned tribute. They know as well as any the way of things. Big Mike is a man to be respected, or at least feared. He's just trying to maintain his hold on things, there's no good in provoking him.*

Liam eyed Johnny. *He has a taste for hurting people. Still, there's no cause to be threatening a woman like that. It don't sit well. For sure, there are better ways to handle things. And why the O'Learys? They barely got a pot to piss in. Stealing from them that's got more than they need is one thing, but squeezing folks like the O'Learys is foolishness. A man as smart as Mike should see that.*

Liam stayed back when he saw Big Mike slap Johnny in the back of his head. He then whispered something to him. Johnny held back and joined up with Liam as Big Mike huffed toward a waiting buggy.

"What was all that about?" asked Liam.

"The fat man was put off that I spoke out. I'll tell you this, if he lays his hands on me again, I'll gut him like a fish."

Sure you will, Johnny, and you'll end up in a pine box for it. "Don't get worked up, he's upset it didn't go well is all."

Johnny hawked a lump of phlegm out of his throat and hurled it out in front of him. "It was going fine until O'Leary showed up with a scatter gun. I would have put a few bruises on her, and she would have come around. They always do."

"You… you would have beaten her? Really?"

"Why not?" answered Johnny. "She wants to run a business like a man; she'll be treated like one. It's all about nothing now, anyway. Things are past that."

"What's that mean?"

"Mike wants you and I to pay them a visit – soon. We're to make an example of them."

Liam only nodded but thought, *Jesus, there is no cause for it. Just talk to Mr. O'Leary in a day or two. Patrick will make her see things clear.* Liam knew better than to argue with Johnny; he got set off too easy – and his blood was up. "What's that mean? – make an example?"

"Not sure, he didn't say. But it won't be pleasant for them. Personally, I look forward to teaching that uppity bitch a thing or two. I can't stand women who don't know their place."

To himself, Liam said, *I won't be party to hurting the O'Leary's – I can't. I'll wait a day or two, maybe pull off that meat job Mike talked about, get in good with him. Then try and explain again that I won't be party to bloodshed. Maybe he'll even let me reason with O'Leary. Surely a man as smart as Mike will see the wisdom in it. I hope so, there's got to be limits as to how far you push people.*

Chapter 8

Standing at the stove, Maggie heard her husband walk into the kitchen; she didn't bother to turn around. "You slept late and reek of smoke - another fire last night?"

"True enough," said Sean.

"You're done in, I'm guessing."

"What are you needing of me?"

"I could use some coal, if you're willing to haul some."

"I'll see to it, in a bit." Sean stretched. "It was a long night. A cottage over on Taylor caught fire. They lost everything, but lived to see the dawn. I suppose that's something at least."

"I've never seen it as bad as this – seems like there's something a flame every day now. Who was it this time?"

"Didn't know them. New folks, I would guess."

"Well, it's a pity. I don't doubt they regret coming here. They'll regret staying even more." Maggie pulled a covered tin from the windowsill. "There's biscuits left, if you're of a mind?"

Sean ignored the remark about regrets. "Biscuits would be lovely. Thank you."

"Your son didn't come home last night."

Sean sighed. "He's *my* son now, is he? Not so long ago, he was *your* little boy."

"Not so long ago, he wasn't running wild. You need to do something about him. He's going bad."

"The boy isn't bad, just confused. He'll come around."

Maggie sniffed. "I am not so sure. I hear things. He's in with a sordid lot."

"I hear the same. I ain't denying he worries me. But I have faith in him."

"Worry ain't doing. You need to *do* something."

"What would you have me do? I've talked to him till I'm out of breath. We both have."

Maggie finally looked at Sean. "I've said it a hundred times, we need to get him to a better place."

"For the love of Mary, can I at least wake up before you start on me?"

"Don't blaspheme. And isn't it just like you to avoid conversation when you know I am right."

Sean sighed. "I've said before, Liam is nigh on to a grown man. Even if we were to pack up all our worldly possessions and wander off to God knows where, he wouldn't come with us. We'd be in a place where no one knows us, or likely wants us. We'd have no money or prospects, or even a home. And Liam would still be here — without us – and still running wild. It's all foolishness, I tell you."

"Even so, we'd be better off."

"You mean *you* would be better off. Or so you believe, anyway. And no thought of what would be best for anyone else, I'll mark."

Yes, you oaf, I would be better for moving. And the more without you along, thought Maggie. She said, "All right then, if you think so little of me. Yes, I would be happier. I've said as much."

"And what of me and Liam," said Sean. "Do you think about what may be best for us?"

"You're a fine one to talk. You took me away from my family in Ballybunion without regard for my happiness."

"Sure I did, Maggie. And are you forgetting the sight of your brother and father hanging from a gallows? And for what – speaking their mind to a landed gent is all."

"Of course, I haven't forgot, and it's a cruel thing to suggest I ever could. I wasn't much more than a child. You took me away and then abandoned me."

"That's rubbish and you know it. I've always done right by you."

"Have you now?" said Maggie. "We were barely off the boat in New York City when you took off with the Army on your grand adventure. You left me stuck in the five points with three children - among strangers."

"Jesus, woman, we've been over this. They would've drafted me, that signing bonus they gave me was our stake in this country. I did what I had to do."

"Don't play me for a fool, Sean. Many a man slipped away and avoided the draft. There's a big country out there. We could've moved the family west, but you chose to leave us. I was alone in a strange place."

"You're playing the martyr. You were surrounded by family."

"Your family, not mine. And you know well that they never took to me. Young and green I was; alone with the boys and you know that too. I was alone when Michael got sick with the fever. Alone, I buried our son, and where were you?"

Sean said, "Vicksburg, getting shot at."

"And where were you when little James died?"

"You know damn well I was in North Carolina. It was a war, Maggie. What would you have me do?"

"Your papers were up in 63. You reenlisted; I will never forgive you for that."

"Is that it then? You blame me for the death of the boys?"

"I blame you for not being there when I needed you."

"The war was raging; how could I have walked away?"

"Others did," said Maggie. "Others walked away when needed by their own. You chose to stay. You wanted to be away… away from me."

"It would have been shameful to leave. I had a duty to the…"

"Don't talk of duty. This country doesn't give a damn for us. You chose it over me, over your children."

"That's a lie and you know it. Was I such a bad husband, after all? Is that why you can't love me?"

Maggie sighed. "You are a good enough man, better than most, I guess. But be honest, we were never a match. We were two green children and had no business getting married. I had dreams, Sean. You've never wanted to do more than get by."

"That's not true. I brought you and the boys here for a better life. I still dream of that."

"Maybe you do, Sean. But you don't have the guts to do it. We got off the boat, and you made it a whole six blocks before you put down roots in the five points. And why? Because there were familiar faces is all."

"That's unfair. You wanted to come west, and so here we are in Chicago. I moved from family to appease you."

"You're thick, aren't you? New York was a seething cauldron of crime and rats and roaches, and you know it. So what did you do? You brought us here is what – just a poorer version of where we were."

"Now who's thick, Maggie. Our life here is grand compared to the Five Points, or Ballybunion, for that matter. You have a cottage and food on the table, and no man is our master."

"It's still not living, don't you see? You just latched on to the familiar. You never put me first. Prosperity is out there, away from the cities, away from this squalor, but you put yourself on a leash."

"Maggie, you keep thinking that happiness is a place. You take your misery with you wherever you go. We could be happy here just as well as anywhere else. But, there's nothing out there that will appease whatever is gnawing on your insides. We could be happy if you tried. At the very least, we could do our best to not make each other miserable."

I won't settle, I can't. How do I tell you that every day I hate this life more, and you with it? She said, "And how am I to be happy when you will not give me what I need?"

"I am not sure I *can* make you happy, or that *anyone else* could either. You want what you don't have, and turn your back on what you do. Still, we are married, and that's the whole of it. It can't be changed."

"No, it can't," said Maggie. "You're stuck with me and I am stuck here - with you. You were wrong to marry me."

"Don't say that, Maggie. You were a Bonnie lass, and I loved you before you turned cold."

"Love? That's nonsense. Neither of us knew what we were doing. I was the first girl who showed you interest, is all. And you, you were… well, it's all about nothing now."

"I was what? Why did you marry me if you didn't love me?"

"Listen to you go on about love like some doe eyed school boy. Love is no bargain for we women. Women marry because we must. What choice do we have? You were going to America - a man with a future, and you were tolerable enough company. Our wedding seemed to be a safe wager. I am paying now for that error."

Sean buried his face in his folded hands. "There was never love then? I don't believe you, that's a piece of cold cunning — even for you,".

"It's a woman's lot. We are what we marry. What you call calculating, I call practical. What's love anyway? Just some silly nonsense for children. Life bleeds it out of you, eventually."

"And you won't try and make the best of it?'

Maggie laughed. "I am afraid, my dear husband, *this is* the best of it. We'll manage to go on because we must, but if you need soft words and a warm bosom, I suggest you keep to your little harlot."

"That again? I told you there is nothing there."

"And I told you…"

A knock on the door interrupted them.

"Are you expecting a visitor?" asked Maggie.

"None that I can imagine." Sean felt a heaviness in his chest when he opened the door. Tom Barnes, his neighbor from a few doors down, stood on the stoop; he held Liam's arm in a firm grasp. Tom was in his police uniform and looked pensive. Liam's eye was purple, his lip was puffy, and flecks of dried blood crusted at the corner of his mouth. His eyes remained fixed on the wooden planks of the stoop. It took a moment for Sean to recognize his expression – humiliation.

Sean asked, "What's this about? Liam, what happened to you?"

Liam said nothing, and after an awkward moment, Barnes said, "I am sorry, Sean, but young Liam got pinched last night."

"Sweet Jesus," gasped Sean. "What for?"

"We caught him around midnight carting off a side of beef from O'Dell's on LaSalle Street."

"And what of the bruises?" It was Maggie.

Barnes kept his focus on Sean. "The boys at the precinct roughed him up a bit. They were trying to get him to turn out whoever hired him to do it. It's clear enough he didn't want so much meat for himself. He's a stubborn one though, I'll tell you that. He never did speak up. I put a stop to the rough stuff when I saw it was your boy."

Maggie stepped toward the policeman. "Oh sure you did. You had no cause to…"

Sean yanked her back from the door. "Hold your tongue. I will take care of this." He turned to Liam. "What have you got to say about this, boy?"

Liam didn't look up or reply.

"Tommy," said Sean. "How is it you brought him here? Why isn't he sitting in a cell?"

From the room behind, Maggie cried, "How could you ask such a thing? Our son shouldn't be caged like an animal."

Sean turned and glared at her. The red face, the vein standing on his temple, and the coldness in his eyes told her he was at his limit and not to be provoked.

Tom Barnes said, "There is the thing. The captain came in this morning and told us that orders came from above to let the boy go. I'll tell you this, it's plain enough your boy has a special angel looking out for him, or some friends with some influence. Either way, he's lucky to be standing here."

"Alright then," said Sean. "I will see to this from here on." He shook the policeman's hand. "Thank you for looking after him."

"Sean, as a friend I'm telling you, I don't know what the boy is into, or how he slipped out of this mess. But I tell you, his luck won't hold. He'll be watched, and it won't go well at all next time. I see it every day; if he keeps on, he'll end up in chains or just as likely buried."

Barnes released his grip on Liam's arm and stepped off the porch. In a rage, Sean grabbed Liam by the shirt and pulled him into the house with enough force that Liam landed sprawled on the floor.

Sean growled, "I am ashamed of you, Liam. You disgraced our name. I've tried reasoning with you. I had hoped you would come to your senses, but I am at the end. If you are to stay my son, this foolishness must stop."

Liam stood and squared off in front of his father. "Foolishness, is it? I got careless, sure enough. But there is nothing foolish about making something of myself. When will you see how things really are? I sat in that jail for only a few hours and now here I am. Why? Because I got powerful friends looking out for me. You're the fool. You think the rules are the same for all of us – well, they're not. That I'm standing here right now tells you that. I'll be an important man soon enough. You never will because you believe in fairy tales and Bible verses."

"An important man? I never took you for stupid, or rotten at your core, but I was wrong. You're not becoming an important man; you're becoming a thief and a liar. There's no shortage of them, and being one ain't no accomplishment."

"Now do you see, Sean?" said Maggie. "It's this place, it's the people surrounding our boy that's doing this. It's settled, we are leaving, and the sooner the better. We'll take our Liam to a proper place and he'll turn around. You'll see."

Liam turned on his mother. "Let it rest mother, I'll not be an excuse for you anymore. And I'll not be going anywhere. Would you have me be some dirt farmer breaking my back six days a week and thanking Jesus for the privilege on Sunday? Should I marry and grow old and miserable like you and father? I won't have it. I'll have a life, I'll have money, and not bow down to no man."

Maggie cried, "Liam, you sound like a fool."

"And you sound like a miserable harpy. Always complaining, making everyone around you miserable…"

Sean snapped, "Don't speak to your mother like that. She only wants you to be a worthy man. What kind of life will you build, boy? Will you be a cheat and thug? Will you be happy being reviled by those who know of you? You won't have to bow down to anyone because you'll be low already – worthy only of the gutter."

"I'll be respected," said Liam.

"You'll be feared. It's not the same. Hurting others is no life, son. You'll end up like your friend McDonald – loathed and shunned by decent people. He was the one that put this evil in your head, isn't he?"

Liam's tone softened. "He's got his flaws; I'll give you that. But, he's not such a bad sort. It's a tough world, and sometimes you have to be a little tough yourself. It ain't no different than those rich lords uptown. They cheat and lie too, but that's just business, they say. McDonald ain't so different."

"You know better. McDonald hurts people, he destroys lives. And for no better reason than it suits him, it's a sickness deep in him. He's a heartless monster and you'll become like him if you don't wake up."

"Better him than becoming some old man, worn down from years of hard work and nothing to show for it."

"Lad, family, friends… dignity… they ain't nothing."

Liam headed for the door. "They ain't enough."

As Liam walked out the door, Maggie said, "Let him go. He's no better than a thug. Damn this place for ruining him, and damn you for keeping us here."

Chapter 9

The rank odor of cigars and stale beer assailed Liam's nostrils. Through the cloud of lingering cigar smoke, he saw Big Mike McDonald sitting at his private table.

As Liam approached, McDonald said, "Well, if it isn't young Liam, delivered from Hades itself. I hear tell the constables gave you quite a time of it."

"I got caught lifting the meat at O'Dells. But then, you know all about that, I would suspect."

"I know a lot of things. For instance, I heard the constables wanted you to give up your partners – and your refusal earned you a beating. They worked you over pretty good too, I'm told. Still, you remained true. Stood up to it like a man, I hear. Good for you Lad."

"I got a few bruises and a cracked rib, but I'll be fine."

"Not surprised, the bastards always go for the ribs. Getting caught was stupid. You should have planned it better – had a lookout posted. I am half tempted to put a few knots on your head myself." His eyes burrowed into Liam's. "It was good you held your tongue. I don't have to tell you that if you had lost your nerve, a beating from the cops would have been the least of it."

"I am no fool, or a snitch; you need not worry about that, Mr. McDonald. I am grateful for your intercession, but it's a night I don't wish to repeat. I'll be more careful in the future."

Big Mike patted Liam's hand. "I know you will. That's why I like you; you're the sort to learn from your mistakes. You remind me of myself at your age. That's why I got a special treat for you. My way of rewarding your loyalty."

A nice crisp twenty would be fair, thought Liam. Instead, he said, "There's no call for that. Loyalty is to be expected."

McDonald said, "Nonsense. Reward and punishment are stock in trade in our business."

Our business? I like the sound of that.

McDonald continued, "Kitty tells me you took a shine to my little Rose when you were upstairs last. Said you were gob smacked."

An alarm bell went off in Liam's head. He had been told that Rose was McDonald's special girl. "I meant no disrespect. I didn't know about her – who she was."

"Relax boy; the attraction is understandable. But you're right to steer clear, she's mine – private stock, you might say. I've only shared her with a few special friends. Hell, I even turned down the mayor when he asked. Although, honestly, that was as much practicality as anything else. He's a rare nasty sort, likes to bruise his girls up. I've told Rose to accommodate you, anything you want."

The mayor is with Mike too? And what the hell kind of man beats a woman whose sole reason for being there is to pleasure him? Even whores deserve better than that. I would expect it from the rabid dogs prowling the alleys, but who would think it of the so-

called gentleman in fancy suits? I suppose I shouldn't be surprised. "Thank you, Mr. McDonald."

"Think nothing of it. Enjoy yourself, and when you're done, find Johnny. There is some business to be done."

*****

Kitty was waiting for him at the top of the stairs. She greeted him with, "Well, I'm not sure how you managed this, but Rose is waiting for you. You got an hour." She added with a smirk, "Though from the look of you, I expect you'll be done shortly. I've got shoes older than you."

Liam bristled at the jab. "They likely are holding up better than you, too."

"Your snippy for a pup. If you knew anything about shoes or women, you'd know the older ones are the most comfortable. I could teach you a few things if you had some manners. Now go on up and try not to make a fool of yourself with her."

Liam slowly made his way to the room at the end of the hall. On opening the door, he found Rose laying on the bed naked except for a silk robe draped over her shoulders – the same robe she wore the last time he saw her. The robe looked more tattered than he remembered, but the girl in it was just as beautiful. A small lass, barely over five feet, she was thin, with flowing red hair and piercing green eyes. He found it hard not to stare, especially at the wispy auburn hair between her legs. His mouth went suddenly dry, and his face felt hot. Mostly, he was aware of the ache pressing in his manhood.

"So, it's you, is it?" she said, eyeing him over. "I remember you – staring at me like an imbecile."

He closed the door and leaned back against it. "Yes, I suppose it is me. I hope it's all right. Big Mike – I mean Mr. McDonald – said I could come up. That is, if it's alright with you."

"As if I have a choice. Well, don't just stand there holding the door up. I was told to accommodate you with anything you wanted, so let's get on with it."

"Just like that?"

"Well, you've been here before; what are you expecting? And why are you staring at me like that? I know you've seen a naked woman before."

"Of course, I have. It's just that you're very pretty. You're maybe the prettiest lass I've ever laid eyes on."

She laughed, but there was no humor in it. "I'll let you in on a little secret, boy. You don't have to flatter me; you'll get what you came for. So what is it you want; should I stay on my back, or maybe get on all fours? I'll put you in my mouth, if you like that sort of thing, but you have to wash it off first."

Liam felt his cheeks burn; her bluntness embarrassed him. "Don't call me boy. By the looks of it, I've got a few years on you. I thought maybe we could talk for a few minutes first – get to know each other."

"Fine by me, it's your time. What do you want to talk about?"

"I don't know," said Liam. "Things… How old are you?"

In a flirty tone, she asked, "How old do you want me to be?"

Missing the innuendo, Liam answered, "I don't know; you look not much more than a child, sixteen maybe – if that."

"Oh, I see it now – you're one of *those.* Mike schooled you on how he likes it, did he? Usually it's the older sods, but you want what you want, I guess."

Almost instantly, her countenance softened, and a wry pout spread across her lips. She slipped off her robe and spread her legs in front of him; her fingers slid down her abdomen. In a voice that somehow was equally childish and seductive, she said, "Papa, I've been ever so good. I want you, papa. Take care of your little girl, please."

"Stop that!" snapped Liam. "I don't like whatever it is you're playing at."

The hard edge returned to her expression. "For the love of St. Peter, I was told to do whatever you want, so tell me what that is, or just climb on and screw me already."

"I don't know what I expected, but not this. This was a bad idea; I should go."

Liam turned toward the door, but Rose sprang from the bed and grabbed his arm. She said, "No, don't leave. If Big Mike finds out that I put you off of me, there will be hell to pay."

"It will be fine. I won't tell him anything."

Practically pleading, she pulled him to the bed. "No, you need to stay for a while. If you leave now, Kitty will tell him something wasn't right and he'll blame me. I can't have that."

Liam saw tears gathering in the corners of her eyes. "What are you so afraid of ? I doubt Mike will care one way or another."

"You don't know Mike, but I do. Believe me, it will go hard for me if you leave. Please, I'm sorry I wasn't acting like you wanted. Just stay, I'll make it worth your while."

"All right. I don't understand, but I'll stay for a bit."

Rose slid off the bed onto her knees in front of him, grasping the button on his trousers. He pulled her hand away. He said, "We're past that now."

Pensively, she said, "I have to, Mike said so. Please don't be angry."

He pulled her up to a sitting position on the bed. "I'm not angry, I promise. It just wouldn't feel right now. Maybe we can just talk. Is Rose really your name?"

She nodded yes in reply.

"And how old are you, really?"

"Why are you asking – what is it to you?" she said.

"I don't know, I just want to know about you. How old are you?"

"I'm seventeen now. I'll be eighteen this winter. How old are you?"

Liam shrugged. "I'm already eighteen."

Rose finally made eye contact and asked, "What's your name?"

"Liam, my name is Liam. Rose, if you don't mind me asking, do you like working here?"

A look of surprise crossed her face. "Do I like strange men, mostly disgusting ones, pawing at me? I hate it here. Mind you, I've got it better than most. I mostly just have Big Mike crawling on me, but now and again he makes me entertain one of his old, fat friends. I'll say you were a bit of a pleasant surprise."

Liam smiled. "I'll take that as a compliment."

"Don't be too proud. You still came for your pound of my flesh, just like the rest. You just look and smell better is all."

"Is it so bad, then? I mean, there's worse things than screwing."

The girl's green eyes flashed in anger. "Is there? And what would you do in my place? How would you take it – dirty sweaty men groping you, drooling on you; sticking it in you. I know of places close by where the deviants would show you what it's like to be violated. You could learn a thing or two from being on the receiving end once. Let those sodomites have a turn with you; then *you tell me* if there's worse things than screwing."

 Liam's face burned. "No need to get your back up. I just never gave it much thought is all. It's a good enough exchange for us men. I sort of assumed it was pleasant enough for the lass as well."

Rose exhaled to calm herself. "It is pleasant, when you got some say in when and with who you lay down with. Here's a secret for you, greenie. Every smile from every whore you ever been with is hiding complete distaste for you. But what do you care? You come and get what you want, then ask Jesus for forgiveness. It must be a fine thing to be a man."

"If it's so bad, why don't you leave?"

"Mike don't let go of his property – not till he's tired of it anyway. Even if I could walk out, where would I go?"

"Don't you have family?"

"They'll have nothing to do with me." Liam saw a tear roll down her cheek when she said this.

"Is it because you work here?" he asked.

"Something like that. It's a subject best left alone. I shouldn't be talking like this. Promise me you won't repeat what I said."

Liam nodded. "I promise, although you took the fun out of my night."

Rose grabbed Liam's arm. "I am sorry I spoke out. I shouldn't have. It's just that you're the first friendly face I've seen since I got here. But, I'm serious, me talking to you like this will have repercussions if it got out. Mike will make me regret it."

"You're really scared of him, aren't you?"

"I have reason to be," said Rose. "And you should be too."

With bravado he didn't really feel, Liam said, "I can take care of myself."

Her eyes found his. "You would be a fool to believe it. Trust me, you'll be the better for steering clear of this place and everyone here. What's making you work for Big Mike? What's he got that's holding you anyhow?"

Liam shrugged, "Money is the short of it."

"Gambling? My father owed him once." Her face tightened in the corners of her mouth and eyes.

"It's not like that. I work for him because I want to earn money – real money."

"Odd you don't look like a criminal, or talk like one either. You look more like an accountant's apprentice, or a lawyer's clerk."

"Do I now, and what do you know of accountants and such? There's none living in this part of town."

"My father has a tailor's shop on the north side. I've seen them come to his place often enough. And you'd be surprised at how many so-called gentlemen come slumming down here too. Men are men. Being rich don't make them any more Christian – worse, as often as not. Anyway, you don't seem cut out for this life you're living."

"You sound like my father."

"Your father still talks to you? There's a blessing. You would do well to pay him some heed."

"He was talking to me … not so sure now."

She sighed. "I'd give anything to see my father again. You'd do well to mend fences with yours."

"I could say the same to you. You don't seem cut out to be a … to be here."

"A whore? Is that what you were going to say? And what do you know about whores – past what you were staring at when you came in?"

Liam blushed at being caught staring. "I know people," said Liam. "This place ain't for you. Go back to your family, talk to your old man."

"That's impossible, Mike wouldn't allow it – even so father turned his back on me – I disgust him."

"He's said as much? You're sure? "

"He doesn't have to, he's never come for me," sniffed Rose.

"He… they – may have softened. You won't know if you don't try."

"I'll give you your own advice back, Liam. You're too soft for this kind of life. Get out from under Mike while you can. Go home."

"You don't know anything about me. I'm not soft."

"You still have some kindness in you, it's not a thing to be ashamed of. You came here with a free pass, and still you treated me like a human. It's more than anyone else has. That kindness is an admirable thing in the proper world, but it will get you hurt where you're heading."

"And where am I heading?"

"This life you're choosing is what I mean. You don't have the cruelness for it."

"It's choosing me," said Liam. "There's few choices for a man in this cold-hearted place."

"So, find a different place. If you could be anywhere, where would you go?"

"I don't know of a place that's better… maybe…"

"Maybe what?"

"Maybe at sea – I miss the ocean. As a boy, I spent hours sitting on the shore. I dreamed of seeing the world – all the exotic places I heard tell of. The sail from home to America was as happy a thing as I've ever felt."

Rose took his hand. "You have a dream, why not follow it? However, it turns out, it will be better than being Big Mike's lackey."

"I could say the same of you, Rose. Where would you go if you could get out of here?"

"You still don't fathom it, do you? The world is a much smaller place for a woman. My dreams are of children and a kind husband. I am ruined now, though. I might as well dream of living on the moon."

"Your but seventeen; how can your life be ruined?" asked Liam.

"You know why, you're just kind enough not to say it. Look where we are. No decent man wants to marry a woman like me and you know it."

Liam shrugged. "Walk out of here and across town, and no one would know where you been or what you did."

"Live a lie?"

"Most everyone does, don't they?"

They fell into a silence. Rose lay her head on his chest, and he instinctively wrapped his arms around her. They lay like that until Kitty knocked on the door. As he got off the bed, she grabbed his arm. "Thank you for your kindness, Liam. You've reminded me of what I was before… before this… what could have been."

"Rose, I'll come back and see you again. We'll figure a way to get you out of here. You can start over."

She smiled, but there was neither joy nor hope in it. "As I said before, you are a green one. You see me naked and now you're in love? You think you can save me like some knight of old. I'll get out when providence intervenes – if at all. There's nothing to be done about it, especially by a moon eyed wisp of a pup."

Her words stung, but he knew there was truth in them. "I'm not falling in love, but I do pity you. I will…"

Her eyes narrowed. "I don't want your pity, though I guess I am a pitiful thing. My life is what it is. And, know this you oaf, with what you're doing, my fate will likely end better than yours. We won't see each other again – Big Mike won't have it. And give up whatever foolishness you're thinking about in helping me – you'll get us both killed. Now go, and remember, say nothing of our talk; you simply came in and took your pleasure and that's it. Better, you would do well to brag about how you gave me a hard turn. I'll put on a show about how repulsive you were. I'll tell Mike you're a nasty prick with a small member. He'll like that. You sure don't want him thinking I enjoyed being with you." She kissed him on the cheek. "It's for the best, especially for me. Now go."

*****

Liam descended the stairs and saw McDonald sitting at his table with two gents he didn't know. From the look of them, he guessed they were bankers or politicians. *Those kinds are easy to spot; they always have that look of self-importance.* McDonald had pulled the waitress – Katie – onto his lap. She was smiling, but he could see the fear. He cupped her breast and even the fake smile evaporated. She gently pulled his hand away, grabbed the empty beer steins, and made a hasty escape. Liam was glad the woman couldn't see the look of pure menace that passed briefly over the fat man's face. *The poor thing, she's scared to death,* thought Liam. *I wonder if she is to replace Rose as his special pet. I feel bad for her, but this may be an opportunity to get Rose away. But where would I take her? It's shameful that her family turned on her. Could I look after her? It's daft, it is, but there's something about her that draws me.*

Johnny Gallagher sat at a nearby table. Seeing Liam, he quickly grabbed him and hustled him out the door. "So, how was it?"

"How was what?"

"Don't play me. How was it with little Rose?"

"Oh, sure. She was good enough, she was. Still, you know how it is. One feels like another."

Johnny used a finger to block a nostril and blew his nose on the ground. "Ain't you the casual one. You should be more grateful for your luck. Lord knows I'd like another turn with her."

A flash of anger ripped through Liam. *It's bad enough that Mike had used her, but Johnny – dirty, crude Johnny?* He wanted to punch Johnny, but knew better. He collected himself and said, "You been with her too? Then I guess you know."

Johnny sniffed. "I suppose, but not really proper. I was only just there when Big Mike turned her out."

"What's that mean – turned her out?"

"You know… that night. It was me and Big Mike and Davey and Willie, too. You had to hear about it."

Liam felt his blood chill. "No, I haven't."

Johnny laughed. "It was a helluva thing. You see, Rose's father got drunk one night and ran up a king's debt playing cards. So, Big Mike is going to take the deed to his building, and the sorry sap pleads with Mike to make an arrangement. They work out that young Rose is to work in the restaurant serving food until the debt is paid."

"Jesus," said Liam.

"Well," Johnny continued. "You know how Mike gets. He gets handsy with Rose. I guess the lass complained to daddy. Next thing you know, the damn fool shows up and starts cursing Mike in front of folks. It was a mistake, that's for certain. Calm as can be, Mike suggests he and Rose and daddy should all go to Mike's private office and talk it over – all civil like. What daddy didn't know was that Mike had given the low sign for us boys to follow. Once we got them in a back room, we beat that poor man half senseless."

"And Rose?" Liam said, hiding his growing agitation.

"That's where it gets good, don't you see? Mike has us tie the poor bastard to a chair and then, with the old man watching, he slaps Rose around a bit. Daddy starts demanding he leave his little girl alone, and that just seems to make Mike even madder. Next thing you know, he rips off all of Rose's clothes – real rough like. Mike then forced himself on her right then and there. When he was done, he told Davey to have a turn, then me and then Willie. The whole time her old man was watching and crying – blubbering stuff we couldn't even understand. She fought like a wildcat at first, but that just seemed to get Mike – us too – all the more worked up. We got kinda rough. After a while, she just sort of went limp and let us do what we wanted. I tell you, the four of us used that girl any and every way you can think of – sometimes two or three of us at a time. She just took it. I ain't no softy, but even I started to feel for her. After maybe an hour, she seemed more dead than alive, and Mike had us untie the poor bastard. He threw Rose on the floor at daddy's feet, laughed and declared the debt paid."

A wave of nausea had risen in Liam. He hated Johnny – Mike even more so. Liam remembered his father's words about McDonald; *he likes hurting people, it's a sickness*. With effort, he managed to ask, "Then why is Rose still with Big Mike?"

"That's the damnedest thing of all. Her old man didn't say a word. He just got up and walked out of the room – just left Rose there on the floor. And Rose didn't say a word, she just lay there while her old man abandoned her. It was the queerest thing I ever saw. Mike told us all to get out, and that was that. Rose has been upstairs ever since."

Sweet Jesus, Rose. Your father isn't disgusted by you. The bastard is ashamed of himself for not being able to protect you from those animals. He can't face you — and with reason. He should never have left you there.

"Why didn't her old man go to the cops?"

Johnny laughed. "Half the police force is in Big Mike's pocket. Hell, the next night, the precinct captain was McDonald's guest for supper. I hear tell Rose was his dessert."

Liam stopped walking and leaned against the building. He hoped he looked casual; in truth, his knees were weak.

Johnny continued, "Anyway, it was a hell of a party. And here's something to brighten your night. If we do good with the O'Learys, you may get a taste of the fun yourself. I think that uppity waitress is heading for the same fate tomorrow night. Mike's getting a taste for it. I hear tell another girl got turned out by Mike and some big wigs from downtown, disappeared after."

"Killed her?" asked Liam.

Johnny only shrugged, sniffed, and sent another wad of phlegm airborne.

Liam's mind raced. *Rape? Murder?* He shivered and asked, "And what is this of the O'Leary's?"

"The fat man hasn't said yet, but it will be tomorrow night." Johnny eyed Liam closely. "You look put out. Are the O'Learys fretting you? You got no stomach for the rough stuff, do you?"

"I'm fine, don't worry about me," said Liam.

"That's good to hear. Get used to the idea. It's what you do now. This ain't no place for the tender hearted." He slapped Liam hard on the back. "Besides, Mike won't likely want them killed. He says blood draws too much attention. I do look forward to paying them a visit, though."

"That's good," said Liam. "I'll meet you here tomorrow at sunset."

As Liam walked off, images of Rose, beaten and used on the floor, flashed in his head, then of the pretty waitress. He ducked in the alley and wretched. *I am done. I'll have nothing to do with any of this – I can't. Big Mike and Johnny and the rest can go to hell. I'll run if I have to – maybe take Rose with me.*

Part Two
Flame

Sketch circa 1871, author unknown

Sunday, October 8, 1871

Chicago, Illinois

This page left blank

Chapter 10

A strong breeze carried unusually balmy air in from the south. Dry leaves and dust swirled between buildings and down alleys. The endless parade of hot, dry days had taken their toll on vegetation and human alike, but the warm fall evenings were a blessing. The neighborhoods came alive in the evenings, friends called on one another, children played in the streets, and the elders sat on their front stoops, greeting those who strolled by.

This was a special night in the neighborhood. The McLaughlin family had invited all their friends and neighbors over to celebrate the crossing of their kin from the old country. A chorus of 40 or more voices sang the Wild Rover, accompanied by a cacophony of laughter and cheerful conversation. Much of the neighborhood had turned out, spilling the party into the yard and street.

With the end of the last chorus of *Wild Rover*, Rory Dougan started pounding out a lively beat on his old bodhran drum. The crowd cheered when Robbie's banjo and Casey's violin broke into a spirited rendition of *Over the Hill It Waits*. To the delight of all, Daniel "Peg Leg" Sullivan moved to the center of the crowd. He had planted his wooden peg in the dirt, and somehow turned circles while his remaining foot managed an intricate series of dance steps – all in perfect time to the music. The crowd clapped in time and cheered him on. When he nearly fell, a young girl dashed forward and caught him by the arm. They hugged and danced a jig together. The McLaughlin's' dusty yard quickly became an impromptu dance floor, as several couples joined the girl and Peg Leg.

Patrick O'Leary took a swig from the jug being passed around and grabbed Catherine's arm, pulling her toward the dancers. "Come along love, let's show them how it's done proper."

Catherine pulled him back. "You're in your cups, dear husband. You forget that you dance like a drunk monkey."

Patrick laughed. "And when have you ever danced with a drunken monkey?"

Catherine reached up and mussed his hair. "On my wedding night, as I recall."

Her jibe roused laughter among their nearby friends.

"Aye," said Patrick. "That was a grand time. We danced the night away and then you took me to our marital bed."

Catherine laughed. "Where you fell asleep right off, you oaf."

The couples around the O'Leary's howled and slapped Patrick on the back. Embarrassed, he said, "Well, I won't fall asleep too soon tonight."

"Alright then, you best be getting me home if you want time for that. I have to wake up near dawn to tend to the cows."

Tommy McCartney poked a finger into Patrick's ribs. "As drunk as he is, Caty, I'll wager he won't be up to it."

With a wry smile, Catherine said, "You'd lose that bet. He's never let me down before. He ain't good for much, but you won't hear me complain about those particular talents."

Patrick beamed and looked at Tommy. "I guess that settles that, then."

Catherine and Patrick said their goodbyes, and Catherine guided her husband toward their cottage. On the way, Patrick kissed Catherine's cheek. "You're a fine wife, darling girl."

She laughed, "No need to butter me up, I'm feeling the itch too. But we need to be quick about it; dawn will come too soon."

"I mean what I say, Caty. It was a blessed day when I married you."

Catherine O'Leary hooked her arm in Patrick's. "So it was, husband. So it was."

*****

Around eight thirty, Peg Leg Sullivan limped up DeKoven Street toward Jefferson. He had noticed Old Man Cassik's absence at the party and thought he should check on him. The old boy wasn't Irish, but he was a good enough fellow, and Peg Leg made a point of looking after him. As he passed the O'Leary place, he noticed the cottage was dark. *Already in bed, I reckon.* He smiled. *Maybe Tommy had it pegged right; it looks as if Patrick is already down for the night.*

Sullivan found Janek Cassik on the front stoop. The old man confessed being down in the back and that he didn't feel up to walking the few blocks to the McLaughlin's. "I would be obliged if you dropped off some spirits on your way home though – if some's left and it's no bother."

Sullivan laughed. "No problem at all." He then lit his pipe and sat on the step. "It's a shame about your back Janek; you're missing a good dust up. The neighborhood is in grand spirits tonight."

A gust of wind pummeled the men. It blew off Cassik's cap. An ember from Sullivan's pipe blew into some leaves; they immediately began to smolder.

"Ain't that something, they took right off," said Cassik as he stomped out the small fire. "Never seen it so dry."

Sullivan agreed. "Longest, driest summer I ever saw – feels like Mexico, that place was as hot as Beelzebub's fanny."

"Never been south," said Cassik. "I hear tell the drought is so bad President Grant is putting a luxury tax on rain."

Sullivan chuckled. "If he can make it rain, I'll pay the tax." Peg Leg took a long draw from his pipe. "I served with the General from the Wilderness brawl right through to Cold Harbor. That's where I lost the leg. I know you were having fun with it. But I'll tell you, if any could order the weather about, it'd be him."

Janek waved off his friend. "Didn't serve, but I hear tell he was nothing more than a brutal butcher. Couldn't find his ass with both hands, some say."

Sullivan bristled. "War is nothing but butchery. He at least saw it. The damn thing lasted so long because the *gentleman* generals didn't have the sand for it. Many a lad would be alive today if Grant had been in charge from the start. We'd of been home by 62."

"As you say, Daniel," said Cassik. "I won't argue politics with you. Let's agree it's a fine night for a drink, and we need rain like Lucifer needs ice."

Sullivan patted Cassik on the back. "Can't do anything about the rain, but I'll see to getting you that drink."

Ten minutes later, Sullivan left Cassik and began the cumbersome trek back to the party. He now regretted the earlier dancing. The last seven years had made him mostly used to the wooden leg, but on nights when he pushed himself, it could be an awful bother. *You'll earn yourself a blister or two in the morning, you damn fool. What was I thinking, hopping around with that young lass?*

Just before nine o'clock, he clomped by the O'Leary barn. He turned when a flicker of light caught his eye. He saw a tongue of flame push out of the barn's hayloft window. "Fire! Fire!" he screamed as loud as he could. *Mother Mary help us. Catherine's cows are in there still.* He hobbled to the barn as fast as his wooden leg would carry him.

Throwing the barn door open, he saw fire consuming the back of the barn. A wave of intense heat and gray smoke engulfed him. Sullivan saw the fire spreading rapidly, and knew he needed to act quickly. He bent as low as he could and hobbled to the first cattle stall. The cow didn't move when he opened the stall gate. In desperation, he grabbed its ear and pulled hard. Still, the cow wouldn't budge. He crossed to the opposite stall, hoping its occupant would bolt. Again, the cow, not much more than a calf, seemed frozen in place. The heat and smoke were becoming unbearable. In desperation, Sullivan wiggled past the animal, to the back of the stall, and tried pushing it out – to no avail.

With breathing growing hard and visibility diminishing, Sullivan realized he had to get out, with or without the animals. As he hobbled past the calf, he stumbled. The near fall wedged his wooden leg between the floorboards. He tried hard to pull it free, but quickly realized it wouldn't budge. In a near panic, he pulled at the leather straps attaching it to his leg. It took several agonizing seconds, but he finally freed himself. As he crawled to the door, he looked on with dread as the fire grew. His escape path was disappearing, and he couldn't stand, much less run.

Near blind in the building smoke, and unable to breathe, Sullivan crawled forward as best he could. Only seconds later, the young cow he had tried to save stepped over him. On impulse, he reached up and threw his arms around the cow's neck. The cow, panicked by the fire, smoke and now a strange human hanging on it, bolted for the door – carrying Sullivan with it. Outside, he lay gasping for air. Looking back at the barn, he was shocked by how fast the fire had grown. Flames now lit the night sky and had reached the O'Leary's coal shed. The thick bed of dried leaf litter and grass near the building had also caught and spread the fire to a neighbor's fence. Worse, the west wall of the O'Leary cottage was smoldering.

Dennis Rogan had heard Sullivan's cry of fire and came out of his house. He ran past Peg Leg and onto the O'Leary's porch. He beat twice on the door and then kicked it in. "Patrick, get up! Your barn is on fire."

A naked Patrick O'Leary threw the bedroom door open. "What are you hollering about, Dennis?"

"Get up you fool, your barns burning, and the house will be next!" was Rogan's response. A moment later, an equally naked Catherine O'Leary bolted past him and into the children's sleeping room. "Hurry, both of you!" Rogan yelled, and ran back outside.

Quickly, the O'Leary's and their children fled to the yard in their nightclothes, carrying some bundles. Rogan, Catherine and Patrick re-entered twice to carry out what possessions they could.

The smell of smoke and the growing glow of the fire had caught the attention of the partygoers. As if they had planned for the occasion, the neighborhood quickly organized two bucket brigades running from the cistern to the cottage. As they tossed water on the exposed walls of the O'Leary home, they sizzled.

While neighbors worked to save the O'Leary cottage, Sullivan lay in the grass watching large, red, glowing embers float from the barn. Several fell on James Dalton's house, some forty feet downwind from the O'Leary barn. It took but minutes for the house to burst into flame. Onlookers ran to help the Daltons empty what they could from the house before the fire consumed it all.

Seeing the growing fire and sensing what was to come, Billie Lee, a neighbor across the street, along with his wife and older sons, quickly tossed anything of value into their basement. As an afterthought, he sent his daughter, Mary, to run the three blocks to Goll's pharmacy and ask him to pull the fire alarm box housed inside.

Breathless, the little girl beat on the door of the pharmacy. She waited impatiently for what seemed like an eternity before Mr. Goll opened the door. "There is a… a fire… a bad one. My father sent me to have the alarm pulled."

"And where is this fire?"

"By my house. Hurry, please."

"Pulling the alarm is serious business, young lady. Exactly what's burning?"

Still catching her breath, Mary panted. "The whole… neighborhood… I think. Please!"

"And is this the right box? Where is this fire? Where do you live?"

The girl pointed in the general direction of her home.

"Show me." said Goll.

Mary took off on a run. Goll followed her at a brisk walk. After only a block, he saw the glow of the fire above the trees and said to himself; *That fire looks a long way away. I'll wager her father must have seen what I see and sent her. It would be a mistake to pull my box and send the fire crews on a wild goose chase. I'll wait and see if someone else comes by.*

Thirty minutes later, falling embers on his street finally induced Goll to pull the box alarm.

*****

Mathias Schaffer looked to the north at the vista of twinkling gas lights below. *A beautiful sight it is,* he thought. Even after all these years working as a fire warden, he still enjoyed the view from atop the courthouse watch tower. Tonight was especially lovely, though. His brother Bernard and sister-in-law Rebecca were visiting him. More to the point, Rebecca's beautiful – and unmarried – cousin Gretchen was there as well.

Gretchen carefully sat on the parapet wall of the tower. Already knowing the answer, she coyly asked Mathias, "What are you smiling about?"

"Just enjoying the view," he said.

She looked around. "It is beautiful up here. Thank you for letting us see it. You're very kind."

Feeling bold, Mathias said, "Your being here makes the view so much more lovely."

Rebecca giggled. "Careful cousin, Mathias can be a rascal."

Beaming, Gretchen chided. "Nonsense. I am sure he is quite the gentleman. So tell me, Mr. Schaffer…"

"Mathias. Please call me Mathias."

"Very well. Mathias, what does a fire warden do exactly?"

"I keep watch for fire, and when one is spotted, I calculate where, and then using that tube there, call down to the alarm man who notifies the correct station. He has connections by telegraph, they set off a bell in the firehouses."

"How impressive that is. And how do you tell a fire when you see it?"

"Oh, nothing but what you would expect, an orange glow and smoke if there's a moon to see it."

Pointing over Mathias's shoulder to the South, Gretchen asked, "Like that?"

The group hurried to the south rail and studied the smallish red glow in the distance. Bernard asked, "Is it something? I hope we didn't distract you."

Gretchen added, "How thrilling! Are you going to send an alarm?"

Mathias studied the glow for a bit. "No, it's not actually a fire. It's but a dying remnant of yesterday's blaze."

Rebecca gasped. "Oh, that was an awful thing. I read four blocks were lost. The whole of the fire department had to be called."

"It was indeed," said Mathias. "The thing will smolder for days. That's what we are seeing – I think."

The three guests continued to talk, but Mathias continually glanced at the small, red glow. The longer he watched, the more he doubted his original assessment. Bernard finally whispered, "I applaud your vigilance, but don't ignore Gretchen; she likes you."

Without turning from the glow, Mathias said, "I think I was wrong. It's growing too fast for smolder, and it seems small because it's at a distance."

"Where do you reckon it is?"

Mathias grimaced. "Hard to say – a distance for sure. Seems in proximity to yesterday's fire, I think." He hurried to the call tube and ordered box 342 struck.

The four watched the growing glow in the distance. Only after the fire had tripled in size did Mathias realize he had miscalculated the location – badly – by more than a mile. He called down to his operator, William Brown, to strike box 319.

Brown grumbled to himself. *Showing off for his guests, I'll bet. 342 and 319 are a fair piece apart. He'll confuse the crews.* He called up the tube for verification. "Are there two fires, Mathias?"

Mathias, Bernard, and Rebecca stood distracted at the south edge of the tower, observing the fire. Gretchen impulsively answered for Mathias. "No, just the one."

Hearing a strange voice reply, a woman's at that, Brown decided not to pull 319. *Mathias should know better,* he thought.

Rebecca said to Bernard, "Perhaps we should get home."

"Nonsense, there is no better place to watch than here. That is, if we're not a bother to Mathias."

Gretchen joined them and took Mathias's arm. He patted her hand. "No bother at all, you're welcome to stay."

"No, we should go," insisted Rebecca. "I'm concerned about our house."

"Don't fret, darling. The fire is far from our house." Bernard put his arm around his wife. "It would have to cross the river – can't be done."

"Are you sure?"

Bernard smiled. "Of course. Haven't you heard? Fires are terrible swimmers."

*****

Sean lay exhausted on a cot near the hose wagon *America*. It was his favorite spot in the station because it was close to a large window. Gusts of warm wind blew in, soothing his aching body. The fire had been a beast, and he was exhausted. All the department had been called up; it'd been hot, nasty work, and his crew had been at it half the night and most of the following day. Nearly four-square blocks near downtown burned. Even so, they had been lucky; the river saved them from further disaster. The balmy breeze was humid and gaining strength. He hoped it promised rain; the town was desperate for a weather change.

A voice called out. "Sean, come eat. Pappy's wife brought corned beef. There's enough for all."

"I'm too damned tired to eat," was Sean's reply.

"Good, the more for me." said young Garland Mercer.

"You'll keep your hands away from his food, you whelp of a pup," an old voice snapped. The remark brought laughter.

"What we need is a woman working here," said Garland. "The place could use a woman's touch, cooking and what not."

Cap scoffed, "Garland, you're touched in the head."

"I don't know maybe, someday you'll see it. Women are changing."

"They seem to be put together same now as always, thank God. Won't happen in a hundred years."

"I'm not so sure," said Pappy. "My old lady is as strong as an ox."

Cap retorted, "No offence, but she sort of looks like one too."

The boys broke into laughter, including Pappy. "True enough. But it's a rare woman who can pull a plow all day and cook supper at night."

"If she hears you talking like that, she'll put knots on your skull."

Sean lay quietly – on the edge of sleep – simply listening. He loved the sounds of a firehouse, especially the banter and laughter. There was little he found more satisfying than the rare sound of men laughing together. Especially the tired laughter of men proud of their hard work. He knew women had friends, close ones at that. But this was a bond that only men who toiled and struggled together shared. It was a connection as close to brotherhood as possible without shared blood. He experienced it during the war, but never expected to find it again. He relished it now.

An all too familiar odor wafted in on the breeze; barely noticeable above the smell of the cabbage. Without opening his eyes, Sean groaned, and said to no one in particular, "I smell smoke."

"I'd be surprised if you didn't." Sean recognized it was Cap's voice. "Everything in here reeks of it, including you, Collins. And the cot now too, thank you very much."

"Sorry Cap."

"Sorry solves nothing. You'll be dragging that thing outside to air out when you're alive again."

Sean said nothing, he just drifted to sleep. Moments later, an old man stumbled into the station. Winded, he bent over with his hands on his knees. He finally panted, "For the love of Jehovah, (pant) What are you sittin' fur? (pant) There's a wildfire up DeKoven way. You…You need to come quick!"

Cap said, "Hold on now, What's burning?"

Panic was clear on the man's face. "What ain't?"

"Where on DeKoven then, damn it?"

"The O'Leary place. Others burning too now."

This page left blank

Chapter 11

The steamer *Little Giant* and hose wagon *America* stormed down Clinton Avenue to the fire in O'Leary's barn. They were met with a wall of flame. The blaze had consumed the O'Leary barn and now four additional properties were burning. Driven by wind, the fire rapidly was spreading east up DeKoven and north toward Jefferson Street.

Sean and the rest of the crew of the Giant secured water and made a stand at the intersection of Clinton and DeKoven while the America traveled a block down and around to Taylor and Jefferson.

"Mac" Collier and Sean advanced a heavy canvas 2 ½ inch hose line to the center of the intersection and began throwing water on two burning cottages on either side of the street – one then the other, back and forth. They quickly realized the position was likely impossible to hold. The heat was near unbearable, and their water stream barely got halfway to the fire before it steamed and evaporated. Looking up, Sean saw hundreds of firebrands lifted away on the wind. Worse, numerous piles of fallen leaves were igniting, and the wind was randomly scattering them in all directions. Although the winds aloft were steadily blowing out of the southwest, the ground winds were swirling. The result was a fire growing in all four directions.

The roar of the fire, the shouts for help, the gusting wind and barking dogs blended into a cacophony of chaos. All was motion and fear. Chickens, dogs, pigs and horses, bolted here and there among the people rushing from their homes, all looking for safe harbor. And everywhere were vermin. Sean had never seen so many rats and mice. The horde scurried between the feet of animal and human alike as they poured out of the burning homes, sheds and coops.

Over the hiss of the nozzle's flow, Mac yelled, "Sean, I don't care for the look of this. There is as much fire getting over our heads as is in front of us."

"I see it, Mac, but there is nothing to be done about it. If we don't hold here, this devil will march right down to the river."

"True enough, but I thought I might point out that if those fires get behind us, we'll be trapped; if that sort of thing is of interest to you, that is."

"Well then, we best hope that the neighbors keep tamping them out."

"They'll be over-matched soon. Where in blazes are the rest of the fellas? We should have 50 men here by now," said Mac.

"You're right about getting overrun. I got this line, pull a second and dowse the next house down, see if we can keep it from burning. If we can stop it from hopping the street, we got a chance of hanging on till help comes."

"Sure we do, Sean. And the wee folk of the forest will be leaving gold in your privy next Christmas as well."

When Mac left him for the second line, Sean absorbed the full recoil of the hose, relentlessly pushing back against him. It nearly knocked him over before he managed to lean forward and plant his feet. The hose pressure up, and it was all Sean could do to stand against it. He knew all too well what happened when a charged line got loose. It would dance wildly, like an angry snake, and all the while the heavy brass nozzle would whip around, striking anything, or anyone, near it. He once saw a man killed when a nozzle struck him on the head, and so he hung on for dear life.

Just as he was beginning to tire, he felt relief from behind, helping him resist the backward force of the water stream. Sean yelled, "What of the second line, Mac? We need more water if we're to hold here."

"I don't know what you mean," came the reply. It was Liam.

Looking back, Sean yelled. "What in blazes are you doing here son?"

"I saw the fire… you looked like you needed a hand."

"You shouldn't be here, it's…"

"You need help. I am staying put."

Sean and Liam stared at each other in a silent battle of wills. Recognizing his son's determination, Sean nodded and returned his attention to the fire. In the minutes it took for Mac, now joined by Garland Mercer, to return with the second line, the fire had gained in intensity. The houses around both corners, north and south, were freely burning. By the time Mac got water flowing, the houses next to them were smoking, and a tree across the street had ignited. Worse, the wind was picking up.

The second line proved too little too late. It seemed to have no effect on the fire at all. They looked on helplessly as the fire ignited a large shed and three more trees. The rising heat forced the men to turn sideways and pull their coats up to protect their faces. Then it happened, a cottage across the street caught fire.

"This won't do, we're getting flanked," shouted Sean. "Garland, go find the America and see if they can stretch a line around the corner and head off this bastard to the north."

Sean could see that Mac was struggling with the line by himself. "Coil it on itself and sit on it," he yelled.

"Can't–it's too stiff," Mac replied.

Without being told, Liam took a position behind Mac, instinctively burying his shoulder in the small of Mac's back; stabilizing him without pushing too hard. Sean watched the grim determination on his son's face. He knew the boy felt the same growing pain from the heat, and the intense, primal instinct to run from a fire. Yet even while the neighbors panicked, his son held firm. *He acts like he was born to it*, thought Sean, with more than a little pride.

*****

More than a mile away, William Brown was getting nervous. After he had refused Schaffer's instructions to strike a second alarm at a new location, he went to the window to watch the fire. After several minutes of nervously watching the fire grow, he took it upon himself to strike a second alarm. However, still convinced two locations might confuse the crews, he sent the additional firefighters to box 342. Nine fire companies stormed into the night, in the wrong direction.

*****

Sean, Liam and Mac stubbornly held their ground, constantly aware of the fire's rapid spread to the north and south. Most disturbing was the steady "red snow" of falling embers behind them. If not for the desperate work of the neighborhood residents, the entire block would be lost. Sean watched as dozens of men and women frantically tamped out embers, tore down fences and sheds, and helped folks carry their possessions to the street, hoping to salvage something — anything — from the ferocious flames. Some faces were familiar, many not. He knew some had already lost their cottages. Still, they worked to help their neighbors. *I hope Liam sees this too,* he thought. *For all his talk about this being a cutthroat world, there's these folks giving all they can to help each other. And isn't he here too? Standing tall, pitching in – this… this is the son I raised, not the liar and thief that…*

"I'm near exhausted," said Mac. "Liam. Trade me spots."

As Sean watched, Liam took the nozzle. When he opened it, it nearly pushed him over – Mac caught him. Instinctively, Liam leaned far forward, out over the hose, until he had it balanced. Liam called to Sean, "Where should I aim?"

"At something orange and hot, it doesn't matter which," was Sean's reply.

"So we just stand here and throw water at the fire? That's the whole of it?"

"For now, son. Yes."

The boy has some stones, I'll give him…

A parade of nine engines interrupted Sean's thoughts. With them, Deputy Chief Snider emerged like a ghost out of the smoke.

Sean was never so happy to see the gruff old German. "Glad you could finally find the party. We were starting to get lonely," said Sean.

"I've no time for your sass Collins," said the burly German. "The dummkopfs working the boxes have us running all over this forsaken town. We're only here now because we saw the glow in the sky."

At that moment, Garland Mercer returned from the America. "The boys over on Taylor are getting singed, and the beast is about to push by them. They can't help us."

Schnider swore something in German and said, "Collins, you can't hold here, you need to fall back to Canal Street. And be quick about it."

"If we leave, we will lose the block."

"You'll lose the block anyway. This thing is spreading in every direction. It's already flanking you. It'll be by us soon enough. We need to throw a ring around the thing and wet down the exposures ahead of it. It'll take a while and you need to fall back far enough that it won't overtake you before we're ready." Snider turned to Garland. "You, go find the nearest box and turn in a code for a 3rd alarm. We need every available man if we are to have a prayer." With that, Snider disappeared into the smoke as quickly as he had materialized.

Sean turned to Liam and said, "Go home and tell your mother to gather whatever the two of you can easily carry. Both of you get over the river as quick as you can."

"No!" Liam protested. "You need help here. I won't leave you short-handed."

"There is no time to argue, son. I don't believe we can stop this thing – not with this wind. You don't have much time. Listen close, soon enough, people are going to panic and run for the river crossing on Madison. It'll get clogged with wagons bottling the whole mess up. You and your mother move north and cross at the bridge on Lake Street – the south branch. Or better yet, use the Indiana Street crossing. That'll put 2 rivers between you and this."

"You don't think it can jump the river, do you?" asked Liam.

"No, we will hold there, I hope. But I tell you, son, I'm afraid Chicago will pay dearly tonight. Many a home will be lost, ours included, I suspect, and many a life too. I'm counting on you to get your mother to safety. And remember, don't dawdle. Get over the bridge as quick as you can. Time is all."

*****

A breathless Garland Mercer turned the corner and found Mr. Goll standing in the street outside his pharmacy. The old man had closed the business and he and his wife were staring, transfixed, at the glowing debris drifting high aloft in the night sky, almost heedless of the embers falling around him. Mercer called out. "I need to use the box in your store."

Without pulling his eyes from the sight above, the pharmacist replied, "No need, I pulled it already."

"I've been told to pull a third alarm. We got ourselves a helluva a mess."

"I'll get my key for you."

"No need," said Mercer. "I got my own." Goll nodded, and unlocked the pharmacy door. Mercer entered the darkened business and pulled the box lever. As he hurried down the street, back towards the fire, Mercer heard Goll shout. "Can you stop it?" "Of course," was the reply. "Don't we always?"

Sitting in the alarm room, William Brown received Garland's alarm for box 319. Unfortunately, in his haste, Garland failed to pull the proper sequence for a third alarm and so only turned in a simple fire notification. At first, Brown assumed this was a case of a citizen making a late report, but the fact it was so far from Box 342 made him nervous. For the first time since the fire started, Brown called up to Schaffer and asked his opinion.

Mathias Schaffer watched the fire for several minutes and, noting the wind, told Brown, "I think the last call was a mistake. Strike a third alarm for box 319."

"Are you sure, Mathias?" asked Brown.

"Do it!" screamed Schaffer. "It's bigger than yesterday's fire, and that was a third."

Rebecca watched the growing flames in terror. To her husband, she said, "Bernard, I fear for our home. That fire is far bigger than I thought possible, and growing so fast."

Bernard looked at his brother. "What of it Mathias?"

Schaffer was silent for a long while, before speaking. "Tonight will be a tragedy long remembered, I'm afraid. There is nothing to do but pray for those on the wrong side of the river."

Gretchen hooked her arm through Mathias's and said. "Thank goodness for the firemen; they'll stop it."

Mathias shook his head. "There over matched tonight. The fire will take what it wants. Only the river will stop it."

Rebecca asked, "Do you think so, Mathias? The river will stop it, you're sure?"

"Let's pray it …"

Bernard cut his brother off. "Of course it will, dear. Fire can't get across a river – never has. It's a tragedy, but let's be thankful it's over there among the slums. God and the river will protect the better class."

I hope you're right brother, thought Mathias.

A floor below, William Brown sat vexed. From his window, he could see the fire was out of control, but didn't believe they had the authority to strike a third alarm. Finally, he concluded that if blame was to be had, it would be on Schaffer. He reluctantly activated the third alarm but again made it for box 342, stubbornly hanging on to the belief that a different location would cause confusion. Fortunately, the box location no longer mattered; the fire had so lit up the night sky crews could simply navigate by sight.

*****

Mac and Sean began the laborious task of pulling their heavy canvas hoses back to Canal Street. Desperately wanting to do something – anything– to help, a crowd of men and women busied themselves dragging the engine and heavy hoses down the street. With their help, the move went quickly but, even so, the fire nearly overtook them. No sooner had they got water flowing again than a nearby fence and tree exploded into flames. The fire had grown intense enough now that it wasn't only growing by falling embers and burning leaves. Now the blistering heat was radiating far outward – greedily reaching for whatever was next- a tree, a shed, a house – it didn't matter. A thing would smolder for a minute or two, then instantly explode into flame. As they wetted the nearby buildings, Sean watched in despair as house after house caught fire in the block they just vacated. The more it ate, the hotter it got, and faster it grew, The fire now consumed everything from Canal to Jefferson and was quickly pushing north and south from Polk to 12th Streets – Four square blocks had become a seething inferno.

Additional firefighters arrived with a third hose. *It ain't enough,* thought Sean. *This thing is already getting close to Maggie, I'll wager. I hope to hell they hurried.*

As the fire grew in intensity, it took on a life of its own. Sean watched in amazement as it sucked in leaves and other debris on a steadily building draft, while simultaneously a blistering hot gale force wind buffeted his face – away from the mounting conflagration. It was something he had heard of but never actually encountered – the fire was making its own wind. It was pulling cooler air in, while expelling a spiraling torrent of super-heated gusts out and upward. As best as he could guess, the winds were at a steady forty – even fifty knots. He watched in awe as the tempest carried away a steady stream of burning leaves and embers, some the size of pumpkins. A flaming shirt soared aloft into the night. It fluttered back and forth as it rose. As a child, he had a nightmare about hell; in it, the tortured souls drifted about on a hot wind as they burned. A shiver ran through him, this night was far too close to the mark. *We won't stop this monster, not with these winds.*

"What the hell?" he heard Garland say. It was followed by a laugh. Sean followed Garland's gaze and saw Dennis Rogan leading a smallish cow with a singed one-legged man on its back.

"Is that you Daniel Sullivan?" asked Sean.

"Yes, and lucky to be alive."

"You seem to have lost your leg – again."

"The damned thing burnt up if you can believe it. Me with it nearly, if not for this beast here."

"So, you're a cattle thief now, are you?"

"This is the O'Leary's calf. I saved it from the fire, or it saved me. A little of both, I guess. This damned fire started in their barn, you know."

"I heard," said Sean. "How is it with them?"

"They all got out thanks to Dennis here. The barn is gone, but their house was still standing when last I looked."

"It would be a miracle if it survived, but they're unhurt and that's the thing."

"Damnedest thing– I went by their house on my way to the Cassik place and all was well. They were in bed, I could tell. Twenty minutes later, I come back and old Beelzebub had opened the gates to perdition. I can't imagine what happened."

"I'm glad you're among the living, Daniel."

"No more than me," said Peg-Leg. "Will you and the boys be able to whip it, Sean?"

"We'll do what we can, but you and Dennis would do well to get across the river."

"That bad?"

"Could be, and Dennis, don't waste time."

Fighting A Fire   Circa 1871, artist unknown

Chapter 12

Pushing through the gathering crowd of panicked onlookers, Liam hustled down Canal Street. His father's insistence on his leaving stung. *He sent me on a goose chase, is all. He's still angry with me about the meat, I suppose – I guess he has a right to be. Still, I just wanted to help.*

He had heard them say that the steamer *America* was at Taylor and Jefferson. That was blocks from their home. However, when he got to Taylor, he could see that the fire had already overrun *America*, and was now pushing north up Jefferson and west, down Taylor toward him. Even from a half block away, he could feel the heat. The fire's progress and the steady stream of falling embers convinced him that what he had thought was a fool's errand to get rid of him was indeed urgent.

At Polk he turned and made his way back to Clinton, where he found crews and private citizens arranging hose lines only two blocks from his house. Looking east, he saw another crew on Jefferson. Now, seeing the peril clearly, he ran to his house.

Liam found his mother standing in the street among a crowd of onlookers. Before he could speak, his mother gasped, "Mother Mary help us. You've singed your hair and clothes. Where have you been?"

"I've been with father; he's at DeKoven. He sent me to…"

A well dressed man holding a notebook and pencil interrupted Liam. "Excuse me, were you down by the fire? Do you know how it started?"

Liam had little use for the hob knobs downtown; the bankers, lawyers and politicians all abused his people, but he especially despised reporters. They lied for a living, blaming the Irish and Africans for anything and everything wrong in Chicago. "Bugger off. I don't know anything about…"

Old man Darcy spoke up. "I don't know how it started, but I can tell you where. Not ten minutes ago, I talked to a gent who had gone to a party close by. He said the thing started in O'Leary's dairy barn."

The reporter asked, "Are you saying some partiers in a dairy barn started this?"

"No – No you fool. I didn't say that. I hear tell they found it; they didn't start it."

Liam asked Darcy, "Are you sure about this?"

"Sure enough. They saw the whole thing. Said they smelled smoke and ran down there quick. Found the thing burning like Hades itself."

It took only a moment for Liam to make the connection. *Johnny! That son of a bitch burnt out the O'Learys. And who knows what with it?* A second realization then came to him. When it did, it hit him like a hammer blow. *And I was supposed to be with him. God, what a fool I've been.*

Liam grabbed his mother's arm and pulled her aside. He whispered, "Listen close. Father is worried that the fire can't be stopped. He says our house may well be lost along with the others. We are to gather what we can carry and head to the other side of the river."

"Nonsense," said Maggie. "The fire is blocks away."

"This wind is driving it hard. I've seen how fast it's growing. He's not wrong – we need to leave."

"We'll watch it a bit, and if it gets to Polk or Quincy, we'll pack up."

"No Mother. It will be too late then. It's near Polk now, and the wind is pushing the thing to the northeast. Father says by the time it gets near us; the bridges will be un-passable. We need to go now."

"I won't leave until I have to, Liam. It may miss us; the wind could change."

"It won't change. And even if it did, there is no harm in getting to safety. Please hurry, we need to go. I promised father."

"No harm you say? You know this neighborhood, and the people who live here. If they see us pack and leave, the lot of them will be robbing us before we turn the corner. They will steal everything I… we have."

"These are your neighbors, you know them. No one will steal anything. Now, come…"

"How can *you*, of all people, stand there and tell me no one will rob us? Tell the truth, son. Were you really with your father, or did you get singed entering someone's burning house?"

His mother's words were like a slap in the face. "You think so little of me?"

"Have you given me cause to think better?"

"I won't argue with you anymore. We need to go."

"And I said…"

"I will make you a bargain, mother. If you do as father says – leave right now, I'll stay and protect the house from all your imagined thieves. If you don't, I swear to Jesus, I will burn the damn place down myself, like the waste of a son you believe me to be."

"You wouldn't dare."

"I swear I will. The damned thing will be lost anyway, and you'll have no further reason to stand and argue with me. The choice is yours."

Maggie spit at her son's feet. "You're as bull headed as your father."

"Thank you," said Liam.

"There was no compliment intended. You're both a spur in my shoe."

Maggie stormed into the house and emerged a few minutes later carrying a knapsack. She glared at her son. "Do you promise to stay and guard the house?"

"You have my word."

"Sure, and gold that is, isn't it?"

As she turned to leave, Liam said, "Father said to avoid the Madison Street bridge. He said we were to cross at Lake or Indiana."

She waved him off without turning.

With a tinge of sarcasm, he called out to her. "Take care, mother." *How does father tolerate her so calmly?* he wondered.

Maggie stopped, turned, and replied. "Guard the house well, Liam. Don't disappoint me."

*****

Joseph Chamberlin watched with interest as the woman and the young man argued. He couldn't hear all they were saying, but picked up something about stealing and protecting the house. Eventually, the woman left, carrying a bundle. He guessed they were mother and son but thought, *you never know with these people.*

Chamberlin hated the poor, especially the Irish poor. He considered them a cancer on the city. Drunk, lazy and stupid, they spread crime and disease in whatever neighborhood they infested. He had joined the staff of the Chicago Evening Post in part because of its vehement editorial stance against immigration. Proper society feared that if stern immigration reform wasn't imposed, the so-called huddled masses would overrun the population. He cared little for the Germans, Slavs, or Nords that were streaming out of New York; most were papists and elbowing their way into business, but at least they kept to themselves. It was the Irish and Africans he hated most. *They are showing up everywhere*, and *they are getting uppity* were common complaints in the downtown parlors and business clubs. Even the preachers in the pulpits were warning of the papist invasion.

He opened his notebook. He had made two notations already, the first read: *Drunken Irish party sets barn on fire and burns down neighborhood.* There was a question mark next to it. The second read, *Drunken couple named O'Leary come home and set barn on fire after party.* He put a check mark next to that one. He knew his editor would like the first story idea the best, but he thought that going with a specific couple who owned the barn would be more authentic.

Below this, he wrote, *thugs going door to door looting houses during fire*. He paused and added an additional note: *Irish thugs stealing from their own during tragedy*. He smiled and said, "Better."

*****

This is foolishness, thought Maggie, as she pushed her way down Clinton Street towards Harrison. *There is no way the fire will get so far. That oaf I call a husband had no right to send Liam to push me off.*

A block down Harrison, a host of embers and a gathering smoke cloud assailed her. Abandoning Harrison, she took Canal to Jackson. Maggie turned back and studied the giant red glow that lit the night sky. *Still, for all his shortcomings, Sean ain't prone to panic. Maybe there's something to it. All the same, I won't be dragging my things all the way to Lake Street – it's just foolishness. I'll go over to St. Paul's and wait till things settle down. If Sean is right for once, it'll be close enough to the Madison Bridge.*

She wondered how much of the neighborhood could burn. *Maybe Sean was right. Maybe it would burn all the way to the South Branch. That has to be over 100 homes,* she thought. *If only it could cross over and burn down the Cheyenne District – Big Mike's place, and all the other whorehouses and saloons. Pity about the poor folks losing their homes, but it would be the lord's work, sure enough. Just like Sodom and Gomorrah, fire cleansing is just what this Babylon needs.* "I'll pray on it," she muttered as she trudged through the gathering crowd watching the distant orange glow.

*****

His mother had only been gone a few minutes when Liam saw the first of the burning embers drop into the street. Only a few for a short while, but soon they fell like red, scorching rain. First in the street, then on the neighbor's roof, then his own house. Almost instinctively, he ran inside, grabbed a broom and, using a nearby tree, mounted the roof. He frantically brushed the constant rain of embers off the cedar shingles. As he worked, he watched his neighbors tamping out fires around their homes and on their own roofs. He noted most of the embers were falling on the other side of the street and watched in horror as house after house caught fire.

The work proved desperate and felt futile, and then, as if by a blessing, the wind shifted almost entirely out of the West. Now, the embers drifted away from his house and down Canal Street. Unfortunately, the near unbearable heat from the burning houses across the street still caused everything around to smolder. He was sure that his own home would ignite soon.

Relief came when a string of fire crews set up at each intersection from Polk Street to Adams. They doused roofs and yards on his side of the street, practically ignoring the unfortunate buildings already burning across from him. From his vantage on the roof, he could see the fire rapidly spreading towards the southern branch of the river only four blocks away, and to the north, to who knew where. He understood what they were doing; they were counting on the river to stop the fire's progress west and were using the engines to stop its spread to the east and north. He guessed another fire line was being set up, at either Adams or Madison. *They have to protect the Madison Street bridge for evacuation;* he thought.

With the immediate danger gone, Liam sat on his roof and watched in awe as the fire relentlessly consumed block after block, unchecked, to the river. He couldn't deny the beauty of the monster as it spread out in front of him, nor could he ignore the growing despair arising from its inhumanity. From his perch, he saw the blind panic among the fleeing people. Some had loaded wagons hoping to save their most treasured belongings. Most just desperately carried whatever they could as they fled. All terrified, all unsure of what to do or where to go, and so they followed each other in a panicked exodus toward the Madison Street viaduct.

He was not conscious of the change within him; it came subtly and there was too much chaos whirling around him. But, for the first time, he felt true empathy – a kindred spirit with the suffering souls desperately trying to flee; he was one with their fear, their sense of loss. He did not know it then, but he would never again have the stomach to cause those feelings in others.

I am glad mother got out early, thought Liam, *Cold as she is, I do love her. Father was right about the fire, about the need to get out early and avoid the bridge at Madison. Father was right about everything. Well, most things anyhow – about Mike – about me. I see it now; Big Mike isn't smart or powerful. He's just too lazy to make a living honestly, and vicious enough to hurt whoever has what he wants. Mike is responsible for all this, I'm sure of it. And for what? So he could take the O'Leary's money? And what Mike did to poor Rose...* Horrible images of that night haunted him, of Mike and Johnny and the rest of them – laughing as they tortured Rose – broke her.

Is that what I want to become? A dupe for a monster and sidekick to a vicious, stupid hoodlum. Is that to be my life – a cancer like them? Look what they've done, nearly set the world on fire. And fool that I am, I can't wash my hands of my part in all this. I could have prevented it – somehow. What was I thinking?

He gazed off to the South, back where he had left his father. The fire had pushed well west and north of where his father had been. It suddenly occurred to him that his father was in the beast's path and that, while the river would stop the fire, it also left his father no place else to run. Soon his back would be against the water. In all the years he was growing up, he had never really considered the possibility that his father could be killed. He felt a sudden urge to go find him. To stand with him.

*****

Chamberlin could not resist the impulse to see the fire, or what the fire crews were doing to stop it. He dodged, darted, and pushed his way back through the fleeing crowd to the intersection of Clinton and Polk streets. He found a line of fire engines stretching from Jefferson down to Canal on Polk. As he watched, he noted the firefighters appeared sluggish and exhausted. *No doubt hung over from the celebration after yesterday's fire*, he thought. In his notebook he jotted down, *Some firefighters drunk?*

Before long, the wind driven fire threatened to overrun the thin line of firefighters on Polk. Even from a distance, he felt the heat punish his skin. He noticed the coats of some firefighters were steaming. *I'll say this, they may be lazy and dull, but they are tough.*

The heat and wind finally proved too much; despite their best efforts, the firefighters hose streams proved futile against the inferno. Chamberlin looked on in disbelief as the fire lines were shut down and pulled back a block to redeploy. He quickly saw it as a strategic error. The fire was faster than the firefighters; before they could reconnect the hoses, the winds had pushed the fire upon them. Like the firefighters, Chamberlin was compelled to make a hectic retreat several blocks north to Adams Street. Chamberlin, the citizens, and the fire crews knew that those abandoned blocks would be lost.

Seeing the firefighters over matched created a widespread panic in the neighborhoods. Chamberlin watched in fascination as panic and chaos spread among the fleeing crowd. Some frantically threw as many of their possessions as possible into carts and wagons, intending to take them along as they fled, only to abandon all when the fire got close. Many simply dragged their possessions into the street, thinking them safer there.

The growing collection of wagons, debris, furniture, and people rapidly clogged the narrow streets. As they became more impassable, panic grew. Watching the pushing and shoving, and hearing the curses, Chamberlin felt disgust at the pandemonium. *Proper folks would no doubt comport themselves with some dignity*, he thought. Look at them, pouring into the street, unsure what to do or what direction to flee, dashing off one way, only to dash back minutes later. *They act like scurrying beetles when their rock is overturned.*

He watched two men fight over the use of a wagon. A woman, indecently dressed in only a sleeping gown, frantically helped her husband herd their sheep into the street. No one, not even her husband, seemed to notice her brazen behavior or offer to cover her modesty. *A proper lady, like my Elizabeth, would rather risk death than let herself be seen like that,* he thought.

There were noble acts of courage and kindness too, but these didn't interest Chamberlin. Neighbors helped neighbors fight the blaze; some ran into burning cottages to help friends remove possessions. The young often carried the feeble to safety on their backs. But Chamberlin made no note of it and had no intention of writing about it. *There would be plenty of heroic stories about proper folks before the night was through.* He would not praise these people who, through their despicable habits, now threatened the city he loved. *This fire is their fault!*

The fire crews finally threw up a line of engines on Adams from the river up to Clinton. The wind had turned mostly to the west, and it looked as though the line would hold. From a safe distance behind the fire line, Chamberlin wrote notes for the morning edition. *The exhausted firemen, many still drunk from the day before, abandoned the neighborhoods to save themselves. In the face of great peril, the hordes of immigrants also showed their true colors. Drunken brawls, looting, and naked women running in the street without shame. Only the sheep and cattle seemed orderly in their evacuation.* He smiled. Yes, the editors will like this.

Chamberlin moved up and down the line on Adams, mostly spending his time close to the river. He watched in fascination as the crowds pushed their way towards the Madison Street bridge, and the relative safety of the other side of the river. He grudgingly acknowledged that the fire line on Adams was effective, and the northern progress of the fire had been effectively stopped.

Around midnight, he was shocked when he saw the firefighters pulling out and taking their equipment to the river. Incredulous, he asked one of the retreating firefighters why they were abandoning the streets to the north. He only caught a part of the firefighter's reply, "… across the river."

This page left blank

Chapter 13

For nearly thirty minutes, Sean and his fellow firefighters stubbornly held the line that Deputy Chief Snider had thrown around the fire. But the searing heat and relentless southwesterly wind eventually proved too much.

Once the fire broke through the circle of engines, it devoured homes, shops, fences, sheds, coops, and even the wooden sidewalks. The updraft created by the inferno lifted torrents of swirling flame hundreds of feet into the air. Discouraged and exhausted, firefighters retreated – regrouped – and retreated again – inexorably pushed back to the river. Realizing that they could not stand in the face of the conflagration, they took up positions on the fire's flank, hoping to control its lateral spread as it burned its way to the water. Their priorities became protecting the escape routes, the Madison Street bridge to the north, and the 12th Street bridge to the south. As Sean had predicted, the panicked mobs soon started fleeing across the river – to safety.

Sean, Garland and the rest of the Little Giant and America crews found themselves on 12th Street just in front of the Fort Wayne rail yards, a massive rail depot and warehouse complex. For nearly an hour, they worked at creating fire breaks – tearing down fences and sheds, and hosing down buildings. Many police pitched in, as had countless citizens. Their efforts had paid dividends; they stopped the fire from getting into the yard. The rail beds helped, as did the wind's persistent westerly push. Now they sat on large fire lines, wetting roofs to hold the falling embers at bay.

From his vantage point, Sean could see that the fire had reached the river across from Taylor Street. He assumed it had reached the water further north as well… *To where?* He wondered. *Van Buren? Jackson, or even Adams? I hope the boys are still holding the Madison Bridge. If not, many a soul will be lost this night.* His thoughts turned to Maggie and Liam. *God, I pray they listened to me.*

Garland Mercer interrupted Sean's thoughts. "It was a hell of a thing watching your boy stand tall to the fire before. You must be proud."

"To be honest, I didn't expect it of him. The boy puzzles me. Just when I think I have him marked, he does something contrary."

"Marked as what?"

Sean shrugged. "Let's leave that be. I'll just say his help was unexpected."

"It's the way with the young," said Garland.

"How's that?"

"Confounding expectations. I remember not being sure of anything when I was his age. Things get jumbled up and confused inside. I surprised myself as much as not, not sure how anyone else was to predict what I'd think or do."

Sean pointed at some smoldering weeds next to a switchman's shack. "Mind your hose Garland. You're about to let that shack light up." Garland trained his hose on the incipient fire, and Sean continued their conversation, "I went through it too," said Sean. "But not like Liam. He's turning his back on the world."

"We all walk our own path. He ain't you – never will be – but he has you in him. Give him time, the young man I saw tonight seemed right enough."

Sean laughed. "And when did you become a sage?"

With a chuckle of his own, Garland replied, "I am still young; I confound expectations too."

"Sorry to tell you Garland, you're a plain enough book to read." Sean paused, then added, "Mind that pile of lumber over there. If it lights off, we'll be toiling all night in this yard."

Garland threw water on the woodpile. "You worry too much. The fire is pushing away from us. This yard is safe enough. I think we got a twist on it now. It's to the river, and we're holding good here. The boys up north are holding their heads high. The bastard is running out of places to go."

They silently watched the fire raging to the north as they dossed a storage shed near the rail yard.

"You may be right," said Sean. "If the wind holds, that is. If it turns hard to the north, I don't know where it goes."

"I never seen such a night like this," said Garland.

"Only thing I saw close was when the cessesesh burned Atlanta – set fire to the warehouses as they skedaddled. They ended up burning the whole town down, never thought I'd see a thing like it again. This looks to be worse – the wind is what."

"I don't care to see it again," said Garland. "It's like one of those old bible stories. Just look at it; as far as the eye can see, its swirling flames leaping and twisting all over, wind howling, fire brands falling like rain from above. I swear to God, a roof got ripped off a shed a while ago. It just got pulled straight up and it was gone. God himself is doing this, no natural thing could."

Under his breath, Sean muttered, *"Father, why have you forsaken me?"*

"What was that?"

"Nothing," said Sean. "Just something from scripture."

"A prayer?"

"Something like that."

"Sean, do you think God is punishing us?"

"Could be. He has a taste of using fire to punish the wicked."

"And what of the innocent children? Many will die or left orphaned tonight. How do you square that?"

Sean moved his hose stream to a small shed close to a scale house. "Let it go Garland. Faith is best taken at face value. Trying to make sense of it gets you nothing."

"You sound like one of them priests when he runs short of answers."

"I ain't your priest, and I got no answers. Believe what you want. As for me, I don't much give a damn why God does what he does. I'm just trying to stay out of his way."

"There should be rain – soon I think."

Sean gave him a puzzled look. "What? Now what in blazes are you talking about?"

"Rain. A wind like this usually heralds a storm. Anyway, I guess we've stood up to the worst of it."

"I hope so. We paid the devil's price tonight. I'm guessing we lost 50 or 60 blocks. Maybe more, maybe much more. God only knows how many lives are lost, and buildings gone. And it's anyone's guess as to what becomes of those put out of their homes."

Garland moved his hose to a large clump of weeds that had caught fire. "They may rebuild… eventually."

Sean shrugged. "Sure, something will get built. But it won't be our kind that does it. Those with deeper pockets than ours will scoop up the burned dirt for pennies and make a pretty profit from our misery. I tell you Garland, the folks that lost homes and businesses tonight won't be back."

"You're a gloomy one."

"There is a mile of fire between me and my burnt-out house. Gloomy is about right, ain't it?"

Garland and Sean continued wetting debris and shrubbery – anything that could burn– near the railroad storage buildings. It was tedious, but it was fruitful. They stopped the southern spread of the fire.

Near midnight, they paused for a much needed break when a fire captain they didn't recognize ran up to them. Above the gusting wind he yelled, "What's wrong with you? Pick up your equipment and get moving!"

Confused, Garland answered, "What? Move where?"

"Across the river. You need to get across the river!"

"For the love of Mary, what's happening?"

"Are you blind?" yelled the captain. He pointed to the north.

In the distance, St. Paul's church towered over the skyline, it was completely engulfed in flame. *The spire looks like a torch held high aloft by God's own arm,* Sean thought. He saw a shower of distant sparks streaming away from the bell tower, off into the night. *Beautiful,* he thought, *how horrible and beautiful that is.* He said, "The church will be a loss to all."

The captain grabbed Sean's arm. "Not the church, you fool. Don't you see? The damned devil has jumped the river."

To his horror, Sean saw what the captain meant. Across the river, the embers from the church steeple landed on distant buildings. Several small but rapidly growing tongues of orange flame were sprouting up across the far bank. "Saints preserve us," gasped Sean. "The whole of the city could be forfeit."

The captain started off, but yelled over his shoulder. "It will be if you don't get your asses moving across that river."

*****

Crossing the 12th Street bridge proved maddening slow. A throng of panicked people, many with carts and wagons, pushed and shoved themselves onto the bridge and both approaches. Sean found the wretched crush of humanity un-nerving. Singed hair and clothes told the story of their escape. Clearly, women and children had gotten the worst of it. The men's duck and canvas work clothes were somewhat resistant to flame; not so for the billowing cotton dresses and night clothes of the women and children. Many were scorched, and some near burned off completely. Blisters and burns were common and ugly. The pathetic sight of injured and terrified mothers and children pushed his thoughts to Katie, Kerry and Mary Sullivan. He prayed they were safe.

Looking at the surrounding faces, he mostly saw fear, but not in all. He also saw what he believed was contempt. Their allegations were unspoken but clear; *You let this happen. You failed us. Now you're running like everyone else.* He wanted off that bridge, and quickly – away from the crowd, and back to the fight, to do something – anything.

Sean, and every other firefighter, understood time was critical. If those fires on the west bank of the southern river took root, they would burn through the downtown to at least the main branch of the river. Trapped on the center of the bridge, he watched helplessly as the fires leaped from building to building. His heart sank; he knew they were already too late. The fire, driven by relentless winds, seemed to consume buildings instantly. In the 20 minutes he stood trapped on the bridge, entire blocks appeared to melt away in a sea of flame. Then came the fire devils – tornado like swirling clouds of flame. They were rare, but he'd seen small ones when large buildings burned. Now several giant ones – some a hundred feet above the ground – swirled in the night sky. Like Saint Paul's church, they were tossing out firebrands over great distances. He could only imagine the winds generated by the monsters.

He saw it before he heard it – or felt it. He experienced it in the war but never expected or wanted to experience it again – the strange suspension of time. First came the flash, then a mushroom cloud of flame rose into the air. Moments later, a solid thud hit his chest, and then the distinct rumble of the explosion. It drowned out the shouts and cursing of the crowd. For a few long seconds, all went quiet, and even the shoving and pushing stopped. All simply stood in stunned silence. Then the city went dark.

"What in the name of Jesus was that?" a voice asked.

"The gas works," said Sean. "The gas works just exploded."

An old woman cried, "God help us."

From behind him, Sean heard a male voice answer. "Not tonight, He won't."

The Aftermath

Photo circa 1871, author unknown

Chapter 14

"…. Holy Mary, mother of God, pray for us sinners, now and at the hour of our death. Amen." Maggie Collins' fingers moved to the next bead on her rosary. Standing among the congregation near the vestibule of Saint Paul's Church, she joined Father Michael and the other faithful in the next prayer. "Hail Mary, full of grace…"

Convinced that Sean and Liam were wrong about how far the fire would spread, she went to Saint Paul's rather than *traipse around in a strange neighborhood at night.* The crowd standing about watching the monstrous orange glow in the distance impeded her progress; still she felt safe. She had no illusions about the fire; she knew it was bad, maybe the worst the city had ever seen, but the idea it could run unchecked so far north was beyond reason. So, Maggie held her ground instead of fleeing. Rather, she joined the others in praying for the souls of those who would perish, and protection of the righteous.

As Maggie recited the rosary, her eye wandered to the prayer card of an elderly woman standing close by. It bore the image of Saint Florian, the patron saint of firefighters. A twinge of guilt nipped at her; praying for Sean hadn't crossed her mind.

He is out there somewhere, facing who knows what? I'm a poor wife for not caring more – I know it. But is he any better? Does he deserve my devotion? Does he care for me, or what I need? What is he but my jailer? I tell him I want different, and does he listen? No, he says. I'm being foolish, he says. When will the oaf learn I know best.

The congregation continued, "… blessed is the fruit of thy womb Jesus."

He'll come home safe and sound – he always does. And my purgatory will go on and on. God protects him to punish me. And for what? Wanting freedom is what.

"… blessed is the fruit of thy womb, Jesus…," said the parishioners.

A thud echoed through the church when a side door flew open. A wild-eyed man covered in soot and sweat yelled out. "Run for your lives, you fools. The church is a fire!" As abruptly as he had appeared, the intruder vanished into the pandemonium now visible outside. The crowd in the church stood in stunned silence for a moment while the warning took root. Then came the rush toward the doors.

The surge of people swept up Maggie so forcefully she barely had time to grab her bundle. Roughly shoved onto the street, she found herself in a sea of swirling chaos. Shouts filled the air. Everywhere, crowds rushed about in all directions. A burning rain of embers fell from above. One landed on a small boy's straw hat, igniting it. His mother knocked the hat off the lad, swept him up, and ran down the street. A woman screamed; her dress had caught on fire. A man threw himself on her, smothering the flames with his body as they rolled on the ground. Without a word, he sprang up and was gone. The stunned woman crawled to her feet and stumbled off.

Maggie looked up and saw the source of the rain of fire. Flames leaped from the church steeple and with them, the wind carried countless fire brands off into the night. She also saw that the once distant orange glow was now nearly upon her. Liam's warning from Sean screamed in her mind's ear, *Get across the river, as fast as you can.*

The surrounding panic took hold. Not sure of what else to do, she joined the crowd pushing to the river bank. At the river's edge, she saw fire pushing near the water to her south and so she kept to the bank heading north. For a few minutes, she made good progress, but as she neared Van Buren, the crowd swelled rapidly. Panic and the crush of bodies packed on the narrow sidewalk reduced the horde into a seething cauldron of pushing and shoving. Cries and curses filled the air. Like waves breaking on a shore the throng pushed forward, then shoved back. Punches were thrown as men tried to clear space for their family. A woman, desperately grasping her young daughter, got pushed off the elevated sidewalk and into the dark foul river some 20 feet down. Maggie knew that sharp rocks and shallow water waited below. *They are as good as dead;* she thought.

If the river bank had been pandemonium, the area around the train depot and Madison Street bridge seemed a scene from Dante's Inferno. The maelstrom of people swept Maggie along as they forced their way onto the bridge. Liam's warning came to her; *Avoid the Madison Street bridge. Get further north.* She understood it now; the bridge was all but impassable. But she was helpless against the crowd's inertia, and so she allowed it to carry her onto the bridge.

She quickly regretted not heading the warning. Wedged into a sweaty, crushing press of bodies, she could barely breathe. The stench of smoke and sweat, and foul breath assailed her. Illuminated only by the fire's distant radiance, eerie faces loomed far too close. Elbows jammed into her ribs, strange hips ground against her. Terrified, her movements were not her own. She was helpless to resist the momentum of the throng. The turbulent wave continued, pushing Maggie forward, only to shove her back again. Had it not been for the crowd pressing so tightly against her, she would have not kept her feet under her.

The crowd behind surged forward, nearly tripping her over some poor soul who had been knocked over and trampled. A man behind her grabbed Maggie around the waist and steadied her. She tried to turn to thank him, but couldn't. He had her in a tight embrace, pinning her arms to her side and pulling her body into him. The stranger leaned over her shoulder; she felt his breath on her neck – he reeked of whisky. He slurred something she couldn't understand. She tried to pull away – he held her tighter, laughed, then began crudely pawing at her breast. Again, she tried to wiggle free; he responded by moving a hand to her crotch. She let out a scream and stomped on his foot. He let her go but roughly snatched for her bundle. She held to it. He snarled, "Give it up, you shrew," and he grabbed at it again.

A deep voice boomed out. "Leave that poor woman be, you animal!" From the corner of her eye, Maggie saw a fist fly by her head. Her attacker released his grip, and she felt him try to punch back, but it was too crowded. Rather, her molester's elbow caught the back of her head. Stunned for a moment, she nearly fell. The scuffle pushed her aside. She nearly fell again, but caught the bridge rail for support.

In a panic, she tried to turn and escape the bridge, hoping to run far north, as Liam had suggested. But going back against the tide of humanity proved impossible. With no other choice, she went with the throng's momentum toward the eastern bank. About halfway across, whispers, then shouts spread through the crowd: *It crossed over. The far bank is on fire. God help us, the whole town will burn.*

With fire now on both banks of the river, the throng on the bridge became unsure of what to do and simply stopped. Maggie suffered no such indecision. The fire on the west bank had spread north, almost to the train depot. Going back was not an option. She would cross to the east bank and then follow the river north until she found safety.

With her back to the rail, and the shoving lessened, Maggie slowly snaked her way toward the east bank. She had nearly made it to the far end when her progress was stopped by a horse pulling a wagon. Attempting to wiggle past the beast, it spooked and pinned her to the rail. She was stuck until whatever was impeding the wagon's progress moved. Maggie took the opportunity to scan the eastern side of the river.

What had been small fires only minutes earlier had practically exploded. Not more than three blocks south, the massive Ogden's lumber yard burned furiously and to the terror of those on the bridge, the intense heat had ignited the thick film of oil waste floating on the water. The south branch of the Chicago River was burning, and the flames were drifting toward the bridge.

The fires would be upon them soon. Desperate to somehow get off the bridge, she considered jumping. Maggie peered down into the dark water. The fire illuminated the grizzly remains of some cattle and other animals floating below. Among them were a handful of dead people. *Good lord, how can this be?* She thought.

Knowing time was short, she tried again to wedge past the horse. A voice tinged in desperation called. "Margret Collins, is that you? What should we do? I fear…"

Maggie recognized her. It was Martha Doyle, Patrick Doyle's wife.

"… we'll be trapped if we…" A deafening explosion overwhelmed the woman's voice. Maggie first felt a blast of hot air hit her from behind, and then the massive weight of the horse slam into her chest. The rail scraped her back as the beast's bulk pushed her up and over. There was falling – then pain – and then nothing.

Chapter 15

From the courthouse observation tower, they had spent the night watching the monstrous fire grow unabated. They saw it, but found it difficult to comprehend how such a thing could actually happen. Seeing it consume everything in its path was awful, yet somehow the swirling clouds of flame were beautiful too.

Bernard Schaffer mused, "It's an almighty terrible thing to see, so much has been lost. Still, I'll never forget the majesty of it."

Gretchen said, "It terrifies me. Nothing seems able to stop it."

"Don't be afraid, cousin. The fire crews seem to have bottled up its sides, and it's near the river now. The worst is over, I think."

"I'm not so sure," said Mathias. "I don't like the look of those fire flies coming off that church steeple."

"Where?"

Mathias pointed. "There to the southwest. They look to be blowing across the river."

Rebecca clutched her husband's hand. "Surely they can't drift so far, can they?"

They all nervously watched for several minutes, hoping – praying – that the river would stop the awful thing. That was, until they spied the first small fire on the east bank of the river.

"God help us," whispered Mathias.

*****

On crossing the Chicago River's south branch, Sean and the other members of *America* and *Little Giant* rushed to the leading edge of the fire at the intersection of Franklin and Tyler. As with their original stand on DeKoven Street, it proved too little too late. The fire had already taken root and was pushing north and east. A fire captain frantically ordered both crews to help set up a defensive line down Wells Street. "We have to hold there or it will take the courthouse and commerce building!" he had said.

As they pulled the Giant down the street, Garland joked, "Drop everything boys, the politicians and bankers are in trouble!"

Pappy gave Garland a playful shove. "Our paychecks are in that courthouse, you dimwit."

"Well then, I'm all for it. Though I don't see the use. We haven't stopped the bastard anywhere else. I don't see us doing better here. It's but a fool's errand."

"Just so, Garland," said Cap. "If it's a fool's errand, there's no better fool for it than you."

Pappy said, "I hear tell both buildings are fireproof."

"Take heart boys, On this side of the river, many of the buildings are brick and stone. We've a better chance here."

"We'll see," said Sean. "I don't put much stock in it, though."

*****

The giant courthouse bell tolled its warning. The deafening sound further unnerved Mathias, and he saw it clearly agitated the already terrified women. He put his arm around Gretchen; she shivered and pressed close to him. For an hour, they watched as the fire relentlessly burned its way towards them.

When the gas works explosion rocked the building, Rebecca had pleaded with Bernard to take her home, to gather their goods and flee. It was Mathias who had urged them to stay. He had warned them the fire was growing too fast for them to make it to their home. He assured them that the courthouse was fireproof, and it was the safest place they could possibly be.

From their perch high above the fire, they watched it consume entire blocks. As it approached, they saw the streets fill with the panicked seeking escape. They heard the shouting, and curses. They saw the chaos. Bernard said, "You were right, brother. Had we left, we would be caught in that fray."

"Our home," said Rebecca. "Our beautiful home will be lost while we sit here like… like cats caught in a tree."

Bernard embraced her. "You are safe. That's all that matters. Our things will be replaced."

Minutes later, the first building near them ignited. Bernard pointed across the street to the Chamber of Commerce Building. Flames were issuing out of the second-floor windows. He said, "My God. it houses the Board of Trade. If that building is lost, it will bankrupt the city."

"I don't understand," said Gretchen.

Bernard replied, "Many invested their life savings in stocks, bonds and commodity futures. They store records of transactions in that building; losing them will wreak havoc on many a family, mine included."

*****

The fire had pushed the crew of the *Little Giant* back from Franklin Street, then Wells, eventually to LaSalle. Despite their best efforts, the Chamber of Commerce Building began burning on the third floor, when embers drifted into a broken window. Sean, Pappy, Cap and Garland immediately set to work, throwing water into the upper floors. They knew it to be fruitless, but it was the best they could do.

Garland nudged Sean and pointed at an older black man who came running out of the building with a large box. He set it down and ran back into the building. "What's that about, do you think?"

"Sean, Garland," barked Cap. "Go see what he is up to."

They suspected theft, but when they looked in the box, they were surprised to only see papers. Garland picked some up and inspected them. Sean asked, "Well, what are they?"

"Damned if I can make a thing of them. Receipts maybe?" answered Garland.

The man returned with another box. "Good!" he said. "I can surely use you boys' help." He turned toward the building. "Follow along now. Hurry."

Sean pulled him back. "Hold on there. Who are you? Help with what?"

"My name is Joseph Hudlin. I'm the head custodian for this here place. And these is the Board of Trade records. They're terrible important. We need to get them to safety before the fire or water, or both ruin the lot. A whole lot depends on it. Now come on, time is a wasting."

Garland looked at Sean, who nodded, and they followed Hudlin inside. They raced across a large, ornate lobby and up an ornate staircase. On the second floor, Hudlin led them into a large office area, and on to a storage room full of cabinets.

Hudlin grabbed a box and tossed some large mail sacks to the firefighters. "Quick as you can, empty these drawers into the sacks."

The three worked feverishly and cleared out most of the drawers in a few minutes. As best as they could manage, they lugged the heavy bags down the steps and to the door. Near exhausted, they dropped their loads in a pile near the building entrance. Sean looked up, then motioned to Hudlin and Garland. The fire had spread rapidly and now was burning freely across the upper floors. Garland said, "If these papers are as important as you say, you did well to get them. This building will be a smoldering pile of bricks by morning."

"They ain't safe yet," said Hudlin. "We need to get these bags and boxes somewhere secure."

"And what are you three miscreants up to?" said one of two very large and angry looking police officers.

Put off by the man's tone, Garland bristled. "What in Hades does it look like? We're with the fire department and we are trying to save these things from that burning building."

The officer pulled his nightstick. "I'll tell you what I see. A nigger and two Irish dogs are stealing anything not bolted down. I'll wager there's money or valuables in those sacks."

"Is that so?" said Garland. "And how about I put that night stick up your ass."

The policeman raised his nightstick. "Hold on there!" a voice called. A short, portly man in an expensive suit rushed up. He pointed at Hudlin and said, "I know this man. He is our head custodian."

"And who are you?" asked the officer.

"I am Josiah Preston, the president of the Board of Trade. This man works for me."

"I caught these three looting the building."

"Nonsense," said Preston. "What have you got there, Joseph?"

Hudlin answered, "These are the papers from the record room. We got nearly all the important ones, I think."

Preston opened one of the bags, then a box. "Thank God! Mr. Hudlin, I wonder if you know what you have done. These papers are more valuable than gold! You've done a great service here – very great. Saving them is nothing short of heroic."

Garland growled at the policeman. "Are you satisfied? Or perhaps you'd like to hold court here on the steps while the building burns down."

To Preston, the officer said, "Alright then, you and your darkie can tend to your papers." He grabbed Garland's arm. "But we have some unfinished business with this mouthy Irish pup."

"And what sort of business might that be?" It was Cap, along with Pappy and Tommy Gwyn. Each held a heavy brass spanner or plug wrench. "Perhaps me and the boys should escort you into that burning building, so you can see for yourself that all is good and proper."

The seven men glared at each other, then without a word, the two policemen turned and walked away.

Sean exhaled and said, "Garland, one of these days your mouth will get you put in a pine box."

"Fuck those two. Coppers in this part of town are all pricks, not like the south side. Besides, I had you at my back if they started something."

"I don't need your help finding trouble."

*****

Mathias, Gretchen, Bernard and Rebecca were watching the fire devour the Chamber of Commerce Building when William Brown crashed through the door to the watchtower. "The building is on fire! Run for your lives, while you can." He then vanished down the steps as quickly as he had appeared.

They stood in stunned silence for several moments. Rebecca said, "I thought this building fireproof."

"So they say," answered Mathias. "Perhaps William got panicked by smelling smoke from the street."

Bernard said, "I'm not so sure, Mathias. I think we should at least go downstairs and see for ourselves."

Mathias nodded agreement, and the four carefully made their way down the steep, narrow stairs that led down from the watchtower platform and bell-tower. They pushed through a second door and found themselves in a hallway near devoid of light. Only the ominous glow of the fire outside penetrated the darkness. Mathias heard Rebecca gasp, "Why are there no lights?"

"The gas works…" said Bernard, "the explosion earlier… it eliminated the lighting."

Mathias reassured them, "It's no bother. I know the way. Come along." He led them down the hallway to the main stairwell. In the dim light, they failed to notice the light pall of smoke lingering at the ceiling. They mounted the stairs and cautiously made their way down.

Only a floor down, they turned the corner and saw the unmistakable orange glow of flickering flames reflected on the walls. In a near panic, Gretchen gasped, "Oh no! The building is on fire."

"It's not," said Bernard. "It's only from the fires outside – coming through a window."

They tentatively continued their descent. As they did, they encountered thickening smoke. They found it increasingly difficult to breathe and noticeably hotter. Bernard said, "I was wrong. I believe the building is on fire."

Mathias replied, "It seems so. We likely have no time to lose. We need to hurry on."

They heard cries for help and people coughing coming from the stairs far below them. Rebecca said, "I won't go down there. We will all get killed."

Bernard coughed, and said, "She's right Mathias, this is no good. We have to find another way."

Mathias took Gretchen's hand and led the group out of the stairwell. "Follow me, there's a service stair at the back of the building. It may be passable."

"We're not going to make it. This can't be happening to us," cried Gretchen.

"Yes, we will," said Mathias. "Come along." Still holding her hand, he led Gretchen down the hall and around the corner. Bernard and Rebecca were close behind. Almost dragging Gretchen along, Mathias led the group down a dark hallway and around a corner. Although he said nothing, he worried he wouldn't find the stairs. He had only stumbled upon them once looking for a water closet. At the far end, they found an intersecting hall leading off into darkness, both to the right and left. He paused, unsure of which to take.

"Do you know where you're going, Mathias?" asked Bernard.

Mathias ignored the question and turned left. As they went, the smoke continued to build. He felt resistance from Gretchen. Breathless, she said, "I have to… stop. Catch my… breath."

"I am sorry, we can't stop, we haven't the time. Everyone, down on the floor, get below the smoke!"

Mathias heard Rebecca whimpering. To bolster their spirits, he said. "I think I remember the stairs being towards the end of the building. They're likely close. This way, hurry now."

Bernard barked, "You think? We can't see a thing, and you have us groping around for stairs that might not even be on this side of the building. This won't do."

"Do you have a better idea, Barney?" replied Mathias. "I'm all ears."

"Hush, darling," said Rebecca, "Your brother is doing the best he can."

Bernard sighed, "Sorry Matty. I'm in a state, is all."

Gretchen squeezed Mathias's hand. She whispered, "I trust you."

He continued leading them down the darkened hall. After they traveled several feet, a memory came to him. Mathias called out, "The stairs are off an alcove, behind a door. The offices will be locked but not the stairs."– *I hope* – "Try the doors and see if one opens."

The hall quickly filled with the sound of doors being franticly jiggled. In moments, they heard Rebecca joyfully call out, "Here! I found it!"

They converged on her voice. Mathias opened the door. The halls had been dark, but at least some faint light filtered in through windows. Behind the door lay only pitch black. He dropped to his knees and felt around the floor. His hand found nothing but wooden planks. His head bumped into a wall, he followed it. It seemed to go on further than a stairwell would. *It's only an office*, he thought. *I've failed!* Panic edged in, he wondered how far in he had gone. *Had I turned? What if I can't find my way out!* He called out, "Bernard?"

"Yes! Did you find it?"

The voice was behind him and close. With relief, he turned to go back. His hand slipped off an edge. He frantically groped at what he knew was a stair tread.

"Mathias! Did you find it?"

"Yes! Yes, it's here. Come to my voice."

His three companions crowded around him. He reached out and his hand found a woman's leg. "Gretchen? Is that you?"

A hand covered his and squeezed. "Yes, it's me."

Cautiously, he slid off the landing and mounted the stairs. He groped with his free hand and found a banister rail. Standing, he felt no great heat and breathed no smoke. "The air in here is safe," he said. "We can descend to the first floor. Let's hope there is an exit to the outside at the bottom. I'll go first, then Gretchen, then Rebecca. Bernard, you go last. Go slow, put a hand on the rail and the other on the shoulder of the one in front of you. Be careful not to shove or we'll all fall."

In his head, Mathias counted the steps, 8 - 9 - 10 - he heard a gasp from behind him. Gretchen's heal had slipped from a step and now her full weight fell upon him. They tumbled a few feet onto a landing; he fell on his back, she on top of him. A hand touched his face. He felt her breath on his neck, then the lightest touch of her lips on his. She whispered, "Just in case we don't survive."

Mathias whispered back, "Gretchen, I…"

"Did you fall? Are you alright?" Rebecca called from the darkness above.

Gretchen answered as she gained her feet. "I slipped, but I am alright. Mathias caught me."

They reformed their line and slowly continued down the five remaining flights of stairs. As they went, it became hotter, but no flame or smoke assailed them. Relieved at finally reaching the bottom, Mathias felt around for the door; it was blistering hot to the touch. He reached for the knob. It singed his hand. "Damn the luck! It must not lead out, and I'm sure the fire is on the other side. We don't dare go out there."

Rebecca cried, "God help us, we are done for."

"No. we are not," said Bernard. "We'll go back up – above the fire and figure something out."

Gretchen said, "Perhaps we should wait here. The fireman will come soon."

"No." said Mathias. "This door won't hold long, and once the fire breaches this stair, it will do us in. We have to go up and find a way out."

"How?"

"We climb until we find a cool door. Go to a room for shelter, and go from there. Bernard, lead the way back up."

As quickly as they could, the foursome re-ascended the stairs. Mathias kept his eyes cast up, even though he could see nothing. The group paused, and in a flash, flames leapt into the stairwell. Bernard let out a scream.

"Close the door!" shrieked Rebecca.

"My God, Barney," said Mathias. "Are you alright?"

"A bit singed, but otherwise fine," replied Bernard. "I think we are trapped in here."

"No, that won't do. Sooner or later, flames will chew through those doors and this stairwell will be our crematorium. Go up a floor. And feel the wood before you open the next door."

On the third floor, Bernard found the door only warm. He cautiously opened it, and found the hallway void of flame, but still quite hot. In the dim light, he could just make out a dense cloud of smoke. He called back, "I don't like it. It feels as though the fire is close at hand, and it's terribly smokey."

Mathias said, "If it's tolerable, we should find an office with a window, preferably with a couple of doors we can shut between us and the fire."

"I don't know, brother. Maybe if we go up a few more floors."

"We're on the third floor, Bernard. If we go any higher, we won't be able to jump."

"Jump!" cried Gretchen. "We can't jump from a third-floor window. We'll break our necks."

"Let's hope it doesn't come to that." said Mathias. "But it maybe our best chance."

A few moments later, the four found themselves sitting on the floor near a window. They had broken into an office reception area, and then into the office proper. An orange glow from outside cast an odd light in the room; by it, they could see the smoke gathering. None mentioned it, but they all felt the heat building. Each new it was only a matter of time.

Gretchen took Mathias's hand. "I wish we had met sooner. I think I would have liked the chance to learn more about you."

"Don't be so fatalistic. This will turn out to be a grand story we tell our children – the night we met and survived the great fire! They'll hang on every word."

"And their cousins will be sitting there listening too," said Bernard as he patted Rebecca's hand.

"That does sound lovely, if only wishing made it so," sniffed Gretchen.

*****

The Chamber building was burning freely, the first and second floors of the courthouse as well. Sean knew both would soon be lost; along with every other nearby building. He expected the order to fall back and re-position to come soon; just as it had again and again throughout the night.

"Collins! Get over here." It was Deputy Chief Snider.

"What do you suppose the Grand Hun wants?" asked Pappy.

Cap replied. "Nothing pleasant, I'm sure. Best go see, Sean."

Snider nodded toward a tall man in a waistcoat and top hat, standing with two police officers. *At least it's not those two pricks from earlier*; thought Sean.

Chief Snider said, "Collins, this is Mayor Mason. He needs your help."

The Mayor said, "There are prisoners locked up in the basement jail. We need to release them before they are burnt alive."

Sean looked at Chief Snider, then the burning courthouse, then at the mayor. "No man alive can get in that building, much less bring people out."

One of the policemen spoke up. "There's a door in the back of the building that leads straight to the cellar. We can get in there."

"So, what am I needed for."

"We don't have the key to the basement door or the door leading to the cells. We're hoping you can break down the doors."

Snider said, "Grab a set of irons and see what you can do."

Sean shook his head. "Sounds foolish, but we can try. Meet me at the door."

As he was pulling an axe and claw hook from the *America*, Pappy joined him. "What are you about, Sean?"

"Would you believe it? They want me to engineer a jailbreak."

"Sounds fun. Can I play too?"

"Glad for the company."

They met the policeman at the back of the building, standing by a staircase leading down to a cellar door. One of them said, "Beings how it's an entrance to the jail, they put on an iron clad door with an extra stout lock. They say it's burglar proof. Do what you can."

Without a word between them, Sean put the claw of the pry bar in the doorjamb and Pappy used the blunt end of the axe to drive it in. Sean re-positioned himself to the side and Pappy swung the axe like a ball bat, driving the pry bar to the side. The door groaned but held. They repeated the process; the door held but part of the jamb splintered away. The third attempt caused the door to swing open.

"I'll be damned," said one of the policemen.

The five men descended into the darkened cellar. One of the police produced an oil lantern. He led them across a smokey store room to an opening closed off by thick iron bars. Obscenities peppered more than few pleas as the caged men called for help. The officer held the lamp next to the door lock. It was solid iron, with heavy plating.

"There'll be no prying that open, I'm afraid," said Sean.

"True enough," said Pappy. "Let me think a moment." He studied the door for a few seconds, then laughed. He took the pry bar and placed it against the top hinge. To Sean, he said, "If you would be so kind."

Sean struck the pry bar, and the hinge disintegrated. In a moment, both hinges were broken, and the door lay on the floor. "Ain't that the way," said Pappy. "A lock for a king and a pauper's hinges."

A policeman said, "You two do little to inspire confidence in our jail."

Sean replied, "Which begs the question, what are you going to do with the jailbirds after you get them out."

"Truth is, we weren't told – Look after them as best we can, I suppose."

"Alright, let's see about the cell doors," said Pappy.

"Were told the cell key is on the wall inside. You two can wait here."

The two officers went into the jail. Sean heard a loud clank, then a shout. "Stop, you bastards!" A moment later, a half-dozen men flew by them and up the steps. The officers emerged with four additional men.

"It appears some of your dogs have slipped the leash," said Pappy.

"They'll turn up. They always do."

Sean and Pappy followed the officers and their charges out of the basement. As they watched the policemen lead the prisoners off, Pappy said, "Well now, there's a new one for the…" A shoe hit him on the head. "What the devil was that?"

They looked up and saw a woman and man hanging out of a third-story window. "Help!" cried the woman. "We're trapped!"

Sean called up, "How many are there up there?"

"Four," answered the man. "Two are women. Hurry, we can't stay much longer."

"Stay put! We'll get a ladder." Sean turned to Pappy. "Round up the 30-foot Bangor ladder and four of the boys!"

Chapter 16

Lost in a fog of fear and despair, Katie fumbled through her work. Big Mike had finally lost patience. An hour before, he had pulled her into the kitchen. In a voice as sweet as honey and as cold as ice, he had whispered that she was to come to his office at the end of her work night. It was not an invitation – it was a command. He had put it to her plain; if she was a good girl, things would go quick and easy. He even suggested he might move her to the morning shift if she was especially good. It was a lie; she knew. The warning followed; if she gave him trouble, it would go much – much worse. A chill ran through her when she thought of the emphasis he had put on the word *much*.

If she quit or he fired her, she would lose the only job she could find. And where would she go? She couldn't re-live the desperate search for money they endured after Danny died. He left her and the girls nothing; if not for Sean, they would have starved. Worse, she risked losing her children if it were known she had no means of support. She remembered well the story of what happened to Rose. She didn't doubt that refusing Mike risked violent rape. Really, what choice was there but to just give in to the awful humiliation.

Memories of the many brutal nights she endured at the hands of her drunken husband haunted her, but holding back tears, she told herself, *what was one more night to endure after so many?* And so, she tried to resign herself to the inescapable. She would submit to the fat, sweaty pig, and hope that once he had his way, it would be done and over. She hoped it, but knew better. The way he looked at her, talked to her – it wasn't a passing interest, it would happen again and again until she found a way out. *It's for my daughters,* she told herself. *For them, I can endure anything.*

As shaken as she was, she barely noticed the customers' chatter all evening about the big fire across the south fork of the river. That was, until one of them said the thing was threatening Union Depot. It was then she realized the fire was close to her home, to her girls.

A much deeper panic took root. She bolted for the door. As always, one of Mike's thugs stood guard there. He stepped in front of her. "And where are you going, love?"

"The fire… it's by… my girls… I have to go home to my girls!"

The man shook his head. "Fire or no, Mike said you wasn't to leave."

"You don't understand, the fire…"

A knowing smirk crept across his face. "It's you that don't understand. He has plans for you later. He said you might try to slip out again, and I was to make sure that didn't happen – and it won't."

"But…"

"But nothing. Look, you seem like a good enough lass. Let me give you some advice. You don't want to make things worse… and they can get worse – I promise. Be a good girl." He shoved her back away from the door.

Stunned, she went to the kitchen. Another of Mike's men stood by the door to the alley. Trapped and scared, Katie's stomach went hollow and her legs threatened to fail her. Not knowing what else to do, she slipped into the storeroom, sat on a crate and began to cry. A faint smell of smoke caught her attention. It wafted from the small window near the ceiling. It took only a moment for her to realize that she might just fit through.

That animal can do his worst to me later, but now I've got to get to my girls. She quickly stacked some produce crates, and as quietly as she could, used them to slip out the window.

In the street, a hot, gale force wind and the stench of smoke struck her. Looking west, she saw the night sky lit by a monstrous orange glow. It reminded her of the Armageddon stories she heard as a girl.

Her normal path home took her west to the river and over the Madison Street bridge. Most nights, the walk was little more than 30 minutes. This wasn't most nights. By LaSalle Street, still four blocks from the river, she had run into a stampede fleeing the glowing fire ahead of her. Her back against the buildings, she pressed forward to as far as Wells Street. Here she encountered the first hints of fire; smoke and falling ash. Realizing that the way west was blocked, she turned north.

To her growing alarm, the fire appeared to travel with her. Eventually, heat and the growing crush of the crowd forced her back to LaSalle. Passing down LaSalle, she saw the Chamber of Commerce and courthouse burning. In the distance, she saw firemen on a ladder; they looked to be bringing people down from a window. It reminded her of Sean. *God protect him,* she prayed.

At Madison, she tried to turn west — to the bridge, but the crowd made it impossible. In growing desperation, she turned north again, hoping to find some other way across. With each step, her panic grew; she was moving further from her girls, not closer. Still, the fire seemed to chase her ever further north, and the crowd made turning west impossible.

Then came the explosion, plunging the streets into darkness. Terrified, she fought the rush of people as she desperately tried to push west to the river, but the crowd's momentum proved too much. As if caught in a massive ocean wave, the stampeding crowd jostled and shoved from one direction to the next. The darkness, the strange streets and abuse of the crowd left her unsure of her bearings.

Alone and terrified, she spotted a well-dressed man in an ornate carriage. *He is a proper gentleman. He will help me*; she thought. She reached up and grabbed the leg of the stranger. "Sir, please, I need your help. I must get across the river to the western bank. It's my daughters… I have to find my…"

The man snarled. "Get away from me, woman. I've my own problems."

Katie pleaded. "Please! It's my girls. I have to get to Canal Street – on the other side, to my girls."

The driver used his foot to push her away from the carriage. "I told you, I can't. Besides, if they're over there, they're as good as dead already. Now get back before I use the whip on you."

Katie grabbed the man's leg again. "I am begging, sir," she sobbed. "I'm in desperate need. Please, I'll pay you what I can."

The whip cracked against her shoulder, near her neck. Stunned, Katie fell back. The carriage lurched forward, nearly running over the people in front.

A scream rang out from somewhere behind Katie. Up the street, only two blocks away, a burning building collapsed. The crowd responded by redoubling its frantic shoving. Katie had no choice but to follow the surge as the throng sought a path not blocked by fire and smoke.

The mob frightened Katie more than the fire. Everywhere was shoving and pushing. An old man had been knocked down and nearly trampled. A frantic woman was dragging a bed behind her. Mothers drug children along by an arm or coat collar. Lost and terrified children pleaded for help – ignored. Young thugs shattered a store window and threw goods into the street. On a corner ahead, a group of unruly men drank from a cask. They were harassing passersby – mostly women. And among them all was the falling embers and gathering smoke.

Katie wasn't sure where she was, but she sensed she was heading the wrong way. Desperate to find a passage across the river, she slipped into a side alley she hoped ran west. If the streets were dark, the alley was near pitch. Still, she was thankful it was free of people. Slowly, she felt her way forward, toward an indistinct glow in the sky.

Not far in, the alley intersected into a winding backstreet. Looking both directions, she only saw darkness. Not sure which way to go, Katie pushed on to her right. The sound of rats scurrying about unnerved her, as did the intensifying orange glow above. She had been so focused on getting to her daughters that she had given little thought to the threat of the fire itself. Now lost in the alley, it occurred to her that she wasn't sure which way was the direction to safety. She decided it wise to rejoin the crowd, hoping they were headed to some safe refuge.

It was with some relief that Katie heard voices up ahead. As she approached, she heard two men cursing, and what sounded like a scuffle. Alarmed, she slipped behind a stack of crates. A third voice pleaded. "Please don't… I have a wife and children!"

A shot echoed through the alley. Startled, Katie tried to run, but her dress had snagged on a nail. She pulled at it frantically; the crates toppled with a clatter. "Who's there?" shouted one of the men. Katie froze. Another shot rang out, followed by a whizzing noise close to her head. Again, she tried to run, but the dress held her fast, another frantic pull and it ripped away.

Katie blindly lurched down the dark passageway, urged on by the footsteps echoing behind her. She tripped over some unseen object and landed sprawled on the slimy cobblestone pavement. Another shot echoed among the buildings. The steps behind grew louder. Instinct screamed *Hide*! She crawled off into the deeper shadows, and into a foul-smelling pile of trash. She lay still as the steps came close, then passed. Close – too close – they stopped. She heard a voice. "Whoever he was, he's gone." Another replied, "Let's be gone too. The fire is getting close."

Katie heard them walk back to where they had been. She lay frozen in place, afraid to make a noise, even to breathe. Then tiny feet crept on to the back of her legs. A second intruder crawled on her back. She suppressed the near irresistible urge to scream – to run. Carefully, she tried to brush the rodent from her leg; it bit her before scurrying off. Thankfully, its companion followed.

She heard running, then only silence. Afraid to move, Katie lay shivering in the trash, until she noticed embers falling close by onto the pavement. Praying the men were gone, she got up and wandered down the back alleys, moving away from where she guessed the fire was. The sounds of the moving crowd guided her out of the back alleys and onto a street – which street, she wasn't sure.

Katie stood at the edge of the sidewalk, unsure where to go. A deep voice said, "Dame geht es dir gut? "

Turning, she saw two men, one short, pudgy, and balding, the other younger. The younger man eyed her with a look of concern. In a thick German accent he said, "Mine father asked if you are good."

Katie was too scared, too shocked, too overwhelmed to answer. She only shook her head.

The young man said, "Is not good… safe… for you alone here."

Katie replied. "Can you help me? I need to get across the south river."

The two men spoke in German for a few seconds, then the younger said, "Is no good getting across south river… bridges gone… cross bigger river, then over."

"Will you take me?" asked Katie.

Father and son spoke in German again. Shaking his head no, the father said, "Nein, unmoglich."

The son replied in something she couldn't follow. He then asked, "My father wants to know what happened to you? Why is your dress torn, and why are you covered in… in filth?"

Katie looked at herself and understood the old man's reluctance. "Some men in the alley. They were after me, but I escaped."

They spoke in German again. After a heated exchange, the old man threw his arms up and nodded.

To Katie, the old man growled, "Sich beeilen!"

The young man grabbed her arm and pulled her to a small wagon hitched to an old horse. "He said to hurry." Without another word, he hoisted her up onto some grain bails in the back of the wagon.

They rode silently. Progress was slow, but steady. The wagon rode rough, but Katie was thankful to be apart from the seething press of people surrounding her. From her perch, she warily kept watch as the best and worst of humanity fought their way to the river. She witnessed acts of kindness and courage. The old helping the young, neighbors carrying possessions for neighbors, and even a man carrying a cripple on his back. Sadly, she too often also saw the desperate push the weak aside, stores looted, and punches thrown. Near the bridge crossing of the main river branch, a man grabbed Katie's leg, either to pull her off or himself up. The young German struck him with a shovel. Katie and her savior locked eyes, but didn't speak.

Once away from the bridge on the other side, the crowd thinned. The wagon rolled to a stop several blocks later. The old man pointed down a street and said something Katie could not understand. Translating, the younger man said, "Father says that down that road is bridge. Goes over the north river. You can work back south once on the other side."

She nodded. He then added, "Much destroyed back south. Better you stay with us,"
She climbed off the wagon. "Thank you, but I can't. Bless you, both."

"Safer here, but still not good. Be careful, hurry quickly… talk to no one."

Katie Jumped from the wagon and set off running for the bridge. The windblown streets were far from empty, but not as crowded. A few residents were loading wagons, but most were simply watching the distant flames and wondering if it would come their way. Few took notice of the filthy woman in the torn dress running past them. Once on the far bank, she followed the river south toward her neighborhood. She had gone but a few blocks when she first saw the leading edge of fire racing past her on the opposite shore. She prayed her rescuers didn't pause on their way north.

As she pressed south, she took heart in the absence of flame ahead of her on the western side. *Maybe my neighborhood was spared. Please God, let it be so!*

It was near dawn before she finally reached the familiar streets of her neighborhood. Two blocks short of her home, she came across a burned-out home and shed. The fires mostly burnt themselves out, with only small pockets of flame still lingering. A block away, she found all the homes on the east side were lost. Buildings on the west were damaged but standing. Shock overwhelmed her when she turned onto her street. All was smokey desolation. A thick pall of smoke issued from every hulk that had once been a home or business. The streets looked deserted, save for the charred remains of animals scattered about.

In shock, she stood before the smoldering shell of the building where she had left her daughters. A singed and dazed woman ambled aimlessly up the street. She carried the remains of a dead dog. In a panic, Katie asked the woman, "Where are the girls who lived here… and Mrs. Carmichael? What happened to them?"

Without stopping, or even looking at Katie, the woman half mumbled. "Gone. Everything and everyone is done in and gone."

Katie fell to her knees in absolute despair and exhaustion. For the first time since crawling through the window of Big Mike's storeroom, she cried

Near the Courthouse

circa 1871 author unknown

Chapter 17

By 3 am, the *Little Giant's* crew found itself at Harrison and Clark. Again, as on the east bank, the crews realized they couldn't stand in the face of the inferno. Regardless of their efforts, it would move unchecked both west and north on the wind. Incredibly, it was gaining in both strength and ferocity, but thanks to a rail bed, they managed to hold a line on Harrison against spreading to the south. As he worked at wetting down nearby buildings, Sean kept a wary eye behind him. It didn't take long for the first tongues of flame to appear.

"Here it comes," said Garland pointing north down Canal Street,

As Sean watched, he saw the first building on Clark Street descend into flame. The fire quickly chewed its way down the block toward Big Mike McDonald's hotel.

Sean's thoughts turned to Katie. He called to Garland, "I should go make sure everyone's out."

Sean charged down Clark to the hotel – to Katie. In a flash, a window exploded. Scorching heat hit him like a wall, driving him to his knees. Bricks fell nearby. Dazed, it was but instinct that screamed, *lay flat, you fool. Cover your head.* Surrounded by smoke and flame, and near unbearable heat, Sean crawled blindly back from where he came. Suddenly, hands grabbed his coat, he felt himself dragged away. Behind him came the awful groan, then crash, of a building collapsing.

"Are you daft, Collins?" It was old Pappy. He and Cap had pulled him clear. "There's no value in getting killed."

Sean coughed, then said, "I know someone who works at…"

Cap said, "At Big Mike's? Lord Sean, I never took you for one to fall into the tender trap."

"It's not like that. It's Danny's widow. She's a cook there."

"Oh Jesus, that's a pity, but there's nothin' to be done about it now. If she has any wits, she got out a while ago."

A growing despair mixed with rage built in Sean. *Katie and the girls, Maggie, Liam – everyone I care about could be dead and here I sit helpless.*

A clearly exhausted Chief Snider rode up on an old draft horse he had commandeered from somewhere. He looked at Sean and sighed. "You boys did well to hold here. We have a solid line running from the river down to State Street. We'll stretch it to the lake in an hour or so. It'll hold I think."

Astonished, Garland asked, "To the lake? The fire will run all the way to the lake?"

"No way to stop it. But if you can hold here, water will do the rest. We'll have the bastard caught up between the lake on the east and the south branch to the west. With the main branch in the front, it'll have nowhere to go."

"Good God," said Garland. "That's near on to three- or four-square miles of the downtown."

Snider closed his eyes and let his chin fall to his chest. "There's nothing to be done for it, boy. We have precious little to stand up to it. Rumor is other towns are sending help, even that federal troops have been called up, but we'll be lucky to see any help before tomorrow."

Garland. "There must be something we can do?"

"Pray. Pray for calm winds and rain. Mostly pray the main channel of the river stops it. If it jumps it like it jumped the south branch, all the city north of this spot will be gone."

"Chief?" asked Sean. "What of the hospital on Water Street?"

"What are you talking about? What hospital?"

"Sisters of Mercy – On Water near Wabash."

Snider removed his helmet and ran his hand through his sweaty hair. "It's standing for now, I suppose. It'll be safe enough for a while. But it's on the wrong side of the river, so fate will have its say, I suppose. Why?"

"Patty is there."

"Patty who?"

"Patty Doyle. He is one of ours, from the Little Giant. He lost his leg last week at the Burlington Warehouse fire – remember?"

"I am sure he's alright. They'll do what they can to evacuate."

"Sure they will, and just so," said Sean. "A handful of nuns will be packing out 20 or 30 beds across the river on but a half hours' notice. Nice and easy as you please."

Snider's countenance stiffened. "And what would you have me do about it?"

"Let me go look in on him, is all I'm asking. The boys can spare me here for a bit."

Snider looked over at a nearby captain, who subtly shrugged and nodded. "Alright," said Snider. "Go and make sure your man is out. Then get your Irish ass back here. No slacking off or I'll make you wish your mother had kept her legs crossed." He reined the old horse around, then added. "Good luck and move fast. I don't know how much time you got."

When Snider was out of earshot, the captain said, "Garland, go with Sean."

*****

Smoke and falling embers foretold of the approaching flames. They filled Michigan Avenue with a panicked horde fleeing the gathering fire storm. Some were pushing west, hoping the lake would offer refuge. Many were running north to the river. Too many just stood in the streets, staring at the coming disaster.

Everywhere, there were carriages, wagons and carts impeding movement. Some were loaded with family members and household goods; most were the wagons of merchants loaded with hastily gathered tools and stock. As the fire made more and more streets impassable, people, wagons and carts converged into a chaotic tangle in the remaining intersections. The growing gridlock further induced panic and frustration among the terrified population. Police, what there were of them, tried to maintain order and keep traffic moving, but with little effect. The increasingly desperate throng eventually took matters in their own hands. Roving gangs unhitched horses, pulled drivers off their seats, and toppled the wagons on their side to create pathways. Resistance earned drivers a beating.

Through the melee, Sean and Garland pushed and shoved their way toward the hospital. With their progress impeded, the ordeal took much longer than they hoped. The fire moved faster than the crowd and reached the hospital before Sean and Garland. On the sidewalk in front of the hospital, they found two Dominican nuns, one old, one very young, tending to a small group of sick and injured.

"What's this then?" asked Garland.

A look of relief graced the young nun's face at seeing the two men in fire coats and helmets. "Our prayers are answered," she said. "These men are too frail to walk. We need aid in moving them to safety. We've been near begging for help, but to no avail."

Sean asked, "Where is everyone else?"

"There were six of us here. When we heard the fire had jumped the river, we began moving the patients. The hospital had two ambulances – wagons really – they loaded up the women, children and sickest men and took them to safety. We were to bring down the rest of the patients and wait for their return."

"They won't make it back from the other side. The crowd will see to that," said Garland.

Sean looked up at the building; fire poured out of the attic and east side windows of the second floor. "Are all out? Is this the lot of them?"

A shadow of remorse passed over the old nun's face. "Sister Agnes and I struggled to bring these few down. It was taxing and I fear we were too slow. Soon after, the building caught fire. We tried to get to the men left on the second floor but it was too hot and smoky, then the roof collapsed soon after. The stairs up are blocked now."

"How many are left, sister?"

"We removed all but six or seven from the West Wing. We left perhaps twenty in the East Wing, I'm not sure."

Looking up at the flames, Garland said, "Sad to say it sister, but those poor souls are all gone now."

Both of the nuns crossed themselves and began saying a Hail Mary.

Sean studied the second floor for a moment longer. To Garland he said, "Patty was on the west side when I visited the other day. There's smoke there sure enough, but it looks tolerable. I think we should see if anyone is alive up there."

Garland shook his head dismissively. "I'll give you this Sean, your testicles are beefy, but your brain is pea sized – begging your pardon for my language sisters. The building is on fire and half the roof has collapsed. The stairs are gone; even if you could get up there – and praise be – someone somehow managed to survive, how the hell would you get them out? It's just daft, and you know it."

"Look here Garland, I have had to leave everyone I care about to fend for themselves tonight while I sit around helpless. My friend is up there, and I'll be damned if I leave him. I'll go look for him. Just help me find a ladder, then busy yourself with helping the sisters and these fellows out of here."

Garland sighed in resignation. "We won't find a ladder in time to do any good, and I'll not have you blundering about by yourself."

"There is no shame in staying down here, lad. I'll go."

"No man will call me a coward." With that, Garland grabbed a nearby drainpipe and started climbing.

To Sister Agnes, Sean said, "We believe there may be some men still alive up there. We'll be back in a few minutes."

"And if you aren't…, are we to fend for ourselves?"

"We can't leave men to die, and to be honest, I'm not sure what we can do to help you, anyway. But I promise we'll do our best when we get back."

Garland called down to him. "Come on then, this was your idea. Mind you, keep your distance. We don't want all our weight on the same part of this rusty old pipe."

With effort, Sean climbed to the second floor. He watched as Garland grabbed a windowsill and swung himself almost effortlessly into the building. Sean reached out with his left hand and clutched the sill, then with his right. As he swung his foot up to the sill in order to roll in the window, his left hand slipped. His heart jumped as he felt the grip of his right hand fail. He was falling. Just as his fingers lost their purchase, he felt two hands grab his arm and pull him up.

Garland and Sean fell in a heap on the floor. Thick impenetrable smoke hanging only a few feet above them left the room near dark. The cloud of smoke mostly obscured the rolling flames at the far end of the room, but their oppressive heat was all too present.

Garland asked, "Are you alright?"

"I'm too old for swinging around on pipes like some playful ape," grumbled Sean in response.

"Well, you're in for a time of it getting out then, my friend. Swinging *out* of that window won't be so quick and easy as swinging in. Have you thought of that?"

"One near death at a time. Let's do what we came for and then worry about getting out." said Sean. He took a brass spanner from his coat and banged on the tiled floor. "Is anyone in here?"

From the darkness came a faint reply. "Ho there. Over here."

Sean called out, "Keep making noise, we'll come to you."

Following the sound of tin striking iron, Sean and Garland crawled low to the ground, trying to avoid the smoke and heat hanging above them. In a few minutes, they found men huddled on the floor between two beds. Visibility was next to nothing and Sean couldn't make out how many men made up the tangle of arms and legs. "How many of you are there?"

"Three," came the reply.

Sean recognized the hoarse voice. "Patty? Is that you? It's Sean and Garland come for you."

"Sean Collins. I sure should have guessed it would be you come to save me. You seem to have a knack for pulling me out of tight spots."

"And you have a knack for getting into them," said Sean.

"Do you believe it? Those nuns left us up here to die. If I see them again, I'll be punching one of them in the nose."

"It's not their fault, they tried. And I encourage you to forego any nun punching. You'll likely be seeing old St. Pete at the pearly gates before the night's done. Considering your history of shenanigans, you have more than enough to account for."

"I see your point," chuckled Patty. "Perhaps just a swat on the fanny would be prudent."

"Patty, this is why the devil…"

Garland interrupted. "Pleasant as this is, perhaps you two can catch up later? We need to get out of this oven on the quick."

Sean said, "He's right. Patty, you said there are three of you. Where are the others? Do you know?"

"Dead I suspect. A while ago, they tried to crawl out through the hall. There was no living out there. I warned them against it."

"Then there's nothing to do for them, let's get you out of here."

Patty said, "Take these two first. They're in a bad way – breathing hard."

Sean and Garland each grabbed a man and began dragging them to the window. It was slower going than they liked. The flames at the far end of the room now tumbled overhead, and it was getting near unbearably hot. Worse, the building was groaning.

"We're running out of time Sean," said Garland. "This room is about to light off, or the roof is going to fall – likely both and soon."

When they reached the window, Sean called out over the rising noise of the fire. "I'm going to go get Patty. Take two bed sheets and tie all four corners together, one on top of the other."

"What? Why? These men are in no shape to shinny down sheets."

"Just do it," shouted Sean, and he was gone.

Not sure of what he was doing, or why; Garland busied himself with the sheets. He finished the last knot as Sean and Patty reached the window.

"What now?" asked Garland.

"We are jumping." Sean leaned out the window and called to Sister Agnes, "Find some men to help you. Hold these like a net." He threw the sheets down to her.

"You first, Patty."

"I think not, my friend."

Sean nudged him to the window. "You've done this before. Besides, you're the fattest. If they hold you, they'll hold us."

"I'd be as well off to flap my arms and fly out the window. You'll have me break my one good leg."

"We don't have time to argue, dammit. Now jump!"

The little nun convinced six men to help. Though not needed, the nuns manned it too. The group caught Patty in the makeshift net without incident. Garland and Sean next dropped the two men down and then jumped themselves.

To the older sister, Sean said, "This is all of them. The others have passed."

"I can't say I approve of throwing our patients out of windows, but thank you all the same." She looked at the sick and crippled men on the street. "Though our burden has grown from your efforts."

Sister Agnes quickly added, "What Sister Martha means is that we somehow need to get these men to a hospital across the river."

"We need a wagon," said Garland.

Sean replied, "And the lord shall provide." He walked toward a nearby freight wagon stalled in the crowded street. A young, well-dressed man of no more than 25 held the reins. On the seat with him was a young woman and child. In the back was a precarious stack of furniture, trunks, and household goods.

Sean said to the man, "You, we need your wagon."

The young man's panicked face went white. He pulled a pistol from his coat and said, "Try and assail us and I'll put a shot in you!"

"Relax, young man…" said a woman in a soothing voice. Sean turned and saw Sister Martha. "… no one is going to harm you. We simply need your help. See the hospital just over there. We have invalids to move to safety. Your wagon is needed."

The young man's face softened, but the gun remained aimed at Sean's head. "I am sorry sister… I am, but I have to take care of me and mine."

Sister Martha carefully grasped the horse's bridal. "And will you let these men die for the sake of some rugs and plates? Is that what you want your child to know of you? How will you face him?"

The young woman pulled on her husband's sleeve. "David, we can't turn our back on them. What choice do we have?"

Sean added, "You're right to be afraid of this crowd. You will never get over the river with this load. Carrying wounded men and a couple nuns is your best chance of getting your family out un-accosted."

The man nodded in acquiescence and climbed off the wagon. Sister Martha scampered up to the seat as he, Sean, and Garland hastily unloaded the wagon. Quickly, several men pitched in. Most of the family's belongings were roughly tossed to the gutter. A few men grabbed boxes, then disappeared into the crowd.

"I've worked hard to provide for my family. Now it's all to be lost," complained the young husband. "What isn't destroyed will be stolen."

With more than a little bitterness, Sean said, "Your family will be alive. That should be enough."

Embarrassed by the rebuke, he nodded. "Of course, you're right."

As the wagon's contents were being discarded, a policeman came up. "What's this then? Get this wagon off onto a side street. It's impeding the evacuation. Be quick about it."

Sister Agnes confronted him. "This wagon is to be an ambulance. These poor souls need to be carried to safety."

The policemen studied the determined little nun and thought better of arguing. "All right then, but be hasty." He pointed to two onlookers. "You two, give them a hand loading those patients."

Sister Agnes patted the burly man's hand. "Thank you."

Sister Martha said to the young husband, "Thank you as well – David, is it? If you'll deliver us to the closest hospital on the other side, we will no longer burden you."

"No," said Sean. "This fire has already jumped one river. There's no promise it won't do so again. You need to get far away."

David said, "I've been fretting about where to go once across. The lake?"

Sean paused, then said. "Listen, if this fire crosses, there will be a panic both north and east. You'll get trapped like you did here. My advice is to go north to Indiana Street and then west till you cross over the north branch of the river. You'll be safe there."

"That's a long way off."

Sean said, "It's a big fire."

"These men will need care," protested Sister Martha.

"Sister, there will be no care for anyone till morning, even if the river keeps the fire at bay. If it doesn't, their fate will be the same as here. Listen to me, get them to safety."

Garland eyed the now fully involved fire in the hospital. To the officer, he said, "If we don't get this crowd moving soon, it won't matter anymore. These walls will fall soon enough, and the fire will spread to the whole block."

An idea occurred to the policeman as the loading was completed. He climbed on top of the wagon and shouted. "Listen all. I am leading this wagon over the Michigan Street bridge. All who want to cross follow behind in an orderly fashion."

As they mounted the wagon, Sister Agnes tentatively waved farewell. Sister Martha silently mouthed, *"Thank you."*

The burly policeman set off down the street, forging a path by the ruthless use of his nightstick. The wagon followed, as did a throng of followers on foot. As they watched the procession move away, Garland asked, "Do you think they'll make it to safety."

"Don't know," said Sean. "But we did what we could, so there's that, I suppose."

"True enough. Sean, I think sister Agnes might have been sweet on me. Is that possible?"

Sean laughed. "For the love of Pete; I swear you're a proper pea wit. She's a woman of God. It'd take more than a skinny pup like you to turn her head."

"Woman of God, sure enough. But there's still a woman under those robes."

"Garland, were you raised by a pack of wolves? Surely, there is some explanation for your depravity."

"I'm hurt," laughed Garland.

"You're unhinged is what you are. Now let's get back to the *Little Giant.*"

Chapter 18

His back hurt. Opening his eyes, he saw only gray and black. At first, he thought he was looking at clouds, then recognized a swirling haze of smoke drifting past. Disoriented, he tried to clear his head. A voice had roused him. At least he thought there was a voice. Unsure of what, if anything, need be said, he ventured, "What?"

A voice from below replied, "I said, are you alright?"

Liam wasn't sure that he was, but answered, "Yes, I suppose I am."

"Are you waiting for Noah's flood?" said the voice.

Again, Liam muttered, "What?"

"Let's try a different tack. What are you doing up on the roof?"

Feeling stiff and sore, he slowly sat up. "I was protecting the house from embers. Then I stood watch most of the night. I guess I fell asleep somehow."

"You did well," said the voice. "Few houses are left standing in this neighborhood."

Liam looked down and saw an old man in tattered clothes standing in the debris-littered street. He found the man more a puzzle than a threat. The hair was snow white, and time and weather had carved deep crevices in the face. But he stood straight – almost youthful somehow. He asked, "You're not out looting, are you?"

The old man spat on the dirt street. "Of course not. And what would I steal? Who around here has anything worth taking?"

"Fair enough," said Liam. "Then what are you doing here?"

"The damned fire chased me away last night. I am walking back to my house – if I still have one, that is. From the looks of things, I got little cause for optimism."

"Where is your place?"

"Evans near DesPlaines."

Liam asked, "It went that far west?"

"I hope not, but it was too close for comfort when I left."

Liam stood. "I watched the fire most of the night. It mostly went north and east. You might be fortunate."

"Luck and I are rarely on good terms," said the old man. "But marvels happen. Well, I best be on my way."

"Wait. I'll walk with you."

"I don't need company, young fellow. Mind to your own house."

"I left my father over that way last night. He's a firefighter, he sent me here to… I want to check on him."

"If he's fighting the fire, he's nowhere close. I hear tell the damn thing jumped the main branch of the river last night. If the stories are true, the thing is burning far into uptown now."

Incredulous, Liam asked, "Are you saying the thing is still burning? That can't be true."

There was a rumble in the distance.

"There's proof for you," said the old man. "That's blasting powder. They took to leveling buildings last night to create what they call fire breaks. Who would've dreamed it, deliberately destroying buildings?"

"Must not be working. If the fire still burns, that is."

"Perhaps. Can't say I know much about it – not my concern either. As I said, I best be on my way."

"If it's all the same to you, I'll tag along. If my pop is off uptown, I'll go to his fire house – see if they've news as to where he may be."

The old man grumbled something to himself, then said, "Suit yourself., but be quick off that roof. I've not got all day."

Liam climbed down and the two trudged south down Clinton Street.

"My name is Liam, by the way – Liam Collins."

"Jacob – Jacob Stanich."

"You're not Irish." said Liam.

"And you're not a donkey. What of it?"

"Don't go getting your back up. It's just that most around here are the sons of Erin."

"Most ain't all now, is it? And ain't we all Chicagoans today? That is, if there is a Chicago tomorrow."

"So, where are your people from?" asked Liam.

"Me mum was from Portugal; my old man hailed from Romania, I think."

"You don't know where your father is from?"

"Never met him. Hardly knew my mother either. I don't have what you would call deep roots. Not that it should matter a tinker's damn to you – I'm from all over, and now I'm from Chicago."

"I'm just asking about your heritage — no need to get defensive. I got nothing against the Romans."

"Romans? There's a good piece of wit. Still, there's the problem with inlanders; you're always going on about where folks are from and don't pay no attention to where they're going. Dirt's dirt, doesn't matter which dirt your mum popped you out onto. Irish, Frenchie, or Hessian, we're all in the same boat and got the same woes."

Liam shook his head. "That's not been my experience. Who your people are has the say in where you're going. For some of us, that means nowhere."

"Not for nothin, but I've traveled the world and I tell you, the same sun shines on all, boy. We're all born. We all eat, drink, fornicate and then get put in a hole and dirt thrown over us. Same for everybody."

Liam shook his head. "It'd be a better world if that were true."

"And what do you know of the world? I doubt you've seen much of it. See off in the distance – the smoke? There's a lot of misery between here and what's getting burnt up now. Do you think the fire discriminates? We all suffer eventually – somehow. Anyway, this is America; I hear tell you can stride on the dirt of your choosing."

Liam said. "Most aren't welcome in most places."

"True enough," replied the old man. "But who said you need an invitation. Nobody is stopping anybody – welcome or not. Where you end up is up to you, nobody else. There's why I put little stock in nationality. The dirt you're born on is happenstance. The dirt you stride tells the story."

Liam gestured to the surrounding ruin. "You're here in this ash pile, just like the rest of us."

"Yes, I am. I chose it. Now let the topic be, you're giving me a headache."

"I suppose where you put down roots says much too. My father won't budge from this place. My mother wants to leave. They fight about it. She says he's afraid, he says she's running after something that ain't out there. He won't take a chance, and she has no choice."

With more than a little exasperation in his voice, the old man said, "Damned if you aren't an odd one. Are all your conversations like this? What's your mom and dad got to do with anything? He chooses to stay, she wants to leave but doesn't… neither you nor me know the truth of why. Only thing for certain is they have their reasons and their choices are *their* choices, and your choices are *your* choices."

Liam considered that a few steps and asked, "Why would my mother…"

"Stop your chatter, son. I don't know your parents, but I'll wager they talk too much."

"Sorry, I have a lot on my mind."

They walked on in silence. The blocks closest to Liam's home suffered extensive fire damage, but a few buildings and sheds still stood. By the time they reached Harrison Street, the devastation was universal. Every structure was burnt. Some smoldering, gutted shells still stood, many had collapsed. Ruined furniture, clothes, and personal effects left by the fleeing victims littered the streets and sidewalks. Smoldering wagons and carts sat abandoned. Dead animals lay huddled in cages and feed pens. The acrid stench of smoke burned their eyes and throats.

"Good lord," said Liam.

"If you say so," replied Jakob.

Liam surveyed the abandoned neighborhood, the once familiar buildings now toppled; even the yards, trees and sidewalks lay wasted and smoking. He thought about Johnny Gallagher and Big Mike, and the utter foolishness of it all. "You can't blame God for this," he said.

"No," said the old man. "It's always us to blame in the end."

They traveled another few blocks and came to DeKoven Street. To Liam's amazement, a few buildings still stood barely harmed. One of them was the O'Leary cottage.

"There's an irony," said Liam. "That smoldering wreck by the cottage is the remains of the O'Leary dairy barn."

Jacob replied, "I am familiar. I've bought butter from them for the bakery. What of it?"

"The fire started in their barn. It's consumed half the city but spared the building closest to its start. How do you explain that?"

"I can't. Luck would be my guess."

Mrs. O'Leary came out of the cottage and stood on the stoop. She fixed a hard stare on Liam, but didn't speak.

She thinks I had a hand in this, thought Liam.

Jacob asked, "Is she a friend of yours?"

"At one time. Not as much now, I'm afraid." Liam walked on. "A bakery – you're a baker?"

"The last few years, I have been."

"What about before that?"

Jacob said, "I spent my youth at sea. Had to go ashore finally; it's not a life for an old man."

"I remember the crossing when I was younger," said Liam. "Happiest two weeks of my life. The sea is a magical place."

"That it is, but she's a cold bitch. It's not a soft life riding her back."

Liam laughed. "Not many lives are soft, I hear. What kind of shipping did you do?"

"Started off on a fishing boat in the Mediterranean, then I came over – whaled out of Nantucket for a good while. Last decade or so I spent on a steamer hauling iron ore across Superior and Erie. I made good money there – could have had my own ship."

"Why didn't you?"

"Lots of reasons. The war played hard on shipping. Then my wife took ill. I brought her here so she could be with family."

"You've a wife then, and children? Where are they – separated in the fire?"

"No. You ask too many questions."

"Sorry, I guess I am a bit off, with the fire and all. It's put a lot of thoughts in my head I can't quite get sorted."

"I've said all I will about me. What about you? How do you keep body and soul together?" asked Jacob.

"After last night, I am at odds, I think."

"Many will be," said Jacob. "Still. There will be plenty of work rebuilding."

"I think I've had my fill of Chicago."

"It may be worth staying. Whatever Chicago was, it won't be again. You never know what new things grow from scorched dirt. There may be opportunities for a young man."

Approaching Wilson Street, Liam said, "Here is where we part company. I hope you find all is well with your place."

"Thank you, Liam. I see little sense in it, but if you decide to search for your father up by the fire, be careful. Getting killed isn't all they say it is."

Liam turned toward the fire station. He had only gone a few steps when he heard Jacob. "Liam!"

Liam turned and saw the old man watching him. "Buck up. Something's plainly eating at you. Whatever it is will pass, all things do eventually. I learned one thing at sea, you never know which way the wind will blow tomorrow."

Odd duck, thought Liam. *Odder still, he would show up like he did.* He waved goodbye and walked on to his father's firehouse.

Except for blistered paint and a few scorched shakes on the roof, Liam found the firehouse undamaged. It had escaped the flames by only a block. Inside, he found a single firefighter. Unlike his station building, the man looked done in and ready for collapse. Hair singed, face blistered, and slump shouldered, Liam could only imagine what this man had endured through the night – what his father had endured as well.

Although clearly exhausted, the man was loading hose in a wagon; each movement seemed ponderous and painful. "Do you need help?" asked Liam.

The man only nodded and leaned forward against the wagon.

With effort, Liam picked up two of the heavy canvas hoses and heaved them into the wagon. "Do you know Sean Collins?"

"Sure, he's with the *Little Giant*."

"Yes. I'm his son. I am looking for him. Where is the *Giant* now?"

"Last I saw, the *Giant* was near the courthouse, but that was a long while ago. Who knows where it may be – or if your father is close by it. It's all a jumbled mess up there; we're scattered all over."

"But you've seen him. He's unhurt?"

"He was in fair shape when last we crossed paths."

"Where should I look for him?"

"As I said, he was in the general vicinity of the courthouse but, that was last night. The fire has taken over that area by now. Your dad could be anywhere, and there is no good in going up there looking for him. Sean is a smart one; he'll be fine."

"I think I'll have a look just the same."

"Lad, the ground between here and the fire front is a blistering, smoldering wasteland the devil himself wouldn't cross. Only chance to go north is to hug the lake shore, and he ain't there, that I promise."

Liam threw the last hose into the wagon. "I'll be going now. Be careful up there. If you see my pop, tell him Liam is about looking for him."

As he walked away, he heard the man mutter. "Damn foolish pup."

Making his way down 18th Street toward the south branch of the river, Liam was struck by the often random destructiveness of the fire. In some blocks, an eye to the right showed the world as it was yesterday; to the left was only carnage and waste. *I wonder if that's the wind at work, or the fire crews?*

He crossed the river using the railroad bridge, only narrowly getting across before a train caught up to him. As it passed, it surprised him to see a large contingent of men and equipment on several flatbed cars. Some stood next to fire steamers, and hand pumpers, most sat or lay down. As a car rumbled by, he glimpsed *St Louis* painted on a chemical engine. *Reinforcements, I suppose,* he said to himself.

At State Street, he turned north. A few blocks later, he ran into a large crowd of refugees huddled in the street. Not far in front of them was the still smoldering wreckage of what had been a thriving business district. Among the desperate souls sat an ornate carriage. In it, Liam recognized the unmistakable bulk of Big Mike McDonald. Next to him sat a thin, bedraggled man in what had once been a nice suit. The coat was filthy and had burn holes in it; the hat crumbled and stained. It took a moment for Liam to place him. It was the reporter he had seen in the street the night before.

*****

"So, Mr. McDonald, any comment on the fire?" Big Mike continued to stare at the desolation in front of him. "None that you could print in the Post, Chamberlin."

"Your hotel is gone. Surely you must have some thoughts about it."

"More than the hotel, but I'll be fine."

"Will you rebuild?"

"In a month, workers will flood in to this town to rebuild all manner of things. They'll get thirsty and lonely after a long workday. Someone has to tend to their needs. Of course I'll rebuild."

"Doesn't it bother you that your own people burnt you out?"

In a voice as icy as the shiver down Big Mike's spine, he answered, "What's that supposed to mean – my own people?"

"I mean no offence. It's just that the fire started up in the Irish ghetto district. As I hear it, in a barn owned by some folks named O'Leary."

Chamberlin's question worried McDonald. *Does he know that stupid Johnny Gallagher did this? The damn fool was to burn the shed as a warning, not the barn. He botched the whole thing, and it cost me my hotel and most of my tenements. Half of Chicago is gone thanks to that fool and it may well be put on me.*

To Chamberlin he said, "Make no mistake, they are my customers, but they aren't my people. On a sober day, their best are stupid and lazy, and sober days are few. Those poor bastards are a blight on the Irish character."

"There money is green though. It's those lazy drunks that's buying your liquor, whoring with your girls and gambling away their paychecks. Now, ain't it?"

"If I didn't supply what they want, someone else would. Besides, I keep them happy and out of the fine neighborhoods you protestant pricks hold court in."

Taking out a notebook, Chamberlin asked, "Would you support some sort of new construction codes, restricting the rebuilding of the shacks up there?"

"Put that notebook down. I told you I have nothing to say to the Evening Post. And if one word of this conversation ends up in print, I'll be paying a visit to that worthless ass of an editor you work for. You'll be on the next train back to Philadelphia or wherever you came from."

"Vermont."

"What's that?"

"I've no interest in visiting Philadelphia. I'm from Vermont."

"Are you testing my patience? I'll send you back to Vermont in a box if you like."

"That won't be necessary, Mr. McDonald. We're on the same side here." Chamberlin slipped out of the carriage and disappeared into the crowd.

McDonald watched him leave. *Maybe I should put him in a box, as I said. He seems close to suspecting something. There will be an inquiry into this disaster, sure enough. And that O'Leary bitch will be casting blame on me. That's not really a concern, but Johnny... he could be a problem. He's not got the sense to keep his mouth shut. If they catch him... In any event, I don't need Chamberlin talking to Johnny. I'll be chatting with that Gallagher fool soon enough.*

*****

Wanting no part of seeing or being seen by McDonald, Liam hustled east to the lakefront. With every step closer to the lake, the crowd of displaced wretches thickened until it had swelled to the thousands. Most lingered on the grassy, littered bank, many stood knee deep in the cold water. Bruises, cuts, and burns were common. Clothing looked filthy and singed. Many were only half dressed and shivered in the morning air. The hollow-eyed look of shock and fear painted their faces, confusion too. All looked exhausted.

There are so many homeless already, and the fire still burns. What will become of them? Where will they sleep, how will they eat? wondered Liam.

"So, it's you, is it? Has Mike sent you looking for me?"

Liam turned and saw a young woman wrapped in a bed sheet, glaring at him. She looked dirty, disheveled, and clearly tired, but defiant. "Rose, is that you?" Liam asked.

"You know well it is, and you won't be taking me back. I'll scream for help if you try and force me."

"I'm not here looking for you. And I'll force you nowhere."

"Good," said Rose. "Then I'll ask you to be on your way and not to tell him you saw me. He'll be trying to find me."

"McDonald and I have parted ways. You were right about him. Your secret is safe with me."

"Good, then I'll be on my way."

Rose turned to leave. "Wait! On your way where? What are you doing here?"

"When the hotel caught fire, I made a run for it. My family lives near here, or did. The house is gone – them as well. I thought I… that they might…. It was foolish. They wouldn't have sheltered me from Mike anyhow."

Liam stood silent for a long while, unsure what he wanted to say. Finally, he suggested, "Well, you can't stand here by the lake forever. And Mike isn't far away. I saw him not more than 20 minutes ago. Come with me. I'll take you to a safe place."

She scowled. "Why would I go with you? I scarcely know you."

"Do you have better options? You're standing here with just the clothes on your back, and from the way you're clutching that bed sheet, I'd wager precious little of those. I can't leave you wandering the streets half naked and hunted. I'll get you a place to sleep and some food. We'll figure out what's next after."

"Let me put your fool thoughts straight. A soft bed and supper won't buy you what you're after. I got away from Mike. I won't be letting you take his place."

"Not all men are out to hurt you. I thought we got past that the last time we were together. I'll demand nothing of you, I promise."

Rose held her ground, obviously pondering options.

"Look, you're in a barrel – you need to trust somebody."

"Why? What's in this for you?"

Liam shrugged. "Damned if I know. I just feel like I need to help you, is all."

"Look here, I am not some helpless waif in need of rescue."

"As I see it, Rose, you kinda are. At the very least, you could use a friend right now. Mike and Johnny are about somewhere. And even if you avoid them, dark comes in a few hours. You'll be on the street cold and hungry without food, clothes or money. Not much good is going to find you, and you know what kinda attention you'll draw."

"Alright, but I'll be sleeping with an eye open. So don't get no ideas."

Part 3
Ashes

Circa 1871, author unknown

Tuesday, October 10, 1871

Chicago, Illinois

This page left blank

Chapter 19

Cold, wet and exhausted, Sean lay sprawled on an altar monument in a cemetery near Lincoln Park. He guessed he had slept a little, but wasn't sure. It felt not much past dawn, and convinced further sleep would elude him, he hoped movement would help ward off the chill. Sitting up proved painful. He hurt everywhere, not the dull aches of muscles protesting a day's hard work, but the sharp, biting pain of a body pushed far too far. He stretched, groaned, and uneasily found his feet.

His space barely vacated, a woman and two small children scrambled onto the dais, desperate for a place to lie down other than the cold mud. A man – likely her husband – eyed him, expecting a protest at his wife's commandeering of the makeshift bed. Sean nodded, and the man relaxed. The little family were but four of the hundreds of wretched, shivering souls seeking refuge in the graveyard, or the thousands scattered in the park. Cold, hungry and confused; none knew where to go, or what to do – so they sat and waited for someone or something to provide purpose. Most were poorly dressed for the weather and few had possessions with them. Such things were abandoned when they had to take flight, often for the second or even third time. They were everywhere he looked; huddled together in tight groups, vainly trying to keep warm, and

seeking solace in that most primitive of human comforts –
proximity to others.

Sean turned up his collar, a futile gesture at warding off the
steady rain relentlessly seeping into every seam of his clothing. It
was a cold rain, one that chilled to the bone. It had been a sweet,
blessed rain – the rain that saved them, saved the city. *And now it
punishes the helpless,* thought Sean. *The fire and now the weather
are great equalizers. Rich or poor doesn't matter a lick now, not to
these poor creatures. We'll all suffer equal for a while – hungry,
exposed to the elements, sick. I fear the worst is yet to come.*

The fire had raged all Sunday night, and through to Tuesday.
Sean watched the wretched people around him, and thought;
*Sunday evening seems so long ago. Yet, it's just a day and night
ago, me and Garland tried to make a stand near the O'Leary barn.
Is it possible that so few hours ago, all was right and normal?*

It had been a time of terror and screams – of frantic work and
falling buildings – of howling winds and a rain of fire. He and
Garland, and the rest of his crew had been pushed to the south
river, then over it. They watched helplessly as banks, churches, and
hotels burned. Still, they fought doggedly to slow the beast, if only
in the vain hope of buying time. Many a poor soul who sought
safety across the south river branch were made to flee again –
across the main branch of the river this time. Then the fire jumped
that river too. The post office burned, the stock exchange too, even
the courthouse fell in a heap. All hope was lost when the
waterworks caught fire. The roof collapsed on the pumps, and with
their demise, every hydrant in the city went dry.

Through the night, the fire gained intensity, growing faster,
devouring everything in its path. The more it ate, the more heat it
produced, the more wind it expelled, the faster it moved. Sean and

the rest of the firefighters could only watch as the wind swept the blaze east, west, and north. At its height, the fire raged along a front nearly three miles wide and two miles deep. With but only 186 exhausted men and no water, the fire department disintegrated into a patchwork of small groups independently working at whatever they thought best. Crews were scattered and unevenly distributed; most had no officers. Still, they fought on.

Monday, help from other communities started trickling in. Departments from Milwaukee, Peoria, Gary, and Springfield sent crews and engines. As the day went on, help poured in from other departments. But without water, little could be done. And so, the terrible war of contrition continued.

Desperate to impede the fire's progress, crews leveled taller buildings using explosives. The attempts were clumsy at first, and ineffectual. Then General Phil Sheridan arrived via train, and with him was an army of troops deployed to maintain civil order. He also brought a contingent from the Corp of Engineers. Experienced in demolition from the war years, the troops set about leveling wide tracks of the city ahead of the fire. It managed to slow but not halt the blaze.

It was late afternoon Tuesday when Chicago got its first glimmer of hope. The weather turned. The gusting southern winds that had driven the fire all night and day abated. Cooler air drifted in off the lake late in the afternoon. Then came the clouds, followed by the first tentative drizzle. That evening, a cheer rose when Chicagoans felt something they had not experienced in nearly three months – rain. Not a light drizzle, rather a heavy, prolonged downpour. With it came the salvation prayed for by so many. It wetted the fuel in front of the fire, stopping its spread, and within a few hours, the once raging inferno had been reduced to isolated pockets of smoldering wreckage.

At first, the rain was universally cheered. It remained so for those fortunate enough to still have a roof over their head. For the newly homeless, the rain and cool temperatures became something to endure rather than celebrate. Huddled under whatever poor shelter they could find, joy over survival turned into worry about food, and lodging, and the coming winter. Overnight, Chicago had become a city of vagrants.

The distant rumble of blasting powder echoed through the cemetery. *General Sheridan's boys leveling another building*, he thought.

"That will be enough of that," Garland grumbled. He was lying on a nearby grave, using its headstone as a pillow.

"Get used to it. It's a sound we'll be hearing often for a while."

"Why, the fire is out. There is no need for breaks anymore."

"How many buildings did you see fall these last few days?" asked Sean. "And how many do you suppose are teetering on the brink. They'll be no rebuilding without clearing away the rubble."

"Rebuild? Are you touched? There'll be no rebuilding, not soon anyway. Chicago died yesterday."

"Your wrong Garland. What built Chicago will rebuild it."

"Sean, you're an optimist. God love you for it. but…"

"All firefighters! Come gather. If any firefighters hear me, gather around," boomed a voice.

Sean and Garland moved in its direction. They found Assistant Chief Thomas O'Neill – dirty, and seemingly exhausted – scanning the crowd. To their surprise, another dozen firefighters answered his call as well.

"Where did they come from?" asked Garland.

Sean recognized none of them. Most wore coats and helmets that didn't match his own or each other. "Damned if I know. Come to help from all over, I guess."

"We don't need their help. Chicago can take care of itself."

Sean replied, "That's just your pride talking. We were no match for that blaze. We needed all the help we could get. Still do, for that matter. It'll be days before we get the department set right again."

"Some help they were. The rain saved us, not those bastards come to the party late."

"You're a proud one through and through Garland. But we got humbled yesterday."

"That may be," said Garland. "But we got nothing to hang our head over. Our boys stood tall these two days."

A large group of citizens had crowded around O'Neill, peppering him with questions: *Do you know where we are to go? Is it safe to go back into the city? Do you have food and water for us?"*

The Chief climbed on a grave marker and raised his hands. "Everyone breathe easy and listen. Men from the Mayor's office and the military will be around soon enough. They will answer your questions. Now move away, so I can talk to the firefighters."

Grumbling, the crowd dispersed. The chief stepped down and motioned for the firefighters to close in. "Listen men, if you're with a fire department come to help from another city, we thank you for your assistance. You are to rally at the train yard near the river docks. It's about a two-mile walk due south of here. Keep the lake in view and you'll run into it. Your respective officers will give you further instructions." In a lowered voice, he whispered, "We're also arranging for you to be fed."

One of the men asked, "Are we to stay for a while, then?"

"I don't know," replied the chief. "You'll hear what's to be done from your own people. Chicago firefighters, you are to report to your own stations…" He shook his head sadly and added, "… if they still stand, that is. If they are lost, temporary quarters are being set up close by – likely tents, look for them. As you go, collect whatever men you pass by and send them back to their stations as well. If you know where your engine or wagon is left, collect it and return it to the station, along with any hose, axes or the sort. You are ordered not to dawdle; it's critical we re-organize the department as soon as is possible. I'll make it clear. Go directly to your station. Stop only to collect our tools and property."

As Garland and Sean stumbled south to their station, Garland said, "I could use a meal in the worst way, and it's a long walk back. If we stopped at the train yard, do you think we could get some food? We're as entitled as our guests, ain't we?"

"The Chief said not to dawdle. We need to get back," replied Sean.

"I can eat and walk at the same time, and the yard is on the way."

Sean clapped Garland on the back. "Come to mention it, I'm hungry too." *Odd thing*, he thought, *I never cared for the kid before. Thought he was all mouth – I sold him short. If our house is gone and we are to be shuffled about, I hope we end up in the same place. He's a good man in a pinch.*

Not far from the park, they passed a family sitting on the burnt porch of what had been a fashionable home. As they walked by, the father called out. "Boys, have you eaten today?"

"No Sir," said Garland.

"Come join us."

Garland started over, but Sean pulled him back. He whispered, "I doubt they have it to spare."

Garland called to them. "Thank you, but we're fine. We'll not put you out."

"Nonsense!" said the man. "It's the least we can do after what you've done for us. We'll not soon forget what you've done for your city boys. Join us."

Sean and Garland each took a small piece of bread, thanked them, and moved on. They were stopped three more times on the way back, once by an old woman who said nothing; she simply hugged them. Many tipped their cap, or waved. Some simply nodded.

Garland later said, "I'm surprised by the way we're being treated. I figured we'd be held to blame."

"I just thought the same," said Sean. "I know we did all we could, but I feel defeated. Their praise doesn't sit well."

"It'll likely be short-lived," said Garland. "Goodwill will falter when they get past being thankful they're alive."

An hour later, the two found their station still standing. A half dozen of the crew milled about, several more were collapsed on the cots. Seeing a number of wives and children gathered on blankets surprised Sean. Visits to the station were no rare thing, even Maggie had come now and again, but so many at once seemed odd.

Nodding at the gathering, Sean asked Donny McCutchen, "Why so many families? Did some of our boys get killed?"

McCutchen replied, "Nah. They've nowhere else to go – burnt out, like the rest."

Sean thought of his own home, his own family, then of Katie and the girls. A tinge of frustration and worry gnawed at him.

The *America* stood in its bay, charred but looked ready for duty. Cap and Pappy were busy refitting her. Cap looked up and said, "Well, the prodigal sons have returned. Where have you two been? We were thinking of sending out a search party."

Garland answered. "We spent the night in a graveyard up north. We just got word to come back a bit ago."

"Slept in a graveyard, did you? What possessed you to do that?"

"We were dead on our feet, seemed close enough to gain admission."

Garland's joke got a laugh and Sean was happy to see the boys still had some spirit. Noting the empty stall, he asked, "What of the Giant?"

Cap shook his head. "The old girl's lost, I'm afraid. Burnt up near the water tower. I hear they're sending the Phoenix over to us. Their station is gone."

"That's a pity. She did well by us. A fine old machine she was."

"No sense in getting misty over it. She saw better days. Speaking of that, you both look done in."

"Were fine," said Sean. "What do you want me and Garland to do?"

Cap replied, "You look like shit, lads. Go home, that is, if you have one. Get some sleep and get back here around nine o'clock. You'll stand the watch tonight. We'll begin regular schedules thereafter. And Sean, if you lost your home, look for someone to take you in. If you can't find something, bring your family here tonight. We'll take care of our own."

*****

The exhaustion, the stress, the desolation; all took their toll as Sean trudged the once familiar, now alien path home. All was wreck and ruin. He wondered if his work was all for naught. Seeing his house still standing caused an unexpected emotional release in him. Something in the smoke rising from the chimney and the smell of food cooking touched him deeply. He tried to choke back the tears, to compose himself – he couldn't. So, he sat on a burnt log lying in the street and did something he hadn't done since he was a small child; he sobbed.

For so long, his home had been a place of strife, now it seemed refuge – comfort. He thought of Maggie and Liam, waiting for him, smiling, happy to see him. At least he hoped it. He sat and looked at his door for a long while, pondering what waited on the other side. *Liam will be gone, doing who knows what. Maggie will be on her high horse*, he thought. *She'll lay into me again about moving away. Maybe she's right. Maybe there is nothing left here. I could appease her, but would anything change? The hard truth is that whatever is out there, it won't make her warm to me – or me her, I suppose.*

Then, an image momentarily flashed in his mind's eye, Katie's girls flying into his arms at the door, squealing with joy at seeing him. He could feel their kisses on his cheek. And Katie… *What of Katie? If I looked in on them, would I be welcome? Why do I torture myself with what I can't have?*

Sean pushed both the fantasy and guilt aside, but resolved to find them as soon as he could. His heart ached at the thought of them out there alone. With effort, he got to his feet and made his way to the door. With each step, his exhaustion grew heavier.

Sean stepped into his home and found a strange woman – a girl really – standing at the stove. On seeing him, a look of sheer panic seized her. She backed away from the stove and pinned herself against the cupboard. She pulled a chair between herself and him.

He demanded, "Who are you, and what are you doing in my house?"

The girl didn't speak, she only stared.

"Answer me. What are you doing here!"

"Liam…" she stammered, "Liam said I… I could stay here. I'll go."

"Stay put. Where is Liam?"

"He… He's out getting…"

"I am right here, father," said Liam.

Sean turned and embraced his son. It surprised Sean as much as Liam. "Thank God you're alright, son. I was worried."

It took a moment, but Liam returned the embrace. "I can say the same. I went looking for you. That's how I found Rose."

"Rose is it? And who might *Rose* be?"

"She's a friend. We met a while ago. She has nowhere else to go."

"She's young. Where is her family? And why is she wearing your mother's dress?"

"It's a long story?"

"Look Liam, it's not proper for a young lady to be here without her family. What's your mother say of this?"

"She hasn't returned yet. She doesn't know."

"All the worse, a young girl alone with two men. This won't do. Perhaps St. Paul's can help her."

"Liam, tell him all of it," said the girl.

Liam looked sheepishly at his father. "Church's won't help. The telling will take some effort."

Sean tiredly collapsed in a chair. "Perhaps you should tell me, young lady."

"As you heard, my name is Rose… Rose Shannon. The truth is, I am hiding from Mike McDonald. He's a…"

"I know of Big Mike. So, you're one of his… ah…alley cats."

"No!" snapped Liam.

"Then why is she running from him?"

Rose replied, "Yes… Yes, I suppose I was one of his girls, but not by choice, sir. My father handed me over to pay off a debt. I won't lie, I was made to do things… I… I am ashamed to say it, but if you need to hear it, yes, I was one of his whores. Turn your nose up if you feel the need – perhaps I deserve it. But it wasn't my choice, and I am terrified of going back."

"Are you saying your own father sold you into… into…"

Rose wiped away a tear. "It's not as simple as that, but that's the short of it. I escaped in the fire, and have no doubt, Mike is looking to have me back. Liam is hiding me. If you make me leave, I'll have nowhere to go."

"Mikes place is gone. I doubt…"

"Mike has other places – worse places, and special punishments for women who anger him. I promise he won't stop looking. If he finds me…"

"Surely your father…"

"He's turned his back on me." sniffed Rose.

Sean turned to his son. "Hiding her from Big Mike? Well Liam, you've stepped into it, haven't you? What will your friend, Mr. McDonald, have to say about this when he finds out you're playing him false?"

"I'm not with him anymore," said Liam. "You were right about McDonald. He's the scourge you said he was. I guess you were right about me as well. I'm a fool and worse, I admit it. Think of me as you will, but we… I…need to help her. I can't turn my back on her. If you turn her out, I'll have to go with her."

Sean nodded in resignation. "No offence young lady, but I reckon we're past worrying about your reputation. You can stay for now, I suppose. Let me think on permanent solutions awhile." Sean turned to Liam. "Still, there's your mother… your mother will be beside herself. I'm not sure how you'll get her to come around. Which brings me to it. Where is your mother?"

Liam shrugged. "I don't know. I expected her home yesterday. I went looking for her, but haven't seen hide nor hair since I sent her off across the river."

"Damn it son! I left her in your care. You were to stay with her. I trusted you!"

"And I tried," said Liam. "She refused to believe there was a danger. I pleaded with her, but she was stubborn. You know how she gets. Wouldn't budge an inch for fear the house would be looted – didn't want to hear about the fire coming."

Sean grumbled, "You should have made her leave – thrown her over your shoulder if no other way."

"As easy as that, is it? When have you ever made her do anything she wasn't inclined to?"

"So then, she wouldn't budge, where is she?"

"I struck a deal with her. She would go across the river, only if I promised to stay and protect the house. As you can see, I kept my end of the bargain."

"She left you in the fire? Alone? You're lucky to be alive. It's God's miracle the house didn't burn."

"Credit the almighty if you want, but I had a hand in it too. I spent hours on the roof putting out fires. It got a bit warm; I'll tell you."

Sean appraised his son as if seeing him for the first time. "Near all the houses in the neighborhood are lost, and you're telling me you stood alone on the roof and held the fire from taking our home? How can that be?"

Liam bristled. "I did. It's not a lie. I stood guard the whole night."

"I'm not doubting you, son. It's just an uncommon act of courage, is all. It seems I am in your debt, though I'm still unhappy about your mother setting off alone – leaving you to cope alone with the fire to boot. It was a fine bit of foolishness all around."

"I tell you; I did my best with mother. It wasn't… she… wasn't pleasant."

Sean nodded. "Liam, you…" He let out a sigh of resignation. "I see it now, on her broom and off brooding, I'm guessing. All the same, she's had time to come home by now. We need to look for her."

"I have. Yesterday, after I got Rose settled in, I spent the better part of the day walking among the crowds along the west bank of the river. I spent this morning on the lakefront."

Sean said, "I have to go back to the station tonight, but we have a few hours of daylight remaining. We'll split up. I'll look west you return to the lake."

"Father, you haven't slept in days. You need to rest. I'll go out, you sleep."

Rose interjected, "I learned some cooking as a girl. I will make something if you like."
Sean sighed, "Thank you, but I need sleep more than food. Perhaps after I get up." To Liam, he said, "You will go out searching?"

"That, I will. What's this about you going back to the station?"

"It's just for the night. I'll be back in the morning. Liam, I have to say; I don't care for the idea of the two of you being alone here tonight. It ain't proper, even considering her… her history."

"We were alone last night…"

"Be that as it may, I won't have you sharing a bed. Promise me."

"Mr. Collins," said Rose, "you need not worry. Your Liam has been the soul of propriety. There will be nothing going on, I assure you."

"I'll have to take you at your word, I guess." *Sure, you two will behave,* he thought. *A prostitute and randy young man alone for the night. If Maggie walks in on them, she'll put a broomstick to the both of them.* "If your mother isn't home by morning, it's because she can't be. We'll need to check the hospitals. I hear there are to be care tents set up about town."

Sean heard genuine remorse in Liam's voice. "I've failed her and you, I suppose. You think she is badly hurt, don't you? Or maybe… she is…"

"Don't get ahead of yourself. She is likely fine. And no matter what, son, know this – whatever her fate, it isn't your doing. She made her choices, not you."

"Father, I swear I did what I thought was right."

"I know you did, son. And who's to say that your going with her would have made a difference. If she is hurt, I'd be looking for the both of you. I am proud of you. You showed me your colors on DeKoven Street, and again here."

This page left blank

Chapter 20

Michael Ahern sweated; his stomach churned, his head hurt and his hands were shaking. He needed a drink badly. He wanted it nearly as much as his desire to be somewhere else – almost. Being around Big Mike always put him on edge. As often as not, it felt playing tag with a rattlesnake. But this was different – worse.

Little daylight penetrated the barn, and it reeked of smoke, hay, and manure. The crate given to him as a chair dug into his thighs. A bottle of whiskey sat on the barrel in front of him. None was offered and, though he wanted it badly, he dared not reach for it.

"How do you like my new office, Ahern?"

"It's… It's… well, rustic."

"Pigsty is the word you're looking for," snarled Big Mike McDonald. "I've suffered from this fire. I lost my hotel, you know."

"Yes, I heard. A tragic loss."

"Tragic… yes, there's a good word. You especially should grieve its loss. You've spent more than your share of time with your foot on my brass rail – and with my girls."

"Mike, why did you ask me here?"

"Ask?"

"Alright. Why did you send for me?"

"Relax, I'm here to help you. I assume you read the Evening Post's stories about the fire. They say it started in the O'Leary barn."

"My paper wrote the same."

"Yes," said Mike. "But I'm going to help the Chicago Republic to tell the story of *how* it got started."

"And how is that?"

Mike poured a glass of whiskey and slid it to the reporter. Ahern snatched at it and gulped it down. McDonald poured another. Ahern sipped, then sighed and set the glass down.

"Catherine O'Leary set the fire."

Ahern finished his drink. "Really? How did you hear that?"

Mike smiled. "You mean how did *you* hear that."

"Alright, you're to be an un-named source close to the O'Leary's."

"No. I'm not to be named at all, understand? You heard it from Mrs. O'Leary herself."

Ahern shook his head in doubt. "I talked to her the day after the fire – or tried to. She had little to say other than she didn't know how the fire started. If I print she had a part, she'll deny it."

"Of course she will; it won't matter. Nobody will care what an Irish bitch has to say. Printing she did it will make it true enough."

Ahern took another sip. "There was a party that night, some suggest a drunk fell asleep in the barn with a cigar or pipe. It's also whispered that the man who claims to have found it – Sullivan, I think – is most likely the culprit. Others say neighborhood kids had a part in the tragedy."

"You're not hearing me, Ahern. Catherine O'Leary started the fire; she told you as much."

"Mike, if I print that… if I accuse her of deliberately setting the fire, she'll be arrested and charged. A criminal investigation will ensue; if no proof is found, it'll play bad."

"I didn't say it had to be deliberate. You say she confessed to getting drunk and setting the barn on fire."

"Doing what?" asked Ahern. "Women don't smoke."

"Who cares how? Say she claimed it happened while she was milking a cow, and the damn thing kicked over a lantern. I doubt they'll arrest a cow."

"And who milks a cow at night?"

"A drunk Irish woman, that's who. Print the damn story."

"Mike, I'm sorry. Putting up false stories about a robbery or a business competitor is all good and fine, but this fire is too big to muck around with. There'll be scrutiny, and not just the local boys. Things could go badly on the paper… and me. I don't think I can go along with this."

"Yes, you will. Ahern. This is no time for you to grow a spine. I own you, and you know how things go with people who disappoint me."

"Mike, I've always been a loyal friend. I want to help, I do. But this is risky – not just for me, but for you, too."

McDonald fixed an evil eye on Ahern. "What did you say? Risky for me? Tell me Ahern, how is your writing a story about O'Leary risky for *me*? Are you suggesting that you would accuse *me* of something? Perhaps I had a hand in creating the story? Is that what you're suggesting?"

"No Mike, of course not. I didn't mean that at all."

"Good. That's good. I'd feel awful explaining how you lied about me to your wife. She's quite pretty, as I recall. You should keep a protective eye on her. Things are dangerous these days."

"Jesus Mike, you're mistaking me. I am just pointing out that such a story might rouse suspicion, is all. There is no need to making threats. I am only suggesting another option. Let me write that rumors suggest the neighborhood party goers are likely culprits. We can even write that some of them think it was the O'Leary's themselves. All that's plausible, but still deniable by the paper. Hell, it was likely what we would write anyway."

Big Mike leaned in ominously close to the frightened reporter. "I don't want unknown partiers blamed. I don't want folks asking around about it either. I want to read Catherine O'Leary confessed to starting the fire; with or without a cow, or a pipe, or what have you. Chicago will want someone to blame, and she'll be it."

Ahern reached for the whiskey bottle, but Mike pulled it away. In resignation, the reporter slumped forward on the table. "Why her? Why Mrs. O'Leary?"

Because the wolves need to be fed is why. The stubborn bitch will tell her story, sure enough. I can only hope to destroy her credibility. And… shut Johnny up. "Who's to say your story won't be true, and never you mind why I have an axe to grind with Mrs. O'Leary. You just do as I say."

"And what of the investigation."

"What of it?"

"She'll deny any part."

"Sure she will, and she may even come up with some story about who or how. But it won't matter, because by the time city hall convenes an inquiry, the story of her involvement will be gospel, and who doesn't believe the gospel as written by the press? Chicago will want to blame somebody. When the smoke clears, it'll be one Irish woman's word against the common belief."

"And what if the authorities clear her?"

"They may not find cause to arrest her, but there'll be no clearing away the shadows of doubt. Take this to the bank, Ahern; the public won't give her the benefit of the doubt – not an Irish woman."

"Alright, I'll write it out as you want. Who knows, the cow story is just crazy enough that people will buy it as truth."

"That's the spirit," said Mike as he stood and moved toward the door. Ahern understood it as his dismissal and followed. As they walked, Mike said, "If I like the story, there'll be something in it for you. If I don't… well, let's not go over that."

Ahern nodded and shuffled out into the still morning. Mike watched the derelict shell of a man amble off. *Well Catherine, let's just see if the fine people of Chicago dislike us Irish as much as I think.*

Mike leaned against the doorframe of the barn, still watching Ahern, thankful for the fresh air. When the reporter reached the corner, a carriage nearly ran him over. Mike recognized it and groaned. *"What in blazes does that lap dog want?"*

When the carriage stopped, a tall, thin man in a tweed suit and bowler hat dismounted. He carried a walking stick he obviously didn't need. Big Mike had always suspected the thing concealed a dagger. To the driver, the man said, "This won't take long. Wait here."

Mike stepped forward and extended his hand. "Mr. Hemsworth! It's always a pleasure to see you."

The man ignored the outstretched hand. "Is that right, McDonald? You're pleased to see me?"

"Of course. Why wouldn't I be?"

"This isn't a social call, and I believe you know why I'm here. The Alderman noted with some disappointment that your weekly donation to the widows and orphans' fund was missing. He asked me to make inquiries."

Big Mike went into the barn and bade the man to follow. "Can I offer you a drink?"

"It's 10am – a bit early, don't you think? And frankly, I don't want to be here any longer than required. About your donation, is there a problem?"

"I am not sure you heard, Mr. Hemsworth, but there was a bit of a fire a few days ago. Perhaps you read about it?"

"That's funny Mike. No, the Alderman is all too aware of your mongrel Irish friends destroying half our city. He's also very aware that the den of depravity you call a hotel burned down."

"Then you understand why I didn't make my usual donation."

"I see," said Hemsworth. "Tell me, McDonald, do you intend to rebuild?"

"Of course. As tragic as the fire was, it presents opportunities. Opportunities I intend to seize."

"Ah, of course. And tell me. What do you intend to rebuild with?"

Mike didn't like where the conversation was going. "I'm not sure I understand."

"You claim to lack the resources to meet your civic obligations; so, with what will you be rebuilding?"

Mike shrugged, hoping he seemed confident. "Loans are out there."

Hemsworth smiled – there was no humor in it. "Money will be available soon, but banks must be very particular about who to lend to. I'm sure they will be working closely with the city. Even those with access to funds will be challenged by the tragedy. So much needs rebuilt, and precious little wood and brick with which to do it. Decisions will have to be made about what gets rebuilt and when. Priorities will have to be set. Banks, hospitals and legitimate businesses will all be competing for access to building supplies and labor. It'll be chaos unless the city controls the process via permits. And land usage must be considered, we can't have buildings popping up haphazardly. Do you understand?"

"Land usage?"

"A lot of prime real estate is suddenly open for development. Many a business will try to – ah – *convince* – officials to support various building proposals. How persuasive they are will depend on who they are."

"I am beginning to see it, yes," said Mike.

"Beginning? Let me be plain. The application of a proposed business will be more favorably looked on if it's from a community supporter, say a man who makes regular contributions to the

Alderman's relief fund. As you know, the fund's is of special interest to him."

"Mr. Hemsworth, I've been a supporter of the Alderman for years and I know which way the wind blows. Still, I am in the barrel here. My hotel, my girls — gone."

"Yes. Yes, you are in a pickle. Fortunately for you, the Alderman is willing to throw you a bone. Ergo, I am here in this festering lair of yours."

"What does he have in mind?"

"Relief supplies are coming in by the trainload. There will be much, but it'll still be thin to start. The bulk of it will go to the better neighborhoods. There'll be shortages in the ethnic areas for a while."

"So, the poor are to be sold short again, is it?"

"And why not? Aren't they responsible for the disaster – living in squalor – breeding like rats? Their shacks and shanties fed the flames, and good riddance. Still, your concern for them is good because you'll be feeding them."

"Concern? I assure you; I have no such concern."

Hemsworth pointed at Big Mike with his walking stick. "Be that as it may, you will be their savior. You'll go to the warehouse each night. Some friendly guards will let you in. You'll load up with food and supplies, then sell the goods to the grimy huddled masses living in the encampments we are setting up to house them. You'll make enough to fund your rebuild and make your charitable donations to the Alderman."

"And how does the Alderman expect the poor buggers to pay for the goods?"

"There'll be more work than workers soon. That and the relief donations will make sales… shall we say, lucrative."

"I like it. Out the front door and back in through the rear. The Alderman is a smart one."

"You like it? Oh, how lovely." Hemsworth slapped his cane on a nearby post. "McDonald, neither the Alderman nor I need or want your opinion. Just do as you're told."

I'd love to shove that cane up your ass; thought McDonald. "And the Alderman will assure my new hotel moves to the top."

"Not quite. Your hotel was becoming a problem – drawing too much attention. The mayor was getting complaints. Plus, we've plans for that neighborhood. No, you'll build a smaller place housing your betting parlor and liquor sales. You can run your girls out of a separate place – no more than five or six rooms."

"That's a bitter pill," said Mike. "Separate buildings will cost more to own and draw smaller crowds. I'll make a lot less money."

"And draw less attention from respectable folks. But you can expand, add more places as demand rises. And Mike, know that each place is to be counted as a separate business, and will make a separate donation to the fund."

"Jesus, Hemsworth. This is too much; you're squeezing me dry. I want to talk to the Alderman."

"You know better than that. He can't be seen with your sort. I'm here, that should suffice. Oh, and one more small detail, your place and those like it, will be moved to the Sands District – near the lake. There are plans for your old block. We can't have your riff raff so close to decent folk."

"You sell me short, if you think I can be pushed around like this."

"Don't be a fool McDonald. You won't get permits to build anything anywhere else. If you try and buy an existing place, the police will shut you down. You'll go along like always, or you'll be run out."

"You're playing a dangerous game."
Hemsworth laughed. "You have a handful of toughs, we have an army of coppers. I like our chances. Be smart McDonald, go along, in time things will work out for you."
"Why am I being treated like this? Me and my riff raff as you call them, got the Alderman elected, and he'll be needing me again soon enough."

Hemsworth started to walk out, over his shoulder he said, "And he knows he can count on your support. Like you said, Mike, the fire has created opportunities. Welcome to the new Chicago."

Chapter 21

"No, I can't say I've seen anyone who fits that description. But then, hundreds wander in and out each day. Feel free to look around if it suits you."

Sean knew and hated the man's expression. The false sympathetic frown that said, *Sorry friend, but if she ain't come home by now, she's dead. Now go on.* He wanted to slap the condescension off the soldier's face. Instead, he said, "Thank you."

At first, he expected Maggie to come home. Soon, he suspected her hurt. So, he and Liam searched. Early on, they looked for Maggie among the sea of tired, dirty faces gathered on the plain west of the city. They had agreed that if she had listened to their warning and rushed away quickly, they would find her there. By Friday, hope faded. Liam grew more despondent each day; he struggled with guilt over not accompanying his mother.

Sean felt guilt too; on the second day of the search, he thought he saw Maggie. There was relief, but not much more. The sad truth shamed him – he searched more out of duty than worry, and while he hoped to find her safe, he somehow couldn't make himself grieve for her. *Walking through the camp, he thought, what kind of man is so callous toward the mother of his child? Is my heart so cold, my life so empty?*

The relief camps sprung up only days after the fire. The newly homeless gathered there, hoping for food, water and shelter. Many of the injured were cared for in the makeshift infirmaries, and so he and Liam had taken to scouring the camps, hoping to find her in someone's care.

They found it hard to fathom the desperation they saw. There was precious little food or water and the air was foul. Men, women and children were forced to relieve themselves in hastily dug ditches with little, if any, privacy. Fights over food and even clean water became common. The air echoed with the cries of children, and the deep hacking coughs of the sick.

To his surprise, Sean felt the greatest sympathy for those from the *better classes.* Those who had never done without, suddenly had nothing. Hungry and exposed to the elements, they had little idea of how to get by, and were now thrown in with the very same poor immigrants they loathed and feared.

Liam shook his head in dismay. "Each day, these camps descend further into squalor. This can't stand; in a week or two people will be dying."

"I see it too," said Sean. "The camps are dreadful and dirty, but what else could be managed on such short notice? The papers claim over 100,000 are homeless."

"Doable perhaps, but look at them; folks can't go on like this."

Sean scanned the misery stretching out in front of him. "I hear they are to build two-room cabins as temporary shelters, starting in a day or two. The promise is that there will be 5000 of them in little more than a week."

Liam scoffed. "And pigs fly. Even if they could manage so many, it wouldn't be enough – that's 20 or more per cabin."

"True enough, but many folks will take in neighbors, and every day the trains are loaded with people fleeing the city."

"And going where?" asked Liam.

"A lot of folks have relatives in other places, and I hear that many a city has offered aid too. Milwaukee, Cincinnati, and St. Louis, just to name a few, all are sheltering our homeless."

"They may be the smart ones – go while the getting is good."

"Perhaps, but relocating will have its own challenges. Different ain't always better."

Liam said, "Look around, father. Different couldn't be worse."

"You sound like your mother. Things can always be worse."

"Mother? Hardly. But short of war, I never thought such things could happen. It's hard to fathom."

"That it is. We should be grateful there are but 300 dead."

Liam looked at his father and took in a deep breath. "You don't believe what they say, do you – about the 300? Many say the number is higher, even a thousand or more."

"I've heard it too. The truth is, no one really knows how many people even lived in the neighborhoods, much less how many died. The 300 is a guess, not much more."

"And mother? Be honest, do you think she is among the lost?"

Sean's shoulders slumped. "I'll tell you plain, son. If she could come home, she would. If she were in a proper hospital, we would have gotten word by now. These tent camps are our last hope."

"Is it time to go to the icehouse; where they… where they are keeping the… the bodies?"

Sean nodded. "There is still hope, but perhaps it is time. It's a thing I think you should avoid, though."

"No. I should come too. I know it will be grisly, but you shouldn't have to do it alone."

"No son, things like that leave a mark on you. If she's not there, you'll have suffered for nothing. If she is, it… it shouldn't be your last memory of her."

"The same is true for you," replied Liam.

"I've been through it before. You're dealing with enough already."

Liam stopped walking and took his father's elbow. "Father, can I share something with you?"

"Of course."

"I am… well, at odds with myself. Is it possible for me to be concerned about mother, to be hopeful of finding her, but maybe… a little relieved at the thought of her being gone?"

"Liam! She is your mother. It's not…"

"I know and I feel guilty that I feel as I do. I love her – I do. It's just very hard to like her."

Sean stared silently at his son for several seconds, not sure what to say. He felt he should chastise Liam and defend Maggie, but in truth, his son had perfectly described his own feelings. "Liam, I realize your mother could be difficult, but she loved you. She did the best she knew how."

"And you?"

"Yes, me too. You're my son, and I've always wanted what was best."

"No. I meant; did she love you? Did she do her best by you?"

"That's improper, Liam. A son has no reason to pry into his parents' marriage."

"Mother – you – me – we've been under the same roof and stayed miles distant. We never talked about what was pulling us apart. I think we should."

"Son, I won't talk against your mother."

"Nor will I. Still, I am not blind. I saw how things were between you. And we both know how she could be. And it wasn't only you that suffered her… her moods."

"It's true, at times our home was – difficult. She and I could have done better by you. What you don't understand is what your mother endured. The death of your brothers, and…"

"I know, and I am not complaining. I am just saying that… I want you to know… to know that since the fire, I see now that the things I thought were true weren't. And things I believed were important, money, possessions, prestige; they are passing – gone in a flash."

"Liam, you don't need to explain. There's no sense in rehashing any of it."

Liam took off his cap and ran his hand nervously through his hair. "Hear me out. It's people that matter. I've learned that these last few days. It's awful saying it – even thinking it – but perhaps I thought those things important, because I believed people cold, like mother… I saw what you bore, and I thought it was the way of things. I thought you weak for putting up with her. I was wrong. I see it now, and I am sorry I contributed to your worry."

Sean swallowed the lump in his throat. "Thank you, son. But why are you telling me all this?"

Liam used the back of his hand to wipe away a tear. "I guess that I want you to know that I suspect your feelings about mother are close to my own, and it's alright."

"Honestly, I am not at all sure what my feelings are, but I doubt they are like yours. It's different between a son and mother, and a husband and a wife. I wish I could guide you better, but I can't."

"Is it only duty you feel? Is there more?" asked Liam.

"It's never that simple. But son, duty is not to be trivialized. Which begs the question; what are you doing with that girl, Rose? Surely there is something there, more than a sense of charity. What's your obligation to her?"

"I guess I am as confused as you are. I 'm not sure what I am going through. I owe her nothing, yet for some reason, I am compelled to protect her."

"Son, sympathy ain't love. You're not doing her or you any favors by letting her believe she can rely on you if you're not in it till the end."

Liam said, "I realize it. It's just so confusing. There may be more there than sympathy; I suspect there is. How can I be sure?"

"I can't help you with that. But you need to figure it out quick. Can you get beyond her past, what she is – or was? Because if you can't, you need to send her on her way. We can get her safely away from Big Mike."

Liam said, "That seems wrong."

"What seems wrong?"

"Letting her go. She confuses me, and I understand I am taking on a lot. Yet, it seems right with her."

"Liam, she is young. She's grown up too soon, but I suspect she still has the tender heart of a young girl. I've seen how she looks at you. Like it or not, you're getting into something beyond just helping out a woman in need. You need to sort that out, or you will hurt her."

"We have something in common then, I guess," said Liam.

"That's not how it was with your mother."

"I didn't mean Mother."

"What are you saying then?"

"I meant you and the widow Sullivan."

Sean said, "Is that what all this talk about your mother and me is about?"

"You've been taking care of her and her children for a long while. Surely, that's something more than pity."

"And how did you hear about that – your mother?"

"Not just her. It's pretty well known. Most consider it kind of you, but some whisper."

"And your mother? What did she have to say?"

Liam shrugged. "Depended on her mood. Most days she said to ignore the whispers. When she was on her warhorse, she accused you of having a second family."

"Liam, I was never unfaithful to your mother."

"I never believed you were. But as you say, sympathy isn't love. To do what you did, to spend so much time… There must be more holding you than duty – or sympathy, for that matter."

"It's true, those little girls are dear to me."

"And the widow Sullivan? What of her?"

"I am very fond of her, but I am committed to my marriage."

"Till death do you part? Even if mother is still alive, I am not sure I could blame you for seeking comfort from another."

"That's enough of that! This is no topic…" Sean took a deep breath to calm himself. "I would blame me. There is the short of it, once you take the vows, you stand by them. Consider that well when you contemplate where you are headed with young Rose."

"And if mother has passed? Then what?" asked Liam.

"Then nothing. We shouldn't be talking about this. This ain't a proper thing between a son and a father."

Liam said, "I'm not a child. And I am not accusing you of anything. If we are to lose mother, I want things right between us. And I want you to be happy. I ask again, if mother is gone…"

"We mourn, each of us as we can. Then we go on. But until we know, we keep looking. Now, go look for her among the tents. I'll talk to the nurses and see if she's been here."

*****

Sean surveyed the poor occupants in the medical tent. Many had broken limbs, a few were burn victims. He struggled to push back images of other tents, of other broken and burned bodies. He wondered if the war would ever leave him.

"Sean Collins! We meet again."

Sean recognized the voice at once. He turned and saw him sitting on a bail of straw. "Patty! It seems you cheated the reaper yet again. How are you?"

"I am well enough, thanks to you and the sisters. They are about somewhere; you should say your hellos. They mention you and Garland now and again."

"I'll make a point of it." Sean noticed the mahogany peg sitting next to his friend. "It seems they've found you a leg."

"Indeed, they have. One of the army lads showed up with it this morning." Patty held the leg up. "Look here, the damn thing is charred on the edges. I'm afraid to ask where the young fellow got it from, but I suspect I'll feel like a bit of a ghoul for wearing it."

Sean chuckled. "I've never known you to be squeamish. I seem to remember you telling me a story about stealing a dead man's boots at Chancellorsville."

Patty laughed. "Not my proudest moment, I confess."

"Tell me Patty, why are you here? None of your family is hurt, are they?"

"No, no. All are well, just homeless like the rest, is all."

Sean said, "Rest easy, I'll find a place for you."

"That's kind, but unnecessary. Tomorrow, the Doyle clan will be taking a train to the lovely city of Boston. The Mrs. has family there."

"Lots of our people in Boston, but it's still not Chicago. What will you do for work?"

"Don't worry, I'll get by." Patty tapped the wooden leg. "Perhaps I'll try my hand at pirating. And what of you? Are you without a roof over your head?"

"No, I was fortunate in that regard."

Patty's demeanor darkened. "Then why are you here? Is it young Liam? I have not seen him, if you're looking…"

"No, Liam is fine, he's here with me. Sorry to say, it's Maggie gone missing. She and Liam got separated the night of the fire. We've been looking for her since."

"Oh Sean, my friend, has no one told you? I am sorry to say your Maggie is gone."

Sean sat down on an adjoining bale. "What do you mean – gone?"

"She's passed on, Sean."

Sean sat silent for several minutes. "Are you… sure? How do you know?"

Patty put his hand on his friend's shoulder. "She fell from the Madison Street bridge on Sunday night."

"That doesn't sound right. She was to go north and cross over at Lake or Water Street. She shouldn't have been near Madison."

"Still, it is what happened. She was thrown from the bridge when the gas works blew."

"How can you be certain? You were across town when the works exploded."

Patty sighed. "I am sorry, my friend. My Emily was on the bridge with her. She saw it with her own eyes."

"Even so, she may have survived it."

"Don't snatch at false hope, Sean. It's a long fall into a shallow, rocky stream. And Emily says the river caught fire – oil I guess – there was no way she survived the fall."

Sean sat quietly for a long while then said, "This will be hard on Liam."

"Sure, it'll be a shock, but he is a tough kid."

"It's not that. We just spoke about… about the chance that she was gone. He expects it. But he'll blame himself for not being with her."

"If he had, you would likely have lost him too."

"True enough, but he won't look at it like that. The boy is sorting out his guilt for not getting along with his mother and me this last year. His head is everywhere. This will be a bitter pill."

"Listen Sean, you have been worried about him for some time. He just needed to grow up is all, and the last week has seen to that. I tell you; he will come out of this a better man."

"Or a broken one."

"Isn't that the way for all? Trouble comes to each; it breaks us or toughens."

This page left blank

Chapter 22

He could feel the hair prickle at the back of his neck. The hour was odd; the place too dark, and far too remote. "What's this then?"

"We need to talk."

"I recall your saying we were to keep a distance from each other for a while."

"It's true, and after tonight, we won't see each other again."

This is off. The fat prick is up to something, thought Johnny. "And why are we meeting in this dark, dirty barn? And in the middle of the night, to boot."

"Relax. We can't be seen together, is all."

"I don't like it. This place gives me the willies," said Johnny.

"You don't like my new office? Whose fault is that?"

"What's that supposed to mean?"

"It means you burned down my hotel, my home, my business. You burned down half of Chicago, you pea wit."

"And who sent me to do it, Mike? It was your idea, not mine. I was for putting a shillelagh upside their heads. You told me to set a fire – I did."

"I told you to set their coal shed on fire. Not the damn barn."

"I found the shed locked. In the scheme of things, it didn't matter; a fire is a fire. Neither of us could have guessed it would turn out as it did."

"That's your problem Johnny; you're as stupid as you are ugly. I wanted to pressure them into paying a stipend for their dairy business. What good would it do me to burn down the damn dairy? And now my own business is gone, thanks to you. This mess is what I'd expect of you, but I figured Collins to have known better."

"Is that right? Well, at least I showed up as I should. Your darling Liam got cold feet. He left me to my own devices."

Big Mike plopped heavily on a nearby barrel. "Collins never showed up? What was his excuse?"

"How would I know? I ain't seen hide nor hair of him since."

"That's a surprise. I expected better of him. Do you figure him dead?"

Johnny Gallagher sniffed hard, then hurled a green wad of spittle toward the corner. "He's alive – I'd wager on it. But I'll have it out with him if I see him."

"Where do you think he is?"

"Probably holed up with little Rose somewhere would be my guess."

"Rose? What's Rose got to do with anything?" asked Mike.

"You should ask her about that."

"Rose is missing, gone since the fire."

Johnny laughed. "That tells you what you need to know, now doesn't it. I tell you this, he was sweet on her. I caught them

making eyes at each other once. And when I told him what you…
we… did to her that one night, he turned green."

"You talk too much, Johnny. Why did you tell him about that?"

"Why not? He's your fair-haired child now, ain't he?"

Mike laughed. "Are you green eyed over Liam?"

"You never gave me a time with Rose, though I asked plenty.
And what of that meat business? Why was I cut out of that?"

"I was feeling Liam out." said Mike. "Tell me, what did he say
about him and Rose?"

"Nothing much. We was talking about how you were planning a
similar thing for that waitress. He seemed bothered by it. So, I told
him how we turned out Rose. I didn't think it mattered none – ain't
no secret."

"You didn't think it mattered? It was a mistake letting you be
part of it."

"Me? You're darling Liam is your problem, not me. He got upset
about what we did to her, I could tell. He didn't like the O'Leary
business, either. That's why he didn't show. It's Liam who you need
to worry about. He ain't cut out for this – too soft."

"I misjudged him, it seems. And you believe Rose is with him?"

"He's lying low, she's lying low. I suspect you'll find both if you
find one."

*Kitty told me he was moon eyed over her. Putting them together
was a mistake*, thought Mike. "Do you know where to find
Collins?"

"I got a general idea. He'll be easy enough to unearth."

"Where are they then?"

"He lives in the neighborhood just down from the O'Leary's. If I ask around a bit, I'll find somebody who knows where. That is, if his house still stands. Even so, someone up that way will know where he is."

"If what you say is true, I'll have some business with him. He'll regret running off with Rose like that – they both will," said Big Mike.

A smile snaked onto Johnny's face. "I'll be happy to fetch the two of them back for you if I can have some time with Rose as payment."

"Just find them. I'll go from there. I'll make it worth your while."

"Speaking of," said Johnny, "there is the matter of payment for the O'Learys."

"Are you tickling me, boy? You fucked that up royally. I am sitting in a barn because of you. You're lucky I don't gut you like a fish."

Johnny stiffened. "You're welcome to try."

A long moment passed as the two men eyed each other. Mike broke the silence. "You're feeling your ginger. You don't want to push me."

Johnny didn't blink. "I want my money."

"We'll talk about it after you track down Rose and Collins."

"Pay me for O'Leary now. Don't worry about those two. I'll take care of it."

Big Mike's always rosy cheeks turned crimson. "I'll pay you when I'm damn good and ready, if at all. Sass again and you'll get nothing."

Johnny spit again, this time nearly on Mike's shoe. "I'm getting fed up with your abusing me. That can be risky."

"Is that so?" asked Mike. "Do you want to try me?"

"I want to be treated right."

Mike's lips pulled into a smile, but the eyes were cold. "Alright, have it your way. I'll pay you, but first find Rose and Liam, then I'll give it to you right before you leave town."

"Where the hell do you think I'm going?"

"I don't know and don't care. But you can't stay in Chicago."

"And why not?" asked Johnny.

"You are a dense one. Let me explain it clear for you, you stupid ox. You burnt down half the city. Hundreds are dead, and thousands are homeless. Worse, important men lost money – somebody is going to hang for it. Right now, the O'Leary woman is in the skillet. But have no doubt, she'll be crying to the authorities that you and I had a hand in it."

"Fine, I'll shut her up – permanent. It's what we should have done right off."

"Don't be daft. That'll set off alarm bells."

Johnny shrugged. "Maybe you should be the one slinking off then."

"I have a hotel full of witnesses who can vouch for me that night. If they can't get anywhere with me, you'll be next on the list. With you gone, the trail goes cold and we're both safe. If they find you, we may both go down. I can't have that. So, you need to disappear."

"What are you worried about? I won't tell them nothing. My neck will get stretched, same as yours."

Mike said, "They're smart, you're not. Sooner or later, you'll crack."

"I won't be tricked into hanging myself."

"You won't if they can't find you. Like I said, you have a loose tongue."

"I know nothing about anywhere but here. I got nowhere to go and you know it."

"Stop worrying," said Mike. "I got friends all over. You'll be looked after."

That's a load of manure, he ain't never took care of nobody but himself; thought Johnny. *Besides, like he said, they'll want to hang me for it – they'd look for me sure enough. He knows that and wouldn't risk me telling my side.* Then it all fell into place for Johnny. *I was never to leave this barn alive – at least until he learned of Liam and Rose. That changed things up a bit. Leave town, my ass. I'll be left for dead once he has his hands on them.*

"You're a fat prick, aren't you?" spat Johnny.

"Mind your tongue, Gallagher."

"You're going to double-cross me, ain't you? It ought to be *me* that guts *you*. You call me stupid, but I see through you clear enough."

"Settle down. I can't abide you in the authorities' hands is all. Just slip away from Chicago and all will be right. You can come back in a year or two."

Johnny shook his head violently. His jaw set and his nostrils flared. "You slimy bastard. If I made it out of town alive, which I doubt, you would give me up the second the coppers put a shadow on your doorstep. With me gone, you'll tell them some tale about me. I'm to be the fatted calf, am I."

Mike knew two things about Johnny. He wasn't very bright, and he was volatile. He slowly slid his hand into his coat pocket and grasped the small revolver. When the blade appeared in Johnny's hand, Mike pulled the gun and fired. In a blink, Johnny lay crumpled at the fat man's feet. Mike looked at the boy and said, "You got no one to blame but yourself, Johnny. Any fool would know better than to come here alone tonight. And, like I said, you talk too much."

From the floor came a muffled groan. "I'll be waiting for you in hell, you… you fat fuck."

"Perhaps, but you'll wait a long while," said Mike as he pulled the trigger again.

This page left blank

Chapter 23

Walking home from the firehouse, a strange sense of displacement settled on him. So much had happened since the fire; the old neighborhood was gone, and it seemed empty now – lifeless. He lived in a home he barely recognized. Gone were the routines and habits that marked the days with Maggie. Rose and Liam were quiet mostly, but for all their troubles, the place somehow felt more alive, even happy. With each day, Rose seemed to come out of the darkness. Sean caught glimpses of what Liam saw in her. Watching them grow closer reminded him of the chasm in his own marriage.

Life is simpler now, but something is missing. Maybe I should have listened to Maggie – picked up and moved. Would it have solved anything? Likely not, I reckon, but at least she'd be alive. Maybe she was right; I feared change. Yet, change found me anyway.

He found Liam at the kitchen table reading the paper, a cup of coffee sat next to him. Sean went to the stove to pour himself a cup. The bedroom door stood open; the bed had not been slept in. He and Liam shared a bed – at least nights when Sean wasn't at the firehouse. Rose slept in Liam's room. He didn't approve of the two sharing a bed, but wasn't naïve enough to expect they honored his rule when he was gone.

Liam tossed the paper aside. "How can they print such lies?"

Sean replied, "The truth can be hard to pin down. So many say different things."

"Rubbish," growled Liam. "The nonsense this Ahern fellow is spewing about Mrs. O'Leary – his claiming she said her cow kicked over a lantern – it's a bald-faced lie. Big Mike had Johnny Gallagher set that fire. I believe it as sure as I know the sun is up."

"You may believe it, but it's Catherine's story to tell, and she's as quiet as a midnight grave."

Liam shook his head. "There's a puzzle. Why doesn't she speak out – put it on Mike?"

"Who would listen to her? People trust what they want, and they like the cow story. It sits well with what they believe."

"And all they know is what they read. That worm Chamberlin at the Post writes that us poor Irish spent the night of the fire drinking, looting, and raping. I saw him skulking around the night of the fire; there was none of that going on. Still, he writes it, and the uptowners accept it as gospel."

"And son, that's why Catherine O'Leary hides in her cabin."

"We all should, all us Irish. General Sheridan has imposed martial law, thanks to those lies. They say they are shooting looters on sight. I hear one bloke got gunned down for nothing more than being in the wrong neighborhood after sunset. Empty-handed he was. I tell you, those that hate us are using the fire as an excuse to put their foot on our necks."

"I'll give you that the papers are harsh on our people. But there's no denying some deserve it. Your Mike and Johnny are examples. I suspect there was looting and drunkenness, but where they got it wrong is judging people by the lot. Race, country, or status have nothing to do with character – good or bad. Getting angry at some imagined group plotting against us is no wiser than bigots fearing and hating strangers. Look around, you'll see acts of kindness all around."

"I don't doubt it, but it gets harder to find. I get bitter. I'm trying to curb it, but it's hard."

"You get your temper from your mother."

"It's a curse."

"Perhaps, but you got her brains too. There is a blessing."

Liam smiled. He found his father's company better than he used to. "If you say so. What did I get from you - good looks?"

Sean sat at the table. "My stubbornness and appetite, I suppose."

"Do you want breakfast? I can burn some eggs and ham. It won't be good, but it won't kill you."

"There is a wonder. Since when can you cook?"

Liam shrugged. "It's a wee bit of a stretch to call it cooking."

"Even so, we should wake Rose. It's time anyway."

"It'd be better to let her be. She had night terrors again. I laid hours with her, getting her back to sleep. I just woke up myself."

"It ain't proper, sharing a bed with her."

"It's the only way she'll sleep. I can guess what you're worried about, father. Nothing happened."

"You're both young. Urges can be…"

"And with her past, of course she'd open her legs readily enough. Is that what you're saying?"

"I said no such thing. I was young once too. I… you two shouldn't be sharing a bed is all."

"She's not like that. It took days before I could even touch her without it scaring her to death."

"She's been often hurt by men, Liam. Some women go dead inside and feel nothing. Others… well, they are like Rose. It's probably why she sleeps so much. She's safe for the first time in a long time. She's trying to heal."

"Proper or not, she needs me and I need to take care of her."

Sean thought, *Such a change. And so fast. Just a few weeks ago, he cared for nothing but himself. Now he's committing his life to… to what?* "Liam… son, I have to ask again. Do you understand what you're getting yourself into? I see you two together; I see the way she looks at you. You need to ask yourself, is she the one for you?"

"We've been over that," said Liam.

"Questions were asked that still wait for answers."

Liam said, "Questions are they, or accusations? You don't judge her worthy of me, do you?"

"I have nothing against her, and I don't look down on her. But son, she has been through a lot. More than a girl of her tender years should ever endure. There will be scars on her heart that will take years to heal, if they ever do. Marriage is a hard thing for all, but for her and you, there will be … problems. I know how hard it can be to live with a woman who…"

"She's not mother."

"I am not saying she is. I'm just saying that…"

"So, you don't approve?"

"I didn't say that. She is welcome here for as long as she wants to stay. And if in time you decide to wed, you're welcome to live here as man and wife. If you choose her, she'll be a daughter to me. I just want you to avoid making the same… well, I just want you to…"

"You want me to avoid the same mistake you made?"

"I suppose I am saying as much. Me and your mum married too young, and too quickly. Your mother and I grew to want different things; it's why she was as she was."

Liam shook his head. "You're being generous. Mother was who she was; she would have been unhappy no matter what she had. It would be different with me and Rose."

"So, you are considering her as a wife, after all."

"Not sure I am there, or if she'll have me. As you say, she needs time. I won't bring it up for a bit."

"Good," said Sean. "You both have been through much. Give her – and you – time to adjust. As I said, she is welcome to stay with us as long as she needs."

"There is the thing, father. I am wondering if Chicago is the place for us. As long as Big Mike is close by, Rose will be afraid."

"You're considering leaving with her – unwed?"

Liam nodded. "We might have no choice."

"Mike's place is burned down. His girls are scattered to the winds. He'll not care about Rose."

"I said as much to her, but it's false. Mike didn't look at her as just one of the other girls. She was his… he used her for… She's sure he will be on the hunt for her, and from what I've seen, it may be true."

"Liam, think hard about this. Here you have a place to live, there will be plenty of work rebuilding, and you'll have friends to stand by you. If you run off, it will be just the two of you – broke and alone. I'll add, it's a bridge you can't come back from. Married or not, you'll be binding yourself to her."

"I have to do what's best for Rose."

A tinge of guilt washed over Sean. *Liam is kinder to a strange girl than I was to my own wife.* "What is best for Rose isn't dragging her to a strange place with nothing to start a life with."

"You and mother picked up roots and left the home country."

"Look around; how did that come out for us?"

"Just because this place didn't work doesn't mean no place will."

Sean said, "They say *the devil you know is better than the one you don't.*"

"Pardon me for saying so father, but you're a pessimist. It's a tremendous world out there, with much to offer."

"You sound like your mother."

"I hardly think so. Mother was bitter and restless, is all. My motives are more practical."

"So what's your thoughts? Have you a plan?"

Liam said, "I always dreamed of going to sea. Perhaps it would suit me – maybe go to San Francisco and catch a job on a steamer."

"That would be a poor life for Rose. Sitting alone waiting for you. The war did that to your mother. She never forgave me."

"I suppose that's so, something else then. Whatever else comes, staying here isn't looking wise."

"Think on it, son. I'd like you to stay."

"You're worried about being alone?"

"I said no such thing. It's just I think you two would be better off with family close by."

"If Rose and I go, you could come with…"

Sean waved him off. "Let's see what plays out, Liam. You have time to weigh options."

"I'm not so sure. Mike is out there looking for Rose. And I may have used up my luck here too."

"You think he could be hunting you, too?"

"He might suspect I'm harboring her."

Sean nodded. "There is the fire too. You say you're sure he was behind the fire. If you know, he knows you know."

"All the more reason to leave Chicago," said Liam

"Perhaps, and perhaps, your association with Mike will put your neck on the block."

Liam's brow furrowed. "I'm not sure I follow."

"If you're missing, or dead, you're easy to pin the fire on."

"I had nothing to do with it, you know that."

"All the same, If your Johnny and Mike get sniffed out, they'll be looking for someone to blame it on if need be. If you run, it makes it easy."

"Sweet Jesus," said Liam. "Mrs. O'Leary already thinks I'm dirty. I may be in it deep."

"Why? How?"

"It's a story I'd rather not tell. But I will say she has cause to blame me."

*****

He knocked on the door again, louder this time – still no answer. He called out. "Patrick! Catherine! It's Sean Collins."

He heard movement and the door unlatch. A smiling Catherine O'Leary opened the door. "Sean, welcome. I thought you…" The smile faded when she saw Liam. "Sean, I'm sorry for your loss of Mrs. Collins; she was a fine woman. You're welcome here anytime, but you had no cause to bring Liam. He's not…"

Liam spoke up. "Mrs. O'Leary, I understand your anger. But I had no hand in the fire. I would never do such a thing."

Catherine O'Leary's expression remained hard – cold. "Is that the message your master has sent you to bring? Well, alright, you have. Now, be on your way." She turned to Sean. "Perhaps it's best if you stayed away, too." She tried to shut the door.

Liam held it open. "Hear me out and we will trouble you no more. You've a right to be angry. That business with Mike and Johnny was a shameful thing. When I saw how things were with McDonald, I parted ways with him. I've come here to help you."

"I've had enough of your help, and McDonald's, too. You can go back and tell him so."

"I'm not playing you false. I am not with him anymore. He may be after me, even. I only want to set things right with you."

"Are you here to build me a barn?"

"No," said Liam. "I am afraid that's beyond me."

"Then there is nothing you can do to help me. I'll take you at your word that you wised up about that pig you were rutting with. Sean, take your boy home and watch him close."

Sean replied, "Catherine, let him speak, please."

She opened the door and said, "Alright, but come inside. One of those reporters will be by soon enough, or kids come to throw rocks."

Sean and Liam stepped into the small cottage. Blankets covered the windows, and even though midday, the room was dark and cheerless. Sean said, "What's this about reporters and rock throwing?"

Patrick answered. He sat on a chair in the kitchen – a scatter gun lay on his lap. "Since those stories in the paper, our life has been nothing but torment. Strangers hurl insults at the house, children rocks. Reporters are the worse though. They hover about like vultures, asking all manner of tricky questions – they make accusations as well. They want to pick our bones clean."

"That's why I'm here," said Liam. "I've read the trash being printed. It ain't right that the blame is being put on you. I want to help set the tale straight."

Catherine answered, "Oh, and how do you propose to do that?"

"I know it was Big Mike who done it. Well, more likely Johnny Gallagher. But at McDonald's bidding."

"And how do you know that? Did you see him do it?"

"No. As I said, we parted ways before the fire. But Johnny told me that Mike wanted you took care of. Surely you believe Mike had a hand in the barn catching fire. It's clear as day."

"Sure, I have my suspicions," said Catherine. "But I got no proof. Sounds like you don't either. You're chattering on about Johnny told you that Mike told him to do this or that – it's weak tea."

"We can talk to the authorities, both of us – together. They'll see it then."

"I've spoken with the authorities already. They'll believe what they want, or what they're told to believe."

"What did you tell them? Did you mention Mike, or Johnny, or me?"

"I told them the truth. That me and Patrick got home and went to bed. We were asleep when the fire started, and have no good idea of what happened."

Sean asked, "Why not tell them about McDonald? Liam says you were at odds."

"There is the thing you see. A man from city hall came to visit, a proper gent he was, but cold as a snake. He asked me what happened, and I told him what I just told you. He was more than pleased with it – said that was all good and fine. I told him I had witnesses too, and that played all well and good too. He then said that there was to be a formal inquiry downtown and I would be called to testify, and the witnesses, too. He said I could tell my story and it would put all those tall tales to rest; that all would be fine."

"That's good," said Liam. "I'll tell what I know too."

"There's the thing. After, he asked me if I had any notions about the fire not being an accident. The way he said it put me off. It's no secret McDonald has friends downtown and all. So, I tell him, I ain't gave that much thought. He's all smiles then. Says that's good, that it wasn't wise to muck things up with suspicions and accusations. He said that would just complicate things, and who knew what could happen then. *'Just stick to what I know is true, and I'll be fine,'* he said. It gave me the willies; the way he said it."

Sean asked, "You felt it a threat?"

Catherine O'Leary pulled at the collar of her dress. "I think they want to hear what they want to hear and don't want to hear what they don't. Your Liam can say or do what he wants, try to clear his conscience if he has one. But as for me, I am not making trouble where there is none."

"So, McDonald gets away with it," huffed Liam.

"God's truth, I don't know for sure he did it; neither do you. But put this in your gospel; if I accuse Mike, people will say I am doing it to push blame away. If they investigate him and find no proof, they'll clear him of it. And then what? I'll tell you, I'll be standing alone, the crazy Irish woman telling tales. Then what do you suppose happens? Nothing good, I'm sure."

"I am sorry you're in this fix, Mrs. O'Leary," said Liam. "But I can't abide with Big Mike walking around free. He needs to pay, and not just for this."

Sean said, "Listen to her, son. Your story won't help. It only puts her at odds with those that can cause her trouble. You too, for that matter."

"I don't care. So long as Mike is around, we all suffer."

Sean said, "Liam, not so long ago you bragged about how the powerful live by different rules, it was how you escaped the jailers."

"No need to shame me for it. I know I was a fool."

"You were a fool for wanting that life. But you were not wrong on the truth of it. The law will not hold McDonald accountable – no matter how loud you scream at the sky."

Catherine O'Leary said, "McDonald will get his justice in the burning pit. The lord will see to it, no one escapes his wrath."

A common depiction of Catherine O'Leary shortly after the fire

Circa 1872, author unknown

Chapter 24

He knew it was foolish, but Liam still felt a little guilty about going across the street to scavenge firewood from the neighbor's burnt-out house. They would eventually tear it down, load it in wagons, and haul it to the fill pile on the lake. Still, it somehow seemed like grave robbing. So, each night, he waited until after dark to do what he half-jokingly called the *dirty deed.*

Things had gone well in the two weeks since the fire. Each day, Rose had become more animated; she talked more, smiled more, even became affectionate at times. Fortunately, the two of them had settled into an amiable domestic routine with his father. That Rose and his father were becoming comfortable around each other was gratifying, especially to Rose. Liam knew how her own father had abandoned her, and he sensed Rose somehow badly needed his father's approval as a sort of reassurance. He saw how much his father's kindness and gentleness meant to her. It meant nearly as much to him.

Happily, he had not seen or heard anything from Johnny or Big Mike. There was talk of Johnny gone missing. Liam supposed he fled Chicago. *Maybe father was right, these things can sort themselves out given time. With his hotel gone, I am guessing McDonald has bigger fish to fry than us. I'll talk to Rose; perhaps she will agree to stay a while longer. I can find work – set some money aside to bankroll our move.*

On entering the cabin, he set the axe and wood on the floor near the Franklin stove. He heard Rose moan, "No, please don't."

Another nightmare, he thought, *poor thing must have fallen asleep without supper again.*

It was then he heard the all too familiar voice growl, "I'll teach you to run away from me!"

In an instant, Liam bolted into Rose's room. He saw Rose half lying on the bed, Big Mike's left hand clinching a knot of her hair, his right delivering a brutal blow to her face.

Liam hurled himself onto the big man's back. McDonald shrugged him off, and Liam landed next to Rose on the bed. He grabbed Liam's shirt and was about to drive his fist into the boy's face when Liam kicked up with all his might. Big Mike reeled back in agony, clutching his groin.

Liam screamed, "Leave her alone you fat fuck!"

McDonald, still bent over, groaned, "You'll pay for that, boy."

Liam lunged from the bed and threw his full body weight into his bulky assailant. They fell to the ground, Liam landing on McDonald's chest. Liam threw a hard right, squarely connecting with McDonald's jaw. He followed with a left that only grazed the side of the big man's head. Before he could land another punch, Liam felt an intense thud impact his ribs; it knocked the air out of him.

McDonald rolled Liam off him. Liam took a fist to the right temple – the room blurred and white fireflies drifted in a swirling haze. McDonald's bulk crushed down on him, then came the vice-like grip of fingers around his throat – he couldn't breathe. In desperation, he tried to throw a punch – it landed weakly on McDonald's upper arm. A vain attempt to kick did little; the big man's bulk was too much.

Panic seized Liam as McDonald's grip on his throat tightened. An intense pressure built behind his eyes, it felt like they may burst. His lungs burned; his chest muscles spasmed as he fought in vain for air. Liam tried to claw at McDonald's fingers, it was useless.

Spittle hit his face when Big Mike grunted, "Imagine how I am going to make her suffer after you're dead, boy. Hold on to that as you go."

The room turned blurry, then light dimmed, and a gathering blackness crept into the periphery. In the long seconds that followed, Liam's world dwindled to a shrinking red tinged light floating in darkness. A last image flashed in his mind; it was Rose. Then there was nothing at all.

*****

It took more than a few moments to comprehend what he was seeing. Rose sat on the floor in a torn, blood splattered dress. She hugged herself as she gently swayed back and forth. A tangled mess of hair stuck to a bruised face, vacant eyes stared at some distant thing. If she knew he was there, she didn't acknowledge it. An axe lay in a large pool of dried and congealed blood. A smeared blood trail let to the back door. The war had taught him well the smell of death; it hung heavy in the air.

Sean crouched down in front of Rose. "Rose, are you hurt?"

She only continued to stare.

He grabbed her shoulders and shook her. "Rose! Look at me!" There was no response. He'd seen this before. In the army, they called it battle stupor. He tried a thing he saw work a few times. Pinching her nose shut, he covered her mouth.

It took a few seconds, but Rose gasped for air, blinked, then shivered. A look of surprise crossed her face. He released her. "Daddy?" she asked. She clutched his arms and pulled herself to him in a tight embrace.

He stroked her hair gently for a few seconds, then said, "It's Sean Collins, darling. Are you hurt?"

"What? No… No, I don't think so." She shivered then went wide eyed. Clutching Sean she gasped, "Where is he?"
"Where is who? What happened here?"
"Mike was here…. he found us… he… he"
"What happened? Where is Liam. "
 "Liam tried to fight him off… he tried…" Rose broke into sobs.
"Rose, gather yourself. Did McDonald hurt Liam? "

"He choked Liam… He… He…"

"Rose – please, What happened to my son?"

"I… I don't know. He ran away, I guess."

"Who ran away – Liam? McDonald? Ran where?"

"I… I… don't know where they are."

"Think Rose! What happened to Liam?"

"I'm alright, father," said Liam in a raspy voice.

Sean turned and saw his son standing at the door. His face and throat were bruised, his shirt soaked with blood. He was pale and short of breath. Rose flew into Liam's arms. She began sobbing uncontrollably. "I thought you left me. Please, don't leave me."

"Are you alright, son?" asked Sean.

Liam held Rose tightly and nodded that he was.

"What happened here? Whose blood is this?"

Liam croaked. "Big Mike found Rose. When I came in, he was attacking her. We got into a fight, and… and while we were fighting, Rose put an axe to his head."

"Sweet Jesus, Liam. What have you two done, and what's wrong with your voice?"

"It was self-defense. The fat bastard got on top of me – he choked me nigh to death. That's what's happened to my voice; he nearly crushed my windpipe." He swallowed uncomfortably and went on. "I was unconscious, I'm guessing; not sure how long. When I woke, his body was on top of me with the axe buried in his skull."

"Dear lord. You're lucky to be alive." said Sean.

"Rose was sitting on the floor, hugging herself, rocking back and forth. I haven't been able to get her to speak. I tried to hold her, get her to lie down, but it just agitated her. So, I let her be. I didn't know what else to do. I spent the night sitting next to her, trying to talk to her. How did you get her to come out of it?"

Sean ignored the question. "She's in shock. You should have called for a doctor."

Liam held Rose tighter and shook his head. "And tell him what? Wasn't it you who said Big Mike has friends on the police force, and city hall too. They know all about him and Rose – he told me once that he even let some of them have at her. The truth wouldn't sit well with them. The story would be I caught Rose in bed with him, and I killed him out of jealousy. We'd be in jail in a cold minute."

"Come Liam, this is different. We need to notify the authorities."

"Is it? Ask Rose how many cops and politicians have abused her? Ask Mrs. O'Leary about the authorities' love of truth."

Sean, sighed and nodded. "This is a deep hole, son. We need to think clear… how long ago did this all go on?"

"Last night – early – when you were at work," said Liam. "Long enough that someone will be missing the big prick. I imagine the police are out looking for him now."

"Where is… McDonald?"

"I drug him outside to the privy. That's where I just was."

"Mother Mary, protect the feeble-minded; that was a bit of foolishness. Dragging a body around in daylight? What were you thinking?"

Liam guided Rose to a chair. "I was tending to Rose all night, then as it got brighter, I got to thinking that the sight of him was disturbing her – me too, truth be told."

"In daylight though? Why didn't you do it last night? Not that I think sticking him in the privy was the thing to do, mind you."

Liam chuckled a bit. "Sorry for it not being up to your standards, but I confess to some inexperience in these matters, it being my first killing and all."

"Really, you consider this is the time to be glib?"

"Maybe not, but I'll confess that I'm more than a little content with him lying dead in the shitter. It seems like fitting justice."

"And tell me, will you be content with your justice when the two of you are in shackles? We can afford no mistakes if you're to avoid the gallows."

"What are we going to do – Run?"

"Not run. Not yet anyway. Even slipping away needs planning."

Liam stroked Rose's hair. "Time is a thing we may not have. Big Mike will be missed soon, if not already."

Sean held his palm up in a gesture suggesting silence. "Let me think a moment." After several long seconds of heavy silence, he said, "Here's how I see it. You're right about important people knowing McDonald, but they aren't his friends. Men like him don't have friends, just lackey's and co-conspirators. His absence will be noted, but he won't be missed. I doubt any will put much effort into looking for him. And those that might care if he's alive aren't the type to go to the police."

Liam said, "Are you suggesting going to the authorities? You think they're to be trusted."

"No one will mourn for Big Mike, but you're not wrong about not trusting the authorities to give you a fair shake. They'll have no problem hanging a murder on a prostitute given a chance… no offense meant to Rose."

"Will you help us?"

"You're my son. Of course I'll help you."

"I haven't been much of a son. It seems I bring you nothing but grief."

"This isn't the time for that foolishness," said Sean. "We have trouble to deal with."

"So, what do we do?"

In barely more than a whisper, Rose spoke up. "I want to get away. I want to go far away and never come back."

Liam said, "Rose, McDonald is dead now. No one will ever hurt you again."

She sniffed. "There will always be another Mike. I can't stay here anymore."

Sean said, "We'll talk about that later. Now, there is the matter of a body in our privy."

Liam suggested, "Perhaps we leave him there. He's fat, but if we take the bench off… we can… you know… stuff him in. He'll fit down there."

"A fitting place," said Sean. "But a poor idea. If he's ever found, we might as well all tie nooses around our necks."

Liam buried his face in his hands. "Not all, just me. Neither you nor Rose will be blamed. I'll stand for it alone if we're found out."

Sean patted Liam on the back. "No need for being a martyr. As I said, no one will lose sleep over Big Mike's disappearance. They'll assume him run off for some reason. And if they stumble upon his body, the authorities won't put much effort into identifying who did him in – could be any of a hundred thugs responsible, or one of his powerful friends had it done. That business with Rose, and the other girls cuts both ways – a lot of shady secrets go to the grave with McDonald. The constables will likely figure some stones are best left unturned."

Liam said, "What if somebody, like Johnny, knew he was coming here. That will put us in the stew."

"McDonald came here to kill you, likely Rose too. I doubt he told anybody where he was going. Besides, if one of his thugs knew the plan, they'd been with him. It figures McDonald told no one where he was going or what he intended."

Rose sniffed. "It doesn't matter. Others will come. We need to run."

"No Rose. No one will come looking. We just need to get his body away from here, and this will turn out fine. In a week or two, Mike will be forgot."

"And how do we do that?" asked Liam? "Wait till night and toss him in the river?"

"Let me think on that. For now, fetch some lye soap and clean water, and we'll see to this blood."

*****

The setting October sun threw long deep shadows in the alley behind the Collins cottage. Sean and Liam carried the last of the charred scrap wood from the adjacent burnt house and threw it on top of McDonald's body.

Rose came out the back door. She looked at the wagon for several seconds and scowled. She asked. "Is he in there?"

Sean whispered, "Lower your voice. Yes, he is in the wagon."

She walked up to the horse and gently grabbed its bridle. Rubbing its muzzle, she said, "I liked the notion of him better in the bottom of the privy, but carted away like garbage is proper too."

Good, thought Sean, *anger is better than remorse.*

Liam whispered. "We rolled him up in an old rug. He's covered pretty good. If no one looks too close, we'll be alright."

"Did you tie those knots secure?" asked Sean. "It won't do for him to come rolling out of that rug along the way. And I don't need blood on the floorboards. I borrowed this wagon from the station house."

Liam nodded.

Rose asked, "Where are you taking him?"

Sean answered. "To the lake. They are using fire debris as fill for something or another at the foot of Randolph Street. People are tossing in wagon loads of brick and lumber from sunrise to sunset. With luck, tons of the stuff will cover him in a day or two."

Rose hugged herself tightly. "What if somebody finds… him… the body, I mean?"

"It won't matter, so long as no one sees who put him there. With luck, the dump site will be quiet."

Liam asked, "Maybe we should wait till late at night?"

"No son, that won't do. Militia are patrolling the streets. We'll come across one or two, I expect. Us hauling scrap so late will rouse suspicion. We need it to look like it's our last load before supper, is all. The fire department markings on the wagon may help pass muster too. Now let's get on with it."

Rose climbed up on the wagon.

Liam asked, "And where do you imagine you're going?"

"I got us in this mess. I'll be going with you to rectify it as well."

Liam shook his head. "This is no business for you to be a part of."

She shot him an icy glare. "I don't need you telling me what I should be part of. Besides, you'll draw less scrutiny with a woman along." She nodded at Sean. "Who brings their daughter to dispose of a body?"

"She's not wrong, son," said Sean.

Liam crossed his arms. "I don't like it. It could be dangerous."

Rose's bravado failed her. Her voice raised an octave as she said. "I won't stay in this cabin alone, not knowing when or if you two are coming back. I won't do it. No, I'll share whatever fate befalls you."

Liam and Sean exchanged glances. Sean nodded, and Liam reluctantly climbed into the back of the wagon. Sean asked, "Are you comfortable? It'll be a bit of a haul."

"No, not at all, come to mention it," said Liam. "I admit to having a bit of the fidgets, sitting on what I am."

"Well, try not to look it. Remember, all is normal."

Slowly and with little conversation, they made their way through the empty, burnt out neighborhoods. Eventually, Rose whispered to Sean. "I'm terrified to near death. I'm not sure I can take this anxiety much longer. How much further?"

He replied, "Do you sing?"

"Sing? You mean… like a song? I can't."

"Try. Something cheery, if you can. You'll feel better with something to occupy you, and it'll seem more convincing to those we pass."

At first, in a halting voice, Rose softly sang the hymn *Amazing Grace*. As they went, the timidity left her voice, though she sang no louder.

"You sing well, child." said Sean. Her response took him by surprise, she hooked her arm in his and put her head on his shoulder.

Approaching near the dump site, a voice boomed. "Halt!"

Sean pulled the horse up short as two soldiers stepped into the street. One held a lantern up to illuminate their faces. The other – younger soldier – moved to the back and passed his light over the wagon bed.

The soldier closest to the front said, "What are you doing out after dark? Stealing, I'll wager."

"Nothing of the sort," said Sean. "We are just disposing of our last load of the day. The damn fire took our work shed. We're clearing out the scrap to rebuild."

"Late, don't you guess? The mayor and general have ordered a curfew – you're not supposed to be out after dark."

Sean kept his voice even. "Not quite dark yet, but it's true; time got away from us. We'll offload this wagon on the double quick and get home."

He held the lantern up again – close to Rose. "And what have we got here? What's a pretty young thing doing with these flea-bitten mutts."

Liam bristled and started to come down from the wagon. Sean held him back. "Stand down, son."

To the soldier, he said, "This is my son and daughter. Come along to help is all."

Never taking his eyes off Rose, the soldier said, "Listen to your old man, boy, or you'll earn a beating. The girl don't look much like you, papa. Are you sure you're her father?" With a snort, he added, "Just because your Mrs. said you is, don't mean she wasn't out and about."

The younger soldier in the back said, "Come on Buck, they're alright. Nothing back here but scrap, just as he said. Let's let them pass."

The older soldier – called Buck – patted Rose's leg. She flinched. "Maybe Jess. Maybe not. I believe they look suspicious. You all get down and unload this wagon right here. We'll make sure you haven't got some stolen goods hid under that pile. But first, Jess, you search these two for stolen property. I'll search the girl – and don't forget to be real thorough."

Liam snarled. "You won't touch her."

Buck pointed his carbine at Liam's face. "Won't I? Get down off that wagon now."

The younger soldier said, "Buck, it's getting late, we've no cause to…"

"Do as I say, Jess. You watch them unload and reload that wagon. I'll keep an eye on the girl."

"Buck, really," said Jess. "There's nothing in the wagon worth stealing. I looked."

The lantern illuminated a malicious sneer on Buck's face. "They'll empty this wagon as I said, then they'll load it back. Every stick of it."

"Why?" asked Liam.

Buck waved the gun toward Liam. "Because I don't like the look of you or your bitch of a sister. If that's what she is."

Liam jumped out of the wagon. Buck cocked the rifle. "Slow boy." He motioned toward Sean. "You and the girl get down too."

"What's this then?" A low voice boomed from behind.

Buck flinched and turned to the officer walking up from an alley. He saluted and said, "Sir, I was just going to check these folks to make sure they weren't looting."

The lieutenant took the lantern from Jess and scanned the wagon. "Aha, and who steals burnt scrap?"

Sounding more than a little nervous, Buck said, "I… I… thought… maybe they had loot under the scrap."

"Did you now?"

To Sean, the officer said, "How about it. Why are you out so close to curfew?"

"As I was trying to explain to your man here, it's our last load of the day. We'd be done and on our way home by now if not stopped."

The officer sized up Sean and Liam, then looked at Rose. He shot a cold disapproving glare at Buck.

"Other than the girl, why are you detaining them?"

Buck said nothing in reply. The officer continued, "Seems like you two have too much time and too little to do. Perhaps you should follow them down to the lake and help unload the wagon for them – get them home quicker."

"But sir, we have to…"

The lieutenant's eyes narrowed as he stared Buck down. "Consider it a gesture of goodwill."

"No, please don't," pleaded Rose. "We don't want any help… not from him."

The lieutenant eyed Rose. "Oh, and why not?"

"He scares me."

"And why is that?"

Near sobbing and in a voice younger than normal, she whimpered, "He threatened to put his hands on me." He eyed Rose, then Buck, and spit. The lieutenant nodded at Sean, and said, "You folks get this wagon unloaded and get home quick. You shouldn't be out after dark." To Buck and Jess, he said, "You two knuckleheads follow me."

When the soldiers walked away, Sean urged the horse forward, sighed and said, "Oh holy mother, that was close. Rose, are you okay?"

She smiled, "I'm fine, I merely thought a girl in distress would convince him to move on a bit quicker," was her reply.

Sean shook his head and smiled. "You have some wits about you."

Liam punched the side of the wagon and growled, "That Buck needed to have an axe planted in *his* head too."

"One axing at a time, son."

Liam said, "This… this is what I was saying yesterday. This town is a sewer."

"And as I said, one place is the same as the next. There's good and bad wherever you go."

Rose said, "Liam, it's time we tell your father."

"Tell me what?"

Liam removed his cap and ran his fingers through his hair. "The thing is… me and Rose talked earlier. We are intending to leave tomorrow."

"How?" said Sean. With what?"

"I've a small amount of money; I'm not proud of where I got it. But, it should be enough to get a start somewhere."

"And when were you going to tell me about this?"

Liam answered, "When this business was over, tonight at supper – when we were all settled a bit."

"Liam – Rose – it ain't necessary. McDonald is gone, and after tonight, the authorities won't be after you."

"This business with Big Mike plays a part," said Liam. "But it's not the whole of it. There are too many bitter memories for Rose here. Truth be told, I have a few things to live down too, as you know. We want a fresh start in a new place."

Sean cleared his throat. "I won't say I'm not disappointed. I hoped we could keep the family together, but I understand the why of it."

Rose whispered. "Family? Am I included in that?"

"It seems fate wants it. I've talked to Liam about plans. What about you? What do you want, Rose?"

"I want to leave Chicago – start over. But stay or leave, I'll do what Liam wants, go where he goes."

"You barely know him. His kindness to you can make you…"

"I know enough," she said. "Who but a good man would treat me as he does, stand by me when he has no cause to do it. I know he has a kind heart. I'll learn the rest as I need to."

Sean nodded in resignation. To Liam he said, "Where are you two going?"

"California… San Francisco likely."

"Alright son. It seems you've two have settled on it. I won't object. But I wonder if tomorrow is too soon. It might look suspicious, your disappearing without cause. Stay a day or two, get packed proper. Maybe tell folks you plan to marry and be with your new wife's family out East. Make it seem all nice and normal."

"We can hold off a day or two," said Liam. "That'll help even, give you time to settle things."

Sean asked, "Settle things? What's that mean?"

Liam took Rose's hand. "We've talked; we'd planned on asking you to join us out west when we're settled. But if we hold off a bit, maybe you could come with us straight off."

"Well, I didn't see that coming. But no, my place is here."

Liam said, "I don't like you being alone here. Take tonight and consider it."

"I'll think on it, but my roots are here."

Rose said, "I'd be pleased to have you come. You and Liam are the only family I have now – You're better to me than my own father ever was."

"That's kind, and I'd be proud to call you daughter. But you two don't need me looking over your shoulder. If you're to do this, you have to do it yourself. Still, I wish you'd both reconsider. You and Liam are welcome to stay as long as you like."

They were mostly silent after they disposed of their grisly load. Sean considered the prospect of living alone. He never had before;

he wondered if he was up to it. *Maybe a change of place would be good?* He watched Liam and Rose. She never let go of his hand, nor he hers. *No, it's their time, mine is past.*

Photo circa 1871, author unknown

Chapter 25

Sean shouted over the sound of a train whistle on the next platform. "Are you sure this is what you want to do?"

"Yes father, I am sure. And you're sure you won't come?"

Sean hugged his son. "I will visit someday. Write when you have a grandbaby for me to see."

"I'll write more often than that. I expect letters from you as well. I'll let you know where we settle out there."

"I thought you decided on San Francisco."

Liam grinned. "California is a big place. And, Rose says she has a cousin in someplace called Monterey. It could be worth looking at."

"You have your itinerary?"

"You're like a mother hen. We got it written down. This train will have us in Omaha late tomorrow. On Thursday, we board the Union Pacific for Sacramento. Ten short days later, we'll be in California."

"I've faith you'll both do well out there. But should the need arise, remember you have a home here – both of you."

Sean was surprised by the warm hug from Rose. She said, "Thank you for your kindness. I'll never forget it. My life would have been better had I a father like you."

He whispered in her ear. "You do now. Remember *that,* should the need arise."

To Liam, he said. "All right, that does it then. Go get on the train before you miss it."

Liam shook his hand. "Remember, if you find yourself in trouble over that business from the other night, wire me. I'll come back and own my share of it."

"There will be no trouble," said Sean. "You and Rose put all that behind you now."

"Thank you, father, for everything. I mean *everything*, not just these last weeks."

"Stop now. This isn't goodbye forever. We'll see each other soon enough."

Liam nodded. "Last chance, to come along. You should be with family."

"Go! Get on the train before it leaves without you."

He strolled down the station platform, thinking about Liam and Rose. He liked Rose more and more, but still worried about them. *I'm probably a fool for not going. Maybe in a month or two of being alone, I'll wish I had. But then again, maybe Maggie was right. I'm just a coward. But something holds me here. Who knows what? But it's as sure as gravity.*

He stepped off the platform and into the rail station; it still reeked of smoke, though repairs were underway already. A cart selling boiled nuts caught his eye. *I could do with some company.*

Maybe I'll take some nuts to the boys at the firehouse – play some cards.

"Out of walnuts, are peanuts good enough?" asked the old man at the cart.

Sean replied, "Peanuts are fine. Sold out of walnuts you say – business that good?"

"Never better. Half the city is on the way to someplace else. Most are hungry too. Where you headed for?"

"Me? Nowhere. I'll likely give up the ghost here."

"Good for you. Chicago is a tough town. We'll be back – bigger and better than ever. That's what the papers say anyhow."

Sean took the bag and gave the vendor a nickel. "You would do well not to believe what's in the papers. But I think it might be true."

As he headed to the door with his bag, he heard a squeal that made his heart skip a beat. "Uncle Sean! Uncle Sean!"

He turned to see little Kerry bolting toward him. Behind her was Katie Sullivan with Mary in tow. Katie called out, "Kerry! Come back here!" She stopped when she saw Sean.

He swept Kerry up in his arms and hugged her. He felt a tear in the corner of his eye; he wiped it with his sleeve and carried the precious cargo back to her mother. "I believe one of your chickens has flown the coop."

Kerry giggled. "I'm not a chicken, silly."

Katie smiled pensively. "Well, Sean… I mean, Mr. Collins, it is good to see you have survived the fire, and unharmed. I've prayed often for your safety."

Sean exhaled deeply as he put Kerry down. "It is so good to see you, too. I've been so worried about you and the girls. I've been looking for you since the blaze. How are you?"

"Things have gone hard on us. If you looked in on us, you saw our home was lost. The hotel was burnt down too – no pity there, but it left me unemployed."

"I saw," said Sean. "But where you have been these weeks? I've scoured every camp and hospital. I feared the worst."

"It's good of you to care. We've been sleeping in the basement of the Blessed Sacrament church since the fire."

"My word, you poor things. Surely there is better refuge."

"The camps?" said Katie. "I think not. Besides, it's moot now."

"Is that what you are doing here at the station?" asked Sean.

Mary chirped. "We're going on a train trip! To visit our aunt and uncle. They live far away."

Sean saw tears in the corner of Katie's eyes. "What's wrong, Katie?"

Katie gathered her girls and said, "Your Uncle Sean and I need to talk. I want you two to go over to that bench and sit. And mind you, stay put until I call you."

"No!" said Kerry, "We've missed uncle Sean. We want to stay with him."

Sean patted Kerry on the head. "It'll be just a minute, I promise. Go on now."

With the girls out of earshot, Katie whispered, "The Christian Children's Society is urging me into placing the children in an orphanage." Katie wiped a tear away. "Being homeless as we are, they may take them from me."

"They can't do that!"

"They can if a judge… [sniff]… says they can. They just have to petition a court. It's been going on often enough since the fire."

"But why would they do such a thing? Much of the city is homeless."

"After the fire, the police found the girls – took them to the church. I thought them lost. I spent days looking for them. I didn't find them until I happened upon a neighbor who told me where they were."

"Again, a common enough struggle, It's no cause to…" said Sean.

"Somehow the pastor caught wind of where I was when the fire started… McDonald's hotel that is. I think he believes I am a … a… women of low morals."

"That's a load of manure!"

Katie sniffed, "It's not true, but what else would he believe."

"So, you're running?" asked Sean.

"Danny's brother and his wife live in Ohio. I've never met them. They and Daniel were at odds over something or another. But I'm hoping they'll take us in – at least until I find work."

"Have you written them? Are they willing?"

Katie sniffed. "I don't know. Danny said they're – well – unpleasant. I figure to surprise them, they'll be less likely to turn a cold shoulder with me and the girls already on their doorstep."

"And if they won't take you in? You'll be on the streets."

Katie sniffed. "What else can I do? At least the girls will be with me."

"Perhaps it's more than a happy coincidence we've crossed paths."

Katie shrugged. "I don't exactly follow."

Sean paused, then tentatively whispered. "You can stay with me."

"That's kind, but daft. Your wife won't stand for it. I hear what she says of me."

"My wife… Maggie… she passed in the fire. I live alone now."

"Oh Sean, I am so sorry for your loss."

"Katie, bring the girls. There is plenty of room."

"You're kind to offer. You always have been good to me and the girls. But no, it's impossible. It wouldn't be proper. Us not married, and you a new widower."

"Since the fire, propriety has become a servant to need. Many a family is housing the displaced. I doubt anyone will notice or care."

Katie rubbed her face in her hands. "Oh, they'll notice – and talk. It will look…"

"Damn how it looks. You and the girls need a place to stay. I have one."

Katie looked at her girls, then at Sean. "There is more to it, and you know it."

Sean took her hand; she flinched but left it. "Katie, your girls need a father. And they need a mother at home to care for them."

"What are you saying?"

"I am saying you should come live with me. I'll put a roof over your head and food on your table. The girls would be safe and provided for. You would be able to care for your children instead of slaving away in some servile position. I'd be proud to stand in as a father to them, if you let me."

Katie studied his face for a long moment. "And me? Are you suggesting I am to serve as a wife to you?"

"I would expect you to cook and take care of the house."

"That's not what I'm asking, and I think you know it. What would you expect of me as payment?"

"I'll demand nothing of you. You can share a bed with your girls. But Katie, I am fond of you – very fond. If you could see me as a husband someday, I'd be honored."

"This makes no sense. It's too quick. Your wife's bed isn't even cold yet."

"That bed has been cold for a long while. Be honest, am I the only one who felt affection between us? Would being with me be such a burden?"

"A burden? You know better than that. But this is… this is too much. It's like something from a penny novel."

"Katie, I understand this is overwhelming. I am not asking you to commit to anything; you have time to sort out your feelings about me. If you can't find affection for me, you can use the time to make other arrangements. For now, I'm offering you and the girls a safe place. You know how I feel about Mary and Kerry. Let me help them… and you. Don't they… you… deserve some peace and security?"

"Are you sure? If you change your mind, the girls will be heartbroken; they love you so."

"You need not worry about that."

Katie took in a deep breath. "I have to say something. The last time we saw each other, I… I treated you badly. You've always been good to me and the girls. I shouldn't have…"

"It's alright, don't fret over…"

"Sean, listen to me. You deserve to know. I was upset because Big Mike… he… you were right about making demands… I was going to…"

"Stop Katie. You owe me no explanation. Whatever happened, you did for the girls. I don't need to know and I don't care."

"Big Mike will…"

"McDonald is gone."

"Gone? What does that mean?"

"I mean McDonald will never bother you or anyone else again. That's all you need know."

Katie stared in disbelief as she processed what he was saying. She nodded and said, "Are you sure? If I come, I will want to stay. The girls… me… You're taking on a lot."

"I am sure. I've dreamed of as much. I know that's shameful, but it's true. I promise to take care of you and the girls like you're my own. Please consider it."

Out of relief and gratitude, Katie wrapped her arms around Sean. She whispered, "I don't need to. I've dreamed it too. And I will take such very good care of you, too."

He laughed and hugged her. "Thank goodness. I'd starve on my own cooking."

Katie blushed and whispered. "If you won't think poorly of me, I would rather prefer to not sleep with the girls."

He sighed. "Let's go home."

*****

Her legs burned. She hadn't expected the place to be so hilly but, then again, what did she know of the country other than Chicago. It all seemed strange – not at all what she heard about the place. Unlike Chicago, everything was spread out. Some houses were half a block from their neighbors. There was a lot of green, even this late in the year. She liked that; although the rest of the town was a disappointment. It all seemed a bit shabbier than she'd hoped and there was an off odor in the air.

The trip had been taxing and being surrounded by strangers was unnerving. Still, it was good to be away from Chicago, and from him.

She sat on a short wall that ran along the crushed rock pedestrian path. Her mind returned to Liam and the guilt brought a tear; *I hope he is alright. I shouldn't have abandoned him as I did, but what else could I do? I must do what's right by me. I can't make anyone happy if I am miserable. And he has his own life to live, his own choices. I couldn't have done anything but hold him back. Still, I should have said goodbye. I owed him that. I suppose it was cowardly, just disappearing like I did. He's probably worried sick. Maybe someday we will see each other again, and I'll make things right by him. I loved him; I hope he knows that and forgives me.*

She willed herself up and walked the last few blocks to the address she had been given. Her cousin had a surprisingly large house, not ornate, but with a stately front porch and fair-sized yard – a mansion by Chicago standards. Still, it looked tired.

With more than a little trepidation, she knocked on the door. *Please lord, make them be sympathetic and take me in. I don't know what else to do or where to…*

A large man she didn't know answered. "Can I help you?"

"I was told Elizabeth Donaldson lives here; may I speak with her?"

"About what?"

"I need to speak to *her*, please."

"Liza. There is a woman on the porch for you. Won't say why."

A small, round woman peered around the man. Her brow knitted in confusion, then recognition. "Oh my word! Margret Collins? Is that you?"

"It is, cousin."

"Oh, this is a shock. What in heaven's name are you doing here in Quincy? Where are your husband and son? Have you all come?"

"No, I am here alone."

"Why, for heaven's sake? And only just a few days ago, we received a letter from your Sean, saying you were killed in the great fire. What's this all about?"

"It's a long story. May I come in?"

The End

Epilogue

The Fire

The Great Chicago fire burned its way into the fabric of American culture, and with good reason. It stands as one of the great tragedies in American history. In only 36 hours, the fire reduced one third of a great city to rubble. The losses were staggering; it consumed an area of over five square miles and destroyed 17,000 buildings.

Remarkably, officials estimated only 300 fatalities resulted from the blaze. *Estimated* is an important word in understanding what happened in those fateful days. Officials recovered 120 bodies; however, many more people were reported missing and presumed dead. At the time, conjecture guessed the death toll was much higher. Many believed that many missing victims remained unreported. Further, Chicago had a large population of poor (especially Irish and African Americans) who were, in today's parlance, *living off the grid,* homeless, migrants, and children without birth certificates. The truth is no one knows the exact cost of the fire – not in lives, nor money.

While the fire was devastating, there was never any doubt that the city would survive. Chicago had been the fastest growing city in the west. When the smoke cleared, the great economic engines responsible for its growth remained intact. The stock yards that made Chicago *the butcher of the nation* survived, as did its grain mills. The city also possessed more railroad connections than any city in the country; they all survived as well. And of course, its location on Lake Michigan assured its robust maritime industry. The fact was that, while Chicago lost much, it had much more remaining. While city hall and a considerable portion of the downtown core still smoldered, the rest of the city opened for business as usual the next day. Incredibly, much of the city went to work on Monday morning completely unaware that the city was still burning.

For over 150 years, researchers have attempted to solve the mystery of how the fire started. It is now an established fact that the common story of Mrs. O'Leary's cow kicking over a lantern is false, but the actual cause is still debated. Popular theories are; Catherine O'Leary set the fire accidentally when checking the barn after a party, Daniel "Peg Leg" Sullivan started it with a discarded pipe ash, milk thieves dropped a lantern, children playing in the barn, spontaneous combustion, and arson. The mystery will probably never be solved.

The Great Rebuild

The city's literal rise from the ashes is documented in several works, and it's an amazing story in its own right. Only a day after the fire, the Chicago Tribune's front page boldly announced *Chicago Will Rebuild!* It was not a hollow promise. Within days, donations poured in from around the world, supporting relief efforts. As importantly, prominent Chicago businessmen went to work securing funds from venture capitalist to finance reconstruction. Rebuilding began even as some building still smoldered. Incredibly, construction began on 5000 one room housing units and nearly 1000 barracks within a week.

Construction supplies and workers flooded into the city, and new commercial building sprung up with incredible rapidity. They rebuilt much of the burned-out area in less than two years. Over the ensuing decade, Chicago had not only rebuilt what was lost, it had significantly grown in both population and economic power. The fire opened up huge tracks of new land for redevelopment. New businesses and industries sprung up – sadly, often at the expense of the poor.

While the fire touched all Chicagoans in one way or another, it was the poor who bore the brunt of the tragedy. Most in the burnt-out slums lived in rented cottages, and the few who owned property often lost their deeds in the fire or never had them to begin with. Developers pushed these unfortunates aside in favor of new commercial construction. The fire destroyed entire ethnic neighborhoods that never got rebuilt. And where low-cost housing was constructed, it was often poorly built. In fact, shoddy construction caused a (mostly forgotten) second great fire in 1874. That blaze destroyed around 800 post fire buildings – mostly tenements.

The often-overlooked element in the fire's telling is the great humanitarian crisis that followed. The fire left 100,000 people homeless (again, an estimate). For weeks, the homeless struggled to access shelter, food or clean water. Although good-hearted people from around the world donated millions in money and supplies towards relief, many of the poorest did without because agencies unfairly distributed resources. "Worthiness" often replaced need as the criteria for disbursement of funds. Businesses and the upper classes were at the front of the line in accessing relief and construction supplies. The poor and infirmed remained a low priority and got placed in barracks, hastily built shanties, or simply given railroad tickets and told to leave.

Bigotry and anti-immigration sentiment ran deep in Chicago. It influenced the city's culture and politics before the fire, during the relief efforts, and in the midst of the rebuilding frenzy. Local Chicago papers routinely printed xenophobic editorials. Immigrants, particularly the Irish were frequently blamed for the city's problems. The intense bigotry aimed at the Irish before the fire only grew because of the tragedy. The press seized the opportunity to further their anti-immigration agenda, blaming the Irish for the fire. They also wrote greatly exaggerated stories of immoral and criminal behavior during the hours of the blaze. A prime example is the vehement attacks made by the press on the character of Catherine O'Leary. Years later, researchers found that fabrications about O'Leary, and the Irish in general, were often deliberate and ruthless attempts to shape post-fire redevelopment policies.

Catherine and Patrick O'Leary

If the story of the fire has a face, it is that of Catherine O'Leary. For over a century, the myth of an elderly Catherine O'Leary's cow kicking over a lantern while being milked has been told and retold in stories, pictures, and even movies.

Long before the fire, the Irish immigrants suffered deep rooted prejudice and distrust. Anti-immigration (and anti- Catholicism), were common policy in politics and editorial journalism. Misogyny was also a social norm of the time; Irish women were particularly maligned as slovenly, and of lax morals. As the fire started in the barn of an Irish woman, it's not surprising then that the press quickly castigated the Irish in general, and the O'Leary's in particular. That Catherine O'Leary was hardworking and successfully running a thriving business never deterred the press from reinventing Mrs. O'Leary into an old drunken fool with a clumsy cow. Once printed, the apocryphal story of her and Daisy the cow (A fabricated name that surfaced weeks after the fire) became gospel. Interestingly, it was Mrs. O'Leary who caught the nation's attention. The press essentially ignored Patrick, her husband. In fact, a few decades later, the common story portrayed Catherine as an elderly widow at the time of the fire.

The month after the fire, the Board of Police and Fire Commissioners convened a formal inquiry into the fire. After gathering and reviewing testimony from a significant number of witnesses, the board found no evidence that Mrs. O'Leary was in any way culpable in the fire's start. Even so, the press remained relentless in fabricating their version of the story. By November, they created the myth of a 70-year-old drunken crone (Catherine O'Leary was between 35 and 40 at the time of the fire) who stupidly started the fire while drunk. One paper even falsely asserted she confessed to starting it.

Many years after the fire, the reporter who originally created the "cow myth" (Michael Ahern) admitted in print to making the whole story up, and in 1997 the city of Chicago officially proclaimed the O'Leary's faultless. Still, the story refuses to die even today. The name O'Leary continues to conjure the image of an old woman and her cow. And the story is still often taught to grade schoolers.

Catherine O'Leary suffered harassment from the press and public until her death. In the years after the fire, she became a virtual recluse, rarely leaving her home. Patrick O'Leary died in 1894, Catherine in 1895. In later years, their son, "Big Jim"

O'Leary, supported them. Ironically, he became one of Chicago's most wealthy and renowned gamblers and a suspected crime boss.

.

Cassius "Mike" McDonald

The reader is again reminded that Mike McDonald's role in the novel is fictionalized. There is no known link between him and the O'Leary's, or any record of him committing the other atrocious acts attributed to him in the story. That said, the historical Cassius "Mike" McDonald was a known crime boss who ran a famous establishment known as "the store." It accommodated a saloon, a restaurant, a hotel, a gambling parlor, and prostitutes. He is, in fact, cited as the originator of organized crime in Chicago. Beyond his legitimate and criminal enterprises, he oversaw a political machine with incredible power and influence.

After the fire, McDonald's business fortunes continued to grow. In the following decades, his political and criminal empire became so deeply entrenched in Chicago society that he operated with near immunity from local law enforcement. He died a wealthy man in 1907.

Joseph Chamberlin

Although Joseph Chamberlin's telling of the *Great Chicago Fire* significantly exaggerated the poor behavior of the Irish victims, his general account of the fire is quite detailed and forms the basis for much of what historians know of the fire's behavior. His notes, along with the accounts of survivors, give one of the most detailed and insightful views of human behavior in a disaster. His work on the fire propelled him to a highly successful and prolific news career.

Post fire, he worked for several east coast newspapers, and even owned a paper himself. All told, Chamberlin's 60-year career as a reporter and author garnered a good deal of respect. He died in 1926.

Michael Ahern

The Mike Ahern in the novel is greatly fictionalized. There is no known connection between him and Mike McDonald and the author exercised some creative license in depicting him as an alcoholic. Still, Ahern created the "cow and the lantern myth." that so harmed the O'Learys. He confessed to the deception years later, though he never fully explained why he did it.

The false story notwithstanding, Ahern remained employed as a Chicago reporter well into old age. In 1911, he published a highly popular serialized article in the Chicago Tribune called *Recapping the Great Fire.* In that telling, he postulates (again without evidence) that milk thieves dropped a lantern in the O'Leary barn, thus starting the fire. Interestingly, the article also claims Ahern as the only surviving reporter of the fire. Joseph Chamberlin remained very much alive at the time, not dying until 1926. Ahern died in Chicago, in 1927.

Legacy

There is no doubt that the great fire is among America's greatest disasters. Yet, an argument can be made that (at least for the city) it did more good than harm. The fire brought the city to the world's attention, and its remarkable resurrection did much to shape the city's reputation as a robust, big- shouldered town and a place worthy of investment. Incredibly, the city grew faster after the fire than before.

The fire was a contributing factor in securing the world's fair only twenty years later. The fire also shaped Chicago's unique skyline, and the Chicago Style of Architecture. The city's vaunted lakefront, parks and public transit system all have roots in the fire as well.

Few scars remain from the horrible weekend in 1871, but one cannot look at the incredible city without seeing its influence.

Fact Versus Fiction

Chapter 1: The Burlington Rail warehouse fire was an actual event. It occurred about two o'clock in the afternoon on Saturday, September 30, 1871, a week before the Great Chicago Fire. As told in the story, an employee (John Sweeney) died in the fire. The description of the fire as two warehouses separated by a rail line is accurate, as is the inclusion of a large store of whiskey in the basement. However, there is no record of the building's sudden collapse.

Chapter 2: The description of Sean Collins's neighborhood is a fair representation of conditions in the slums near the O'Leary dairy on DeKoven Street. It should be noted that the description of Catherine O'Leary is much closer to the truth than the traditional characterization of the woman. Myth depicts her as a foolish elderly spinster woman. In reality, Catherine O'Leary was between 35 and 40 years of age. She ran a dairy barn and sold milk, butter and eggs. A woman running a business was a rarity in 1871, and people who knew her described her as smart, tough and kind. Her husband (Patrick) worked both in construction and in a meat packing house.

Chapter 3: All characters and their conversations are fictional. Quincy was (and is) an actual community in west central Illinois. As described in the chapter, the village was a rapidly growing community in 1871, with a robust German catholic community.

Chapter 4: Big Mike McDonald moved to Chicago in 1862. He became a proto mob boss, specializing as a gambling kingpin, and pimp in the vice district called the *sands*. Chicago lore credits him with originating the phrases "There's a sucker born every minute," and "Never give a sucker an even break." The characters of Rose, Johnny and Liam are fictitious, as is the Shannon distillery.

Chapter 5: All the characters and their conversations are fiction.

Chapter 6: All the characters and their conversations are fiction.

Chapter 7: As stated above, Catherine & Patrick O'Leary were real people. They did, in fact, own a dairy farm on DeKoven Street. Big Mike McDonald was a contemporary of the O'Leary's, and as depicted, he was a career criminal. However, there is no documented relationship between McDonald and the O'Leary's. Their meeting in chapter seven is pure fiction.

Chapter 8: All characters and their conversations are fictional. General references made about famine and social unrest in Ireland occurring 1857 to 1860 are accurate. Sean references actual

American Civil War battles in the western theater (Shilo and Vicksburg.) Many Irishmen comprised Sherman's army in his *march to the sea.* A significant portion of the western army was from the Midwest. After the war, many Irish civil war veterans settled in Illinois, Ohio, and Wisconsin.

Chapter 9: All characters and their conversations are fictional.

Chapter 10: This chapter is an *essentially* accurate depiction of events. The McLaughlin's did, in fact, have a party the night the fire started, although some histories (not all) suggest the family actually lived in a rental behind the O'Leary cottage. Daniel Peg Leg Sullivan was the first to find the fire while returning from checking on a friend – although the character of Mr. Cassik is fictitious. The story of Sullivan saving the calf and losing his leg in the fire are recorded in the official fire investigation record. As is the fact that the O'Leary's were asleep and had to be wakened by Dennis Rogan when the fire started. The real-life efforts of neighbors did, in fact, save the O'Leary cottage – ironically, the only building on the block to escape significant damage.

The first citizen alarm came from Goll's pharmacy; however, it was delayed by as much as 30 minutes by Goll's unexplained reluctance to activate it. In reality, it was an adult male, not a young girl who roused Goll.

Mathias Schaffer was the watchman on duty the night of the fire. He did have visitors, although it's not recorded who they were. He did, in fact, mis-identify the fire, and send the fire department to the wrong address. The character of William Brown is also real, as are his actions as described in the novel; though his thoughts and motivations are unknown. The story of a man running into the firehouse is fiction, although there were reports of similar occurrences throughout the night.

It should be noted that as referenced, there was an actual huge fire the day before, and as depicted in the story, the entire department was exhausted when the *Great Fire* started.

Chapter11: The Giant and America were the actual first companies at the fire. The fire conditions described are fairly accurate, although stories from eyewitnesses vary somewhat regarding details. Wind, blown embers, and trees full of dead leaves made fire control near impossible. Brown did activate a second alarm of his own volition, and in fact, sent crews to the wrong address. A firefighter was told to activate a third alarm, but entered the wrong code. After some delay, Schaffer and Brown did so of their own initiative, but again to the wrong location.

Chapter 12: Liam and Maggie are fictitious characters; their conversations and actions are likewise fictitious. However, their described experience of the fire, the panic and evacuation are consistent with witness accounts. The reporter, Joseph Chamberlin, is an actual historic figure, who did in fact cover the fire for the Chicago Evening Post. Both the paper and Chamberlin had reputations as strong opponents of immigration. In his account of the fire, Chamberlin was highly critical of the Irish immigrants, and firefighters, and those accounts are generally dismissed as skewed. Still, his reporting on the actual fire, its growth and timeline are praised as the best record of events.

The description of the early fire and fire suppression efforts are consistent with (but not exact) those documented in the post fire investigation notes.

Note: The character of Big Mike McDonald is real, but there is absolutely no evidence that he was in any way associated with the start of the fire. Further, there is no documented connection between him and the O'Leary's. This plot element is entirely fictional.

Chapter 13: As described in the chapter, the fire jumped the south branch of the Chicago River. This was caused by burning embers from St Paul's church steeple that were carried on the wind to the other side. After the fire jumped the river, the "Gas Works" exploded. It essentially left most of the city without lights. Note: The gas works explosion occurred around 1am. About 20 minutes later than is inferred in the novel.

Chapter 14: St. Paul's church was lost in the fire. Stories from survivors described the pandemonium experienced by those fleeing to the believed safety across the South Branch of the river are consistent with Maggie's misfortunes. Also, eyewitness accounts described the ignition of waste oil on the river, as well as the many deceased human and animal bodies floating by the bridge. The bridge eventually burned.

Chapter 15: William Brown and Mathias Schaffer were at the courthouse during the fire, as were Schaffer's unknown guests (Bernard, Rebecca and Gretchen are fictional.) At some point they fled the courthouse when it caught fire, although the account of their escape in chapter 15 is fictional.

The story of Joseph Hudlin saving important records from the Chamber of Commerce Building is true, except that he had no recorded assistance from fire crews; nor was he confronted by police. Hudlin received a commendation for his efforts.

The Chicago Mayor at the time of the fire, Roswell Mason, did order the release of prisoners from the basement jail of the burning courthouse. The involvement of Sean Collins and Pappy is fictionalized. Several inmates escaped and were never apprehended, a few stayed and assisted with firefighting efforts.

Chapter 16: Katie is a fictional character. However, her experiences in trying to get home to her daughters accurately reflect eyewitness accounts of the city streets during the fire.

Chapter 17: The Sisters of Mercy Hospital is fictitious, as are the two sisters described in the chapter. Although McDonald was associated with gambling and prostitution, the hotel on Clark Street is a fictional location. However, he actually ran a very similar establishment, commonly called "the store," in the "sands" area of Chicago, near the lake.

Chapter 18: The reference to the use of blasting powder in chapter 18 is true. Late Sunday night, a group of private citizens (generally with the approval of a few Chicago alderman but not in cooperation with fire officials) began leveling buildings ahead of the fire in order to create firebreaks. The practice was only marginally successful. Again, McDonald's involvement in the fire's start is pure fiction. In fact, the exact cause of the fire remains a mystery to this day. One of the true ironies of the fire is that the O'Leary cottage (not more than 50 feet from the barn) survived the fire.

As described in the chapter, thousands gathered at the lakefront during the fire, hoping it would provide refuge from the flames.

Note: The historical Joseph Chamberlin was born in Vermont and moved to Chicago as a young man.

Chapter 19: As described in the chapter, Lincoln Park and the nearby graveyard sheltered thousands of refugees. The fire's progress, as described in chapter 19, is consistent with records from the post fire investigation.

Chapter 20: Michael Ahern was a reporter for the Chicago Republic at the time of the fire. Although the relationship between Ahern and McDonald is fictional, Ahern did fabricate the story of Mrs. O'Leary's cow kicking over a lantern as the fire's origin. Even though Ahern later recanted the story, admitting he made it up, the myth took root and is still believed by many today. Note: Reference to Ahern's drinking is an exercise in literary license.

Hemsworth and the "Alderman" are fictional, as is the plot to pilfer relief supplies. However, there were reports of misappropriation of funds, irregularities in permitting, and unfair distribution of relief resources relative to the rebuilding effort.

Chapter 21: Charitable donations from around the world quickly arrived in Chicago. Even so, the first few weeks after the fire were hard on many of the nearly 100,000 displaced. Like most modern disaster survivors, access to food, shelter, water and sanitation was elemental to survival. Remarkably, even with the reported graft surrounding relief efforts, Chicago managed to build thousands of temporary shelters in just a few weeks. The speed at which the city rebuilt remains a marvel even by modern emergency managers.

As stated in the chapter, only 120 bodies were recovered after the fire. The reported death toll was estimated at 300. Many disputed the number as too low, as residents in the poor neighborhoods were often not officially documented, and it's assumed many missing were not reported to the authorities.

Chapter 22: All the characters and their conversations are fiction.

Chapter 23: The chapter references the imposition of martial law under General Phil Sheridan. This is historically accurate; however, Liam's accusation of abuse is fictional. It is noteworthy, however, that a special commission was convened by the city of Chicago to investigate the fire. The commission ruled the cause of the fire to be undetermined and exonerated the O'Leary's. Unfortunately, the official commission findings did little to dispel the myth of a drunken Mrs. O'Leary and her cow starting the fire. Even so, the contemporaneous records of the commission proceedings have been invaluable to historians in researching the fire.

Chapter 24: This chapter is nearly all fiction. The real Big Mike McDonald was not murdered. Rather, he died of natural causes in 1907. Two historic tidbits in the chapter are accurate; much of the fire's debris was dumped in Lake Michigan and nearby marshes. Chicago's famous Grant Park is built on fill from the fire. Also, as described in the chapter, martial law was imposed by General Sheridan in the weeks following the fire, and as a precaution, troops enforced a curfew for a short while.

Chapter 25: All characters and their conversations are fictional.

Sources

- The great Fire Exhibit – The Chicago History Museum

- The Great Fire, by Jim Murphy (2001)

- The Great Chicago Fire, by James Lowe (1979)

- The Great Chicago Fire of 1871 and Other Devastating American Fires, by E.J. Goodspeed (2019)

- The Chicago Historical Society and Northwestern University, The Great Chicago Fire & the Web of Memory

- https://greatchicagofire.org/

- WTTW Chicago Public Broadcasting, Chicago shall rise again,

- https://interactive.wttw.com/chicago-stories/chicago-fire/chicago-shall-rise-again-rebuilding-a-better-city-after-the-blaze

-

- WTTW Chicago Public Broadcasting, A cow, a lantern, and a myth

- https://interactive.wttw.com/chicago-stories/chicago-fire/a-cow-a-lantern-and-a-myth-mrs-oleary-and-19th-century-immigrants-in-chicago

- National Geographic, The Great Rebuilding by Mary Schons

- https://education.nationalgeographic.org/resource/chicago-fire-1871-and-great-rebuilding

Other Books By

H. Scott Walker

Novels

- *Man Down - A firefighter's story of loss and redemption*

Textbooks

- *Fire Service Ethics - College level text*

- *Data Driven Fire Administration*

For more informationm visit

https://www.hscottwalker.com/

www.ingramcontent.com/pod-product-compliance
Lightning Source LLC
Chambersburg PA
CBHW040854010826
48978CB00013BA/1017